The Chimera Collusion

A Novel

by

D. J. Knedgen

ISBN-13 978-1482634754
ISBN-10 1482634759

Note: Knedgen is pronounced as 'ka **ned** gin'

The Chimera Collusion is a work of fiction. Names, characters, places, and events are the product of the author's imagination or are used for purely fictitious purposes. Any resemblance to reality is purely a coincidence.

www.fictionauthor.wix.com/djknedgen

This book is dedicated to my fellow citizens of the world and to my children, Steve and Leslie, and my grandson, Nova. I hope they will inherit an America worthy of them.

A special thank you to my significant other, Max Taylor, for his patience and technical help throughout the writing process, and also for the original cover design that he produced with the image from istockphoto.com, and TypeStyler by Ken Stillman and technical assistance from Dave Stillman, both of Strider Software.

"The individual is handicapped by coming face to face with a conspiracy so monstrous he cannot believe it exists."

— J. Edgar Hoover
Former Head of the FBI

"Power concedes nothing without a demand. It never did and never will. Find out just what any people will quietly submit to and you have the exact measure of the injustice and wrong which will be imposed on them, and these will continue till they have been resisted with either words or blows, or with both. The limits of tyrants are prescribed by the endurance of those whom they suppress."

— Frederick Douglass
Abolitionist, Author, Diplomat

"Our lives begin to end the day we become silent about things that matter."

— Martin Luther King Jr.
Clergyman, Civil Rights Activist

"Do not assume anything Obi-Wan. Clear your mind must be if you are to discover the real villains behind this plot."

— Yoda
Jedi Grand Master

Prologue

Detroit, Winter

"It ain't Maxwell House coffee sweetheart, but some women claim that it's good to the last drop." Laughing at his cleverness, the big guy grabs two handfuls of thick long hair forcing her to her knees.

Slowly regaining her wits, the metallic taste of blood mixed with the bitterness of the small crystals coating her tongue sickens her. Through dazed, crossed eyes she peers down the short slope of her nose, now deviating rudely to the left. Morbid curiosity compels her to raise a hand to further assess the damage. She stops short, her elbow screaming in agony.

"I can't let this trash take me out," she thinks, watching the big guy's hands free his rigidness from the safe confines of his jeans. Even in the frigid winter temperature of the abandoned warehouse, his foul stench assaults her nostrils like a rude slap across her face. A wave of sour nausea ascends from gut to throat, and back again.

"Open wide. Don't make me have to bitch-slap you."

Another wave of nausea hits her. In defiance, she projects the contents of her stomach forward.

"Fuck!" the big guy curses as he raises his hand in a threatening backhand gesture, and then suddenly stops short. "I'd love to rearrange your pretty face but it's going to be tough enough to explain that broken nose."

Grabbing her hoodie, he scrapes the vomit from himself. "You're nothing but a two-bit whore. That's all you've ever been. That's all you'll ever be. Don't ever forget it. If you do, you'll find yourself choking to death on the business end of this." Kim averted her gaze, but his meaning was clear. He zipped his pants up over his filthy, limp threat and then balled up the hoodie, taking aim at her broken face. At such close range, he hit his mark. Her nose succumbed without a struggle, the broken cartilage too weak to care.

With that said, the big guy calmly and deliberately walks out of the warehouse, disappearing into the darkness.

Sprawled out on the cold, filthy floor, she fights to hold onto consciousness while wondering who she is and how she got there. In the distance, she hears a single gunshot piercing the silence of the cold, dark night. It's the last thing she remembers.

1

Detroit, Early Spring

Winter was officially over and had been for weeks, but its harsh, damp chill still descended over the Motor City every evening when the sun went down. Between the weather, the economy, and the crime rate, Detroit was no place for sissies.

Street paced back and forth, trying to create some body heat and cursed himself for not dressing warmer. A hometown boy, he knew the nights could be colder than a frigid bitch in an ice storm. Another hour or so in the dank coldness and it would take just as long to shake off the chill even after he had left it behind. Shoving his hands deep in his pockets, he nervously fingered the baggies with numb fingertips.

Even with the downturn in the economy–and Detroit was hurting more than most cities–business was usually still good on a Friday night. Folks just wanted to smoke some pot to mellow out and forget the broken promises of a change for the better. They wanted to relax for a while. Forget the stress of bills piling up, no jobs, and the threat of eviction always hovering knowing they had nowhere to go and no means to get there.

Street figured he'd push what pot he had left in the next hour or two for some easy money and then call it a day. No sense pushing his luck. Knowing the limits of what the local cops would overlook in exchange for the occasional tip only he could provide, he wasn't about to take a chance and ruin the good thing he had going. Getting greedy could ruin everything.

Working the corner would have drawn unwanted attention in another neighborhood, but not this one. Having been born and raised there, Street had long been a familiar sight to the locals. He knew every back street and alleyway and could vanish in seconds. He could also spot a stranger three blocks away and he carefully made mental notes of anyone or anything out of the ordinary. Those were the skills that kept him alive on the streets. Those, and some warm clothes.

Even from four blocks away and with no headlights on he recognized the approaching car. He watched as it slow-crawled deliberately in his direction. Finally, the police cruiser pulled up to the curb alongside Street, stopped, and waited patiently. Street casually looked around and then edged closer to the cruiser's open window.

"What's up?" he asked.

"You tell us," a uniform replied.

"Ain't heard a thing Donnelly."

"See anything?"

"Ain't seen nothing Branson."

"You'd tell us if you did, right Street?" Donnelly asked.

"You're both in my faves list," Street said, sarcastically.

It was the usual chatter. Sometimes they shared, sometimes they didn't. If information needed to be exchanged though, someone always gave in and got the ball rolling. It was a game of mental chicken. There was much at stake on both sides and everyone played it cool.

Street looked around nervously, biding his time. With Branson and Donnelly holding their ground, Street finally said, "Well, if there ain't nothing else, it ain't exactly good for my reputation to be seen hanging with guys like you."

Continued silence.

Branson and Donnelly stared stone-faced and straight-forward through the windshield and into the dark emptiness of the deserted neighborhood. Street made a small move to back away from the car. That small threat forced a break in the silence.

"We got a body dumped over at Hyacinth and Azalea," Donnelly finally announced before Street went too far. "We figured one of the girls might have some info."

Street fought hard to suppress a smile. He knew that the winner was always the one who didn't need anything. He took a couple of steps forward and leaned in closer, his forearms resting on the window ledge, his head half in, half out, of the open window.

"Now, what makes you think that?" His casualness belied his interest. There wasn't much that went on in the neighborhood that he didn't hear about, and usually before the cops came looking for information.

"Male. Butt-naked. Looks like he died happy if you get my meaning," Branson said.

"I get your meaning but I got no info. Shit!"

Spotting the black Mercedes slowly rounding the corner, Street backed away from the car like he'd been hit in the chest by a twelve gauge shotgun at close range.

"Gimme some help here, guys," he pleaded as the Mercedes came to a stop at the adjacent corner. In seconds, the door opened and the beefy driver of the Mercedes climbed out from behind the wheel.

Both cruiser doors flew open and Branson and Donnelly were on Street like flies on shit. All hell broke loose. Within seconds they had Street pinned on the hood of their car.

"You got anything in your pockets that could hurt us? Any needles or sharp objects?" Donnelly asked loudly. The cops proceeded probing pockets and frisking him down. When Street protested, they slapped the back of his head for effect. They all knew they were being watched so it needed to look legit.

"I ain't done nothing. I swear. I'm just waiting for the cross-town bus."

"Let me take a wild-ass guess," Branson interrupted, "you're on your way to that fancy, black-tie fundraiser at the Mayor's mansion."

"How'd you guess?"

"We got word that you're dealing!" Donnelly shouted, cutting Street off.

"It's just a matter of time and you're going down, punk!" Branson added. "We didn't find anything tonight, but we'll be watching you."

"Oh yeah? Well maybe I'll just move to Washington State or Colorado! Those people got the right idea about legalizing pot!"

Amidst Street's cries of protest, they got back in their car. Branson discreetly tossed the confiscated contents of Street's pockets on the seat between him and Donnelly and then yelled through the window, "A young, tight-assed thing like you will have more prison suitors than you'll know what to do with. You probably won't have a minute to yourself, if you get my meaning."

Both cops laughed loudly as they drove off, but they didn't go far. Circling the block, they turned the headlights off, kept the engine running, and got out of the car. They cautiously made their way to the corner of a deserted building. Peering around it, they watched as the driver of the Mercedes descended on Street.

"I told you. I sold it all. If I had any left my ass'd be on the way to county lock-up right now," Street said indignantly, as the man gave Street a thorough going-over.

"Just checking you out, my man. It's nothing personal. I'm checking everybody out. Word on the street is that there's word on the street. Not saying it's you doing the talking. Just being cautious. It's us against them. No one crosses that line. No one. If the cops want info, they can get it the good old-fashioned way–they can pay for it or beat it out of someone."

"Is that any way to talk about Detroit's finest?" asked Street, pushing the insides of his empty pockets back into his pants.

"Just doing my job, Street. No hard feelings. You're the man," Mercedes said. Looking past Street, he caught sight of one of the girls strutting her stuff in their direction. Reaching behind Street, he pulled Street's jacket collar up snug around his neck.

"Better get in out of the cold, Street," Mercedes advised, tightening his grip just enough to get the message across. "You're finished for tonight anyway. And, stay out of trouble. I can't be watching your ass day and night, you know. And by the way, Washington and Colorado will have no use for your business skills."

Mercedes turned and walked back to his car as Angie approached from behind.

"And don't you forget it!" Street shouted as he postured with clenched fist waving in the air for added effect.

As slowly as it had arrived, the Mercedes pulled away. When the text signal came in, Street ignored it until the Mercedes rounded the corner and was out of sight. Then, he pulled it out and with a quick flip of his thumb he opened his phone to view the one word message.

"Walk with me, talk with me, Angie, while I retrieve my inventory." Falling in step beside him, she could see his amused disgust.

"Dumpster?" she asked. Not waiting for an answer she continued. "Doesn't this make three dumpster dives in a row? What happened to 'gutter' or 'newsstand'?"

"Gutter fell off and they moved the newsstand two blocks over. It's a small price to pay, Angie. I help them, they help me. It's a symbiotic relationship. It's what keeps things in perfect balance. It's the way business gets done."

The dumpster was only half full so Street shimmied up the side and went in head first, just far enough to keep most of his weight outside the dumpster so he wouldn't fall in. Looking around the assorted mess within, he tried to catch sight of the baggies. He spotted them, strewn about and shiny in the moonlight.

With his goods back in hand, Street knew he couldn't take up his usual post on the corner in case Mercedes came back. If caught with the marijuana, his credibility with his supplier would be ruined. His only interest now was getting rid of the pot, and quickly.

"It's your lucky day, I'm in a generous mood," he told a familiar young couple as he offered them his merchandise at a discount. After a little negotiating, the couple scored themselves a mellow weekend at a deep discount. Afterwards, Street and Angie hustled across the street to get a beer at The Library.

2

"How's tricks, Angie?" came the greeting when they walked into the dimly lit neighborhood bar.

"Real original, Jay," Angie bantered.

"The usual?" he asked, ignoring the sarcastic jab. Not waiting for an answer, Jay turned to get two beers. Street and Jay exchanged their customary silent nods of acknowledgement as Street hoisted himself up on the bar stool. That's when Street noticed Angie's look of disapproval.

"You and me need to talk," she said, tilting her head toward a table in the far corner. Taking her cue, Street slid down and followed her.

"Either you've suddenly got some serious competition on your corner or you can't give it away for free," Street teased, falling in across from her in the secluded booth. He couldn't ignore the grave look on her face and tried to lighten the mood.

"Competition is what keeps people on their toes, little man. It's what makes this country great. I don't fear it. I welcome it. But this isn't about me. I'm happy with my little lot in life," she said. "But, I am concerned about Kim. She's been acting pretty strange lately."

"How so? I ain't seen her in days. Besides, I wouldn't know if she was acting strange or not and I don't think you know her well enough to know that either."

"Trust me, Street. I've got a sense about this stuff. Something's up with her. Something bad."

"Even if you're right, it ain't none of our business, Angie. The secret to our success on the street is MYOB-mind your own business and let others' mind their own too. Don't ask, don't tell. She just dropped into our lives a couple of months ago. If she's got issues they're hers, not ours. Don't get me wrong, I like her too, but we don't need no attention on ourselves by getting ourselves mixed up in her problems. End of story."

"Speak for yourself," Angie said. "Something's up and I'm going to hang out for a while and see if she shows up. You just go ahead and run along and don't let the door hit your skinny ass on the way out."

3

The dead weight of his leg across her thigh woke Kim. Sitting up, she looked around as her eyes slowly adjusted to the dimness of the room. As she got her bearings, she carefully shoved the leg aside, then slowly inched her way to the side of the bed. The pulsing displays from the neon sign near the street threw a rainbow of colors through the silky window sheers, casting her surroundings in an eerie glow.

She silently berated herself. She wasn't supposed to fall asleep. No sleeping on the job. That was the rule. But, what the hell. A double Bloody Mary, some very satisfying sex, and besides, she thought, she was ahead of schedule anyway.

Her toes disappeared in the plushness of the carpet as she quietly padded her way across the room and into the bathroom. After flushing the toilet, she returned to the bed and carefully climbed back in. She turned her attention to her partner. Aided by the neon glow, she studied his face intently. He looked so peaceful. Was that a slight smile on his lips? She hoped so. Carefully, she once again inched her way to the edge of the bed and got up. She dressed quietly and quickly, picked her phone up from the nightstand, and dialed.

"I do believe it's true what they say," she said softly into the phone.

"You know, what they say about men dying happy when they die during sex," she continued.

Kim shot back, suddenly edgy. "Because he wasn't a quickie or a one-time johnny. Besides, he deserved to get his monies worth."

Casting another glance at the man she thought to herself, *What a waste*. For a few seconds she had the unsettling experience of wondering who she was and why she was there. Then, fleeting images of recognition, of having seen him before.

"Mick, this guy, there's something about him. He looks vaguely familiar." Kim sounded confused. "What's going on?"

Five long seconds of silence on the other end and then the conversation resumed. Kim listened intently to what she was told. Then, just as quickly as it had come, the unsettling experience of confusion had passed. She knew who she was and what she had to do. The dead man was, once again, nothing but a stranger.

"Yes Mick," Kim said, very businesslike. "I know the routine. I'll be in touch."

Mick hung up, then sat back and closed his eyes. "Sheeple. The country's full of them," he muttered disgustedly. But the disgust was tempered by a larger sense of elation. Empowered by a feeling of being in control, he let his muses run wild. He'd come a long way but still had a long way to go. From the sanctity of his corner office, he had discreetly garnered control over so much. Self-satisfaction was interrupted when his private cell phone broke in on his thoughts. Annoyed, he glanced at the caller ID. He was tempted to ignore the incessant ringing, but that would be unacceptable and could prove costly. Begrudgingly, he answered it before it quit ringing. In his business no one let anything go to voicemail.

"Mick here," he spoke with confidence to the faceless intruder on the other end.

"As planned and right on schedule," he responded to a short inquiry.

"Everything's golden. Our star player's performing even better than expected. Far better." Mick had already forgotten about Kim's little memory jolt. After all, everyone had a sense of deja vu once in a while.

The call was brief, cryptic, to the point, then ended quickly. Sitting back, Mick closed his eyes once again and with the phone call behind him, he allowed himself to fully relax for the first time in days. *Kim should be preparing to leave the hotel any minute now, as if she had never been there. Everything was falling into place, exactly as planned,* he thought.

After quickly wiping down the toilet handle and the few other things she may have touched, Kim took in a deep breath, picked up the hotel phone and dialed the front desk. "My date isn't breathing! Call

911!"

With the call made, she used a kleenex to open and close the door as she stepped into the hallway. To keep her face out of the range of the surveillance cameras, she lowered her head and wasted no time leaving the same way she had come in two hours earlier–the back stairwell.

Kim hustled across the four long blocks on foot. She was well-muscled and in excellent shape but couldn't remember any effort to get that way. Not even slightly winded from the exertion of her four block jaunt she, nevertheless, leaned against the brick facade of The Library as a fleeting collage of disjointed, vaguely familiar images once again played through her mind like a kaleidoscope. Then, just as suddenly as the images came, they vanished. She'd had a handful of these experiences in as many days. Shaking off her uneasiness as stress, Kim pulled the wig from her head and shoved it into her bag. Then, as if nothing had happened, she walked into The Library.

4

Seated at the bar, Kim started to look around for her friends and then realized that it was early so Angie and Street would still be working their corners. She decided to hang out until they showed up.

"Jay, what's the word?" she asked the bartender as he spotted her.

"Eight words, actually. Birth, taxes, broken campaign promises, death, more taxes. What else is there?"

"The eternal optimist," Kim said with good-natured sarcasm. "Your skeptical pessimism is going to buy you an early grave, my friend. Studies show that an optimistic outlook can improve one's health, not to mention one's life span."

"With the way this country's going, there's not a hell of a lot to look forward to. But of course, that's just my opinion."

"And, as usual, we're all entitled to hear it," she said. Jay laughed.

"Seriously, Jay, if you don't like the way things are going then try changing them," she continued. "Pardon the cliche but, be the change you want to see."

"How many times do I have to tell you that you can't fight city hall," he shrugged, pouring a drink.

Glancing around the room again, Kim spotted Angie and Street already huddled in the corner. She placed her drink order with Jay, then walked over to join them. Her sudden appearance surprised them and they looked embarrassed, as if she was intruding on a private conversation. Suddenly, she felt confused and uncomfortable. She turned to leave. Angie lunged across the table and grabbed her arm.

"Now, just where do you think you're off to, girlfriend?" Angie said, trying to make her voice sound as casual as possible.

"Sometimes three's a crowd. No problem, though. I'll just keep Jay company at the bar," Kim announced, trying to keep it light.

"Oh no you don't," Angie said firmly. "As a matter of fact, we were just talking about you."

Suspicions confirmed, Kim thought, as she let Angie pull her toward the table.

Looking sheepish, Street silently slid over to make room for her. As a diversion, he pulled the sports section out of the newspaper that someone had left behind on the table.

Kim suddenly felt an unexplainable leeriness. Angie and Street were strangers just a few short months ago. She really didn't know much about them. *Where is this paranoia coming from?* she wondered.

Jay put her drink on the table and spied the front page of the newspaper. Pointing to it he said, "Looks like they ID'd the body found dumped across town a couple of days ago. Some political type. But this'll be the last we hear about it. It'll be hushed up and swept under the rug because half of America doesn't care about what's going on or where we're headed, a fourth are too scared to question anything, and a hundred years from now who's gonna give a rat's ass anyway? Hell, ten year's from now no will care. John F. Kennedy's assassination is proof of that. One of the biggest cover-ups of modern times and it hardly caused a ripple of unrest."

"You're wrong about that, Jay," Angie said. "People cared then and they care now."

"Maybe. But it's in the cold case file because, like I said, you can't fight city hall."

"In case you didn't know this, Yasser Arafat's body has been exhumed in an effort to prove or disprove Polonium-210 poisoning as the cause of death, which would indicate assassination. That proves people do care."

"That only proves the Palestinians care. I still say Americans don't."

Kim was glancing at the newspaper and listening to Angie and Jay debate the issue when suddenly her attention was elsewhere. Angie was the first to notice Kim's reaction to the picture of Senator Madsen gracing the front page of the Crier. Recognition followed by shock.

Kim grabbed the newspaper and her eyes skimmed over the text. "Just days short of announcing his candidacy, the death of presidential hopeful, Senator Madsen, has robbed the country of the chance for much-needed reform through push-backs of the most economically devastating regulations in this country's history." *Senator?* she thought to herself. Disturbing flashbacks flooded her mind.

She was naked, straddling the sixty-something, paunchy, sweaty "john". Even with Viagra his erection was functioning at half-mast and she felt cheated. Her pelvis was working overtime to keep him and his heart rate on task.

Poor guy. He'd had enough Viagra to give a cadaver a boner. Having difficulty riding something that small and limp and wanting to get the job over with as soon as possible, she slid down until she was on all fours between his legs. Like most men he responded readily to her mouth and within minutes his heart was pounding in his chest. As if on cue, he suddenly clutched his chest in agony. Undaunted, she continued on and completed his orgasm with her hand until both the orgasm and his life came to a simultaneous end.

An hour earlier, her pimp had justified Kim's high price to the eager politician by explaining that he was going to be on the receiving end of some drop-dead sex enhanced by a very safe triple dose of Viagra. "It's done all the time," the "john" was assured when he voiced concerns about his ticker. "And when you wear this bitch out I've got a couple more lined up to step in." Hearing that, all worries about his heart were fast forgotten in anticipation of a night that a lifetime of religion-suppressed fantasies were made of.

Eager to get to the promised drop-dead sex he gulped down the handful of pills, washed them down with a scotch on the rocks, and then quickly ushered the pimp to the door. Little had he known that he should have taken the pimp's promise of drop-dead sex literally, not figuratively.

Kim was so engrossed in the flashbacks that she never noticed Angie's efforts to get her attention.

"Kim!" Banging her fist on the table, Angie broke Kim's trance.

"Girl, you look like you just saw a ghost!"

Kim had also captured Street's attention and he was highly curious as to what she was fixated on. Before she could answer, he was on his feet and peering over her shoulder at the newspaper.

He let out a long, slow whistle. "Oooweeeee," he finally uttered. "Married with children, active in his church, upstanding citizen, respected politician, man, that's one lucky stiff."

With both girls shooting him a confused look, Street explained. "Try to keep up here. The man was found naked in an active section of town, if you get my meaning. Any man would be better off dead than face the little woman, the kids, the in-laws, the neighbors, the church, the constituents, the press…"

"Spoken like a man," Angie cut Street off before turning her attention back to Kim.

"Let's keep it real, here, Kim. You know something about this." Her tone brooked no denial.

Again, Street jumped in before Kim could respond. "Listen up Angie. I thought we were straight on this. Not. Our. Business. We've got a smooth ride through life going on. No need to involve ourselves."

"Look who's talking. Every time you lean through the window of a police cruiser you involve yourself."

Angie's point was valid, but Street would not concede. Looking at her intensely, he explained. "It's all part of my carefully thought out plan, Angie."

"By all means, enlighten us," Angie said sternly.

"I let people think I'm playing their game, but I'm really getting them to play *my* game."

"*Your* game?" Angie asked.

"Yeah. *My* game. Everyone knows I've been on the streets most of my life. It's how I got my nickname. So I see a lot. Hear a lot. Both sides of the law think I'm down with them so they slip me a little info here and there as they're trying to get info from me, and that lets me stay on top of the street news. I work both sides that way. Gets me in some doors, keeps me from even trying to get in others, if you get my point.

"I give a little. I get a little. I help them, they help me. I got it worked out for myself and I ain't about fucking it up by asking questions about what's none of my business. I say live and let live and stay the hell out of the spotlight. It's all just a process going on anyway, Angie. In the end, none of it's gonna matter anyway. We're just the little people. We're never gonna accomplish anything great. We're never gonna make a difference except to the few people closest to us," he said, as he thought about Grandma Mae.

Angie started clapping as she stood to give Street a standing ovation. "My, my. Aren't you the Patrick-fucking-Henry of the neighborhood," she said, with just the right tinge of sarcasm. "You can high-tail that skinny ass of yours right on out of here if you want to. But Kim looks like she just might have something on her mind and I, for one, am willing to disrupt my self-indulgent status quo to step outside of myself to lend an ear, a hand, whatever!"

Angie and Street had been going at it so strong that they barely noticed that Kim was gone. Bolting from the table, Angie was off and running with Street close behind her. Jay waved his hand toward the front entrance signaling the direction he saw her go.

5

Outside, they heard an uncontrollable sobbing coming from around the corner of the building. They found Kim sitting on the sidewalk, head in hands. Street was the first to join her. Sitting down on the cement he put his arm around her shoulders and pulled her close to him.

Angie slid in close on the other side. "Kim, whatever it is, it can't be all that bad. Most of the time things seem worse than they really are."

"I'm not sure things could get any worse," she answered between sobs.

"You know something about Senator Madsen," Street said, getting right to the point.

"I don't know. I'm not sure. I think so."

"What the hell kind of answer is that?" he said in a half-joking manner.

Kim continued to quietly sit.

"You either know the man or you don't," Angie said softly, trying a different approach. "You can trust us."

The three sat in silence as each waited for someone else to make the next move. Realizing that her friends were not going to give up, Kim finally broke. "How can I know if I really know anything about the senator when I don't know if I really know anything about myself?"

"Girl, what the hell are you trying to say?" Street asked.

"You're not making any sense, Kim," Angie agreed with Street.

Kim looked from Angie to Street, then back to Angie, trying to make up her mind if, and what, she should tell them. Just when she had decided to open up to them, her mind suddenly started playing out another collage of seemingly unrelated events.

She was sprawled out in a dimly lit warehouse, broken and bleeding, wondering who she was. Then, little flashbacks of herself, naked, watching her client–Senator Madsen!–clutching his chest while his body spasmed with the last orgasm he would ever have. Then, somehow, she was at a shooting range, headset on, firing round after round into the heart of a cardboard target. Just as quickly, her mind jumped track to her appointment earlier that evening and her phone call to Mick. Tonight was nothing more than a repeat performance with someone else who now felt oddly familiar as if she should know him. *His face was familiar, but how? What is going on?*

Angie and Street sat helpless as Kim's mind tripped back in time. Her breathing had become labored and whatever she was thinking about was causing her serious distress. They were both scared.

"What's happening to me?" she moaned to herself, coming out of the episode. She was unaware that she was not alone.

"You tell us, Kim," Street shot back in sudden realization. "I thought you were clean."

"I am clean," she said emphatically, now fully back in the present.

Angie gently voiced her agreement with Street. "You do act like you're tripping. Maybe somebody slipped you something. Once in a while you'll get a creep who'll do that. You know, he wants a wilder, wetter ride. I had it happen once. Now I don't take anything from anyone I don't know. I order a beer, in a bottle, open it myself, and never pick it back up once I take my eyes off of it."

"It's nothing like that," Kim said, both fear and anger showing through. "I'm probably just tired. It's been a busy week." She pulled herself to her feet and took the handbag that Street held out for her. "I'll see you around."

Not knowing what to do, Street and Angie stood helplessly by while Kim walked away then Angie turned to Street. "Now can you agree with me that she's acting strange?"

"Yeah, except she ain't acting. But, like she said, she's probably just tired. A good night's sleep and she'll be okay." Anxious to dismiss the whole episode as nothing more than fatigue, Street started back toward the bar.

"I sure hope you're right," Angie said as she watched Kim disappearing into the distance.

Within seconds, a scream shattered the quiet of the night. Jay tore

out of The Library and joined Street and Angie as they ran toward it.
What they witnessed stopped them in their tracks. Kim was flattened
up against the wall of a building, breathing hard, her face contorted in
terror.

6

Drained of energy, Kim put up an unconvincing struggle before allowing herself to be led back into the bar. Jay quickly took control of the situation. Discreetly guiding Kim into the small, cluttered back office of The Library and away from the prying eyes of the patrons, he motioned to the cot in the corner.

Angie and Street gently led Kim to the cot and coaxed her to lay down. When she weakly struggled to sit up, they pushed her back down. They didn't know what else to do. Within minutes, too exhausted to fight them, she settled down and quit struggling.

Jay pulled out his cell phone and flipped it open. Street grabbed it from his hand.

"What the hell do you think you're doing!" Jay yelled.

"You're not calling 911!" Street shouted back, holding Jay's phone behind him and out of reach.

"The hell I'm not!" Jay lunged for his phone. The two engaged in a push and shove contest. Street was no match for Jay in size, but he was quicker on his feet.

Angie sat on the cot, cradling a passive, exhausted Kim and watched Street and Jay struggle for control of the phone.

"Stop it!" Angie ordered. Her tone caused both men to stop in their tracks. Having their attention, she continued. "There's something wrong with Kim, but I don't think it's anything that we need 911 for. I read about post-traumatic stress disorder and…"

"You mean like the war vets have?" Street caught on.

"Yeah. Kim is showing all the classic signs."

"You're a hooker, not a fucking psychiatrist! Besides, she's not a vet," Jay said. "At least not that we know of," he added, reminding everyone how little they knew about each other.

"I may be a hooker but I'm not stupid. PTSD can happen after any

stressful trauma. I read that somewhere. Obviously the late Senator
Madsen figures into this somehow. We just have to figure out how."
Angie had cast her lot with Kim. Now she just had to get Jay and
Street to join her. With Jay's cynical, skeptical nature and Street's
reasoned avoidance of interfering with the status quo and other
people's affairs, the two were going to be a tough pair to sway.

"If she's involved somehow with the senator, then we definitely
need to stay out of it," Jay responded emphatically. "At the risk of
sounding like one of those paranoid conspiracy freaks, we're going to
find ourselves involved in a game we can't win, and the losers end up
dead. If we have no chance of winning, why play?"

"Much as I hate to agree with Jay," Street said, "I have to go along
with him on this one. If Kim knows something about Madsen's death
then we need to stay as far away from her and the situation as we can.
I don't claim to be a current events expert but I'd have to be deaf,
dumb, and blind to not notice all the commotion about how Madsen
was planning to run for president and how he was gonna shake things
up real good. Seems like he was gaining a whole lot of unexpected
support from people who are sick and tired of this country going to
hell in a hand basket and taking us along for the ride."

"Jesus H. Christ, Street! You sound like you're writing a fucking
editorial!" Jay snapped.

"I'm just saying that we're gonna get sucked into a whole lot of
front page news. I've spent years making sure I fly under the radar."

No one noticed that Kim was alert and listening. "They're right,
Angie," Kim said weakly, struggling to sit up. "I can't let any of you
get involved in this. Whatever this is."

Angie wasn't about to give up. "Not so fast. If one of us was
having a problem, would you bail on us?"

"Of course not." The answer came without hesitation.

"Then it's done. End of story. Who's in? Who's out?" Angie said.
She made eye contact with Jay, then shifted her penetrating gaze to
Street. "In or out?" she demanded, firmer.

"In," Street answered unconvincingly under Angie's withering
look. "But we'll probably live to regret it," he quickly added under his
breath.

"I'm in, not that it's gonna make a rat's ass of difference," Jay
conceded.

"Then it's settled." Turning back to Kim, Angie made it clear that there was no room for compromise. "Start talking, Kim. And I mean at the beginning and don't leave anything out."

Spellbound, the three listened as Kim began with the flashbacks of her brutal attack in the warehouse. Cautiously, she did her best to piece together the disjointed memories that were plaguing her the past few days.

"My god," Angie muttered with tears in her eyes.

Kim shared her suspicions about being hired to entertain two particular gentlemen in the past few days and how she feared she was responsible for their deaths. Fielding questions from Angie, Street, and Jay, Kim swore that she had no idea until she saw the paper earlier that one of them was the senator.

In her line of work, discretion was top priority. If a client wanted to keep his identity a secret it would be honored. Now, however, it seemed that the client she had so thoroughly enjoyed earlier that evening now seemed vaguely familiar, as well. But the memories that were trying to break through were being suppressed.

"Jesus H. Christ! You're a contract killer!" Jay, drawing the obvious conclusion and getting right to the point, looked seriously impressed.

"It would seem that way, but don't ask me why or how because I don't have the answers. Based on what memories I've been having, I can only say that at the time it all felt so right, so justified. Like I didn't even have a conscience about it. And now these little flashbacks, and nothing makes sense. Everything seems wrong. It's like I'm living someone else's life, not my own. I'm not even sure who I really am." Tears fell steadily down her cheeks. "Sad to say, but except for the flashbacks, I have absolutely no past recollections of any previous life. It's like every day is the first day of my life."

Hearing this Jay said, "Now it's my turn to agree with Street. If we get involved with this we probably *will* live to regret it. If we're allowed to continue to live, that is." Before getting up, he looked at each to make sure that what he was saying was sinking in. The look on their faces assured him that his statement had left its mark. "Sit tight. I'm just going to check to make sure that everyone is going about their business and not eavesdropping on ours."

Leaving them in silence to ponder their dilemma, he made his way to the door, opened it a crack, and peered into the crowded bar. Satisfied with what he saw, he rejoined the others and got right to the point.

"If what you're saying is true and your hunches are correct, and I'm not saying it isn't and they're not, but if it's true then we're all getting involved in something way over our heads. And, like I always say, you can't fight city hall." Jay looked at each one in turn. When he saw that he had their full attention, he continued.

"Street is spot on about Senator Madsen. The senator was really kicking up some dust across the country. I'll admit I was damned glad he was stirring things up but I figured it was never going to amount to anything. He was bringing a lot of attention to things that most people don't know about and obviously don't want to know about or they'd make it their business to find out. His election would have been a long shot but, if elected, he was going to bring down a lot of very powerful entities. Even if he lost, what he threatened to bring to light on the campaign trail was enough to cause serious concern among the power elite. I can't imagine any of them sitting idly by and letting that happen. I know I wouldn't."

Street uttered a long, low whistle. "Oooooweeee. Kim's a paid assassin."

"Hold everything!" Angie cut in. "You two are assuming that these flashbacks are reality."

"You're the one who was acting like a fucking psychoanalyst! Post traumatic stress syndrome and all that crap!" Jay was, once again, on a short fuse.

Kim spoke up. "There's only one sure way to find out."

"How's that?" Angie said.

"If my memory breakthroughs are reality based, then there should be a very well-built dead man either in a hotel room four blocks away or on the way to the county morgue."

No one spoke as the implication of her evening's work became obvious.

"I'm not so sure we have the skills to cope with something of this magnitude, if you get my meaning," Street spoke and all eyes were on him. He knew what they were thinking and wished he were anywhere else at the moment.

"According to you, you're the man with all the connections,"

Angie said. "So get your ass out there and see what you can find out."

"Okay, but I ain't promising anything. I sure the hell ain't Kojak, and these sure aren't the Streets of San Francisco," Street grumbled. "Besides, what's it gonna prove?"

Jay agreed. "Street has a valid point. Digging into this mess is just going to stir up something that might be better left behind. Let's say, for the sake of argument, that this is exactly what it appears to be. Maybe the best thing that Kim can do for herself is to just walk past this like it never happened and then figure out how to break away and make a new life for herself. You know, let sleeping dogs lay and if it ever reappears to bite her in the ass, she can deal with it then."

Kim started to make a point but Angie cut her off. "You guys don't get it because you weren't listening. Kim said that except for the flashbacks, she has no hint of a past life. That, for some strange reason, every day for her is a new beginning. But, she does seem to have memories of certain things. Like us, for instance. Certain other things are being blocked out but for some strange reason they're breaking through. It's hard to get on with a life when you don't know who you are and what that life is. If her flashbacks are real, they hold the key to who she is and what's happening. If we can break through that then we'll have some real answers that will help her move forward."

Kim looked at Angie with gratitude for her grasp on the situation. She knew she couldn't do this alone and was reluctant to enlist the help of her newfound friends and put them in jeopardy.

"Hold everything! We're all gettin' way ahead of ourselves. Once I find out if there's a stiff or not, then we can go from there." Street continued, "Until then, let's not jump to any conclusions. Agreed?"

"I'm pretty sure you won't come up empty-handed," Kim said, regretfully. "My recollections of getting attacked and my interactions with the two clients are becoming more frequent and vivid. Less like out of body experiences and more real."

She ran her fingers over the small bump on the bridge of her nose. "This is real. It's obviously been fixed but I have no memory of that. The attack seems to be the turning point when my life did a one-eighty. It must have been a planned attack, not random. I've been set up. But, by who?"

"Let's not forget the 'why'," Jay added. "The political implications are endless."

Street got up to leave. "I'll be in touch. But remember, I ain't promising nothing. Sometimes the street gives it up, sometimes it don't."

7

Agent Jensen's office looked like a mini law library with some very impressive titles lining the bookshelves. Some titles were job related, some were simply his personal favorites. Standard issue file cabinets were clustered together in a corner, each one locked tight. Jensen's earlier bravado had faded so he kept a nervous eye on the video monitors on his desk. Kim's unexpected behavior in the hotel room earlier had him on edge. Though he had tried to ignore it and deny the possibility that something was going wrong, it seemed to be the only logical explanation. Any further attempt to relax was useless so he picked up his cell phone.

It hadn't been easy for him to make the call and he had put it off as long as he dared. So much was at stake. Years of dreaming, of planning. Forcing himself to appear calm and in control, he spoke quietly into the phone.

"Listen up. We've got a problem. Kim appears to have had a temporary breakthrough.

"As in, she was wondering what the hell was going on!" he screamed into the phone.

"Don't tell me to calm down, god dammit!"

Pacing the floor like a caged animal, Mick was beside himself with frustration and all too eager to lash out at anyone or anything. She was his safe haven. She liked it rough and could give as good as she got.

Settling back at his desk, he opened the bottom drawer and pulled out the silver flask. Sixty seconds later he felt the warming calmness course its way through his bloodstream and into his brain where each cell responded to the relaxing warmth like dominos being knocked over, one by one.

"You're right. It's not your fault," he said, much calmer. "No, don't come over. I probably couldn't get it up right now anyway. Too upset."

Mick's eyes had temporarily strayed from the video monitors so he listened intently for the sound of approaching footsteps signaling the need to end the call. He should have played it safer by leaving the premises to make the call. Confident that no one was coming, he watched the monitors and continued talking.

"I'm not sure," he answered the inquiry. "The drug she's been given was tested over and over and the results were flawless. And don't forget that it's not just the drug that's key here, it's her personality as well. She's a mouse. She goes along with whatever she's told. The years of monitoring her past and my own working knowledge of her affirms that after her parents died she found out that she got along easier by going along with things than by fighting them."

Mick closed his eyes and sucked back another swallow of whiskey as he tried to quietly reassure himself that the plan had not gone bad. It couldn't have. Too much was at stake. Kim was the sacrificial offering being served up for a cause bigger than herself, bigger than him, even bigger than the whole damned country. He comforted himself with the fact that she had no surviving family. No one to miss her and come looking for her. He listened intently as Lacy laid out some ideas for his consideration.

"Sounds good Lacy. I knew I could count on you to come up with something." His relief was evident.

"No, she won't recognize you. You met only briefly and that was years ago. The beauty of CRP-24 is that it gives one a very selective memory based on what's programmed into the brain as memorable or not. And I, and I alone, make that determination. In a nutshell, every day's a brand new day for everything not acceptable for Kim to remember. Hence the name, Can't Remember Past, and 24 stands for the hours in each new day. And I want to assure you, my dear Lacy, that you are most definitely not acceptable for her to remember.

"No! I don't think it's a permanent breakthrough!" he screamed at her implication. "Forget what I said earlier! There must be some other explanation!"

Then, in a much calmer response to her next question, "Because a further refinement to her memory protocol allows her to remember me either as Mick Jensen, her mentor and boss or Mick, her pimp, depending on the situation. Sounds complicated but it's really very simple, which is why it works.

"Actually, Lacy, that's not a possibility," Mick responded. "We never have to worry about our demented pharmaceutical guru betraying us. After he "indoctrinated" Kim–his words, not mine–at the warehouse a few months ago, his head had the misfortune of being on the receiving end of your .38 as he got into his car.

"Because you're on a need to know basis," he answered. "You don't need to know the identity of your 'hits', you just need to get the damned job done!" Mick's answer was curt, his patience wearing thin. He liked to give orders, not explanations.

He thought about how glad he was that he had only temporarily considered Lacy for this very special mission before giving it to Kim. She had all but begged him for it, relishing the idea of sex and murder all wrapped up in one kinky, climactic encounter. But Lacy was a much tougher nut to crack. It would have been an unpredictable challenge to keep her under control. Though she had punished him by withholding her unique brand of favors from him for several days afterward, he knew that it was the right decision for the good of the project.

"Here's what I need you to do Lacy. Get out on the streets and see what you can find out, and do it sooner rather than later. Kim works a four block circuit and generally stops by a little neighborhood bar near the corner of Patton and Lehigh." As Lacy listened, Mick continued.

"If you have to use some of your special powers of persuasion, so be it." Mick was confident Lacy would understand. Sexually, she was insatiable. He could attest to that. Inventive and insatiable. On top of that, her weapons and martial arts skills were unparalleled. If she couldn't seduce the information out of someone, male or female, she had no problem resorting to a more persuasive approach.

Lacy considered both approaches wet work and found them equally satisfying. Just thinking about it gave Mick the stirrings of a hard-on that just minutes before had seemed out of the question. For a brief few seconds he thought about taking Lacy up on her offer to come up and relieve some of his tension. He then thought better of it. She no longer had security clearance.

It had been an ugly scene and everyone was on notice about her new status. Anyone caught letting her anywhere near the premises would be considered an accomplice and would suffer the same consequences. No. It would be better if their alliance remained a secret. Better for his career and definitely better for the project. Lacy was his very secret weapon and he planned to keep it that way.

On the other end of the phone, Lacy was already miles ahead of Mick. She had a plan formulating in her mind and her adrenaline was at full peak just thinking about it. She gave Mick a brief overview as she turned on the shower and stripped out of her sweater and jeans.

"Yeah, sounds good. And Lacy? Don't call with excuses. We wouldn't want that to be the last call you ever make, now would we?"

8

Street was, once again, pacing back and forth on the corner. He had nothing to sell but promises at that point. Promises for high-grade product the next evening. But he wasn't there to make a sale. He needed to make a contact that would get him the info on a possible "stiff" found at a hotel a few blocks away.

It would be better if the contact came to him. It wouldn't look as suspicious that way. If he had to jog four blocks to the hotel and then start asking questions, now that might look peculiar as anyone who knew him knew he wasn't an inquisitive guy. He liked to mind his own business and preferred it when others did the same.

In a short time the temperature had dropped a few more degrees and the dampness had him chilled to the bone. He was hoping that some info would come his way soon. And he had promised Grandma Mae that he would check on her, as he always did, before she went to bed. In the scant light of the streetlight, he strained his eyes to see the hands on his watch. It was later than he thought.

"Got a light?" A sultry female voice broke the silence of the night.

"No. Ain't you heard? Smoking's bad for you," Street answered.

She had materialized from nowhere, cigarette in hand. Street had been startled but he kept his cool. Not an easy thing to do as he checked out the finest piece he'd ever laid eyes on.

"You're not from around here," he said, thinking to himself that he sure would have noticed. "If you were from around here," he continued, "you wouldn't be so overdressed," he followed up, sarcastically.

After she pushed the cigarette back into its pack, she slipped the black beret from her head and put it in her bag.

"Better?" she asked.

"Much. Looking for something in particular?" Street asked her. It was his usual question for new prospective customers. The fact that she didn't ask him something similar told him that she might not be a street girl. *What a waste,* he thought.

"Depends. What do you have?" she asked.

"Who wants to know?"

"Lacy."

"I can see that," he answered as his eyes roamed over her very scantily lace-clad body. "But, what's your name?"

"Lacy's all you need to know," she said, moving under the streetlight to afford him a better view.

"I got nothing you need, Lacy."

Street was wary of strangers and too much talk. The two didn't mix well for someone like him. Too much talk to the wrong stranger could get you in county lock-up or dead, or county lock-up wishing you were dead.

"I'm not vice," she tried to assure him, "though I sure have my share." Lacy laughed, trying to lighten the mood. Street laughed with her as he tried to figure out her game.

He was sure he'd never seen her before. She would have been hard to forget. She had the softest curves over the most well-muscled frame he had ever seen. Her name didn't ring a bell either. And she was too high-end for the neighborhood. Nobody that looked like her needed to be hitting on him, that's for sure.

"State your business Lacy, and be specific." Street decided the tough, direct route was the way to go with this one.

Lacy did the same. Playing coy was wearing thin. It just wasn't her style. "I'm looking for a hooker named Kim."

Street was the epitome of cool and calm. "The hookers I know don't swing your way."

"For your information, I've never met a woman I couldn't seduce, but my interest in Kim is business, not pleasure."

"Kim's a real popular name on the street. You're gonna have to come up with more than that." Street feared he already knew the answer, but wanted to make sure.

"About my size, overall. In good shape but not as muscular as me. Blonde, blue-eyed, smaller breasted, but then who isn't?" she said as she ran her hands over her obviously implanted breasts. Lacy enjoyed watching people squirm.

Street found it hard to keep his eyes off her hands. "Don't know her," he said firmly, finally looking away. Street had a feeling that this stranger wasn't going to bode well for any of them, especially Kim. There was something unusually cold about her. Then, too, her showing up tonight in the midst of all of Kim's drama was not likely to be coincidental.

He wasn't sure if he should be relieved or nervous as he spotted the police cruiser making another pass. With the shift change he wasn't sure who was in the car and the newer recruits were usually strictly by the book. Just as the patrol car did a U-ey to circle back and pull up to the curb, Street turned to tell Lacy that she needed to be hightailing it out of there. She was way ahead of him. As quietly as she had come, she was gone. Only the provocative scent of her lingered on.

Maybe she is just a hooker, Street thought to himself. That would explain why she was afraid to be seen, dressed as she was. The car pulled to a stop directly in front of him and he tried to look as nonchalant as possible. The window slid down but he stood his ground, making no move to approach.

"You Street?"

"Yes sir."

"Donnelly said you're the man."

Hearing that, Street relaxed a little.

"Yep, Donnelly said you're the best dumpster diver in town."

Street relaxed a bit more. Walking over to the cruiser, he leaned in the open window. Donnelly only gave that bit of info to new recruits he felt he could trust and since Street had learned to trust Donnelly, that was good enough for him.

After a quick flurry of introductions, they got down to business.

"We're hearing that the black Mercedes has been seen cavorting with some real bad element from across state line. People who don't deal in the lightweight crap you do. Got any thoughts on that?"

"Definitely don't know nothing about that. Definitely." The emphasis was not for effect. Street had his principles. Nothing heavy. His relationship with Mercedes was bonded on that premise. No. Street definitely knew nothing about any of that. Furthermore, he didn't want to know anything.

"Well, word just came in at shift change and Branson and Donnelly thought you should know. We said we'd messenger it on over here.

We'd all hate to see you being an unwitting accomplice. If you hear anything..."

"Yeah, you'll get the word. I ain't looking for trouble." That was no lie. If Mercedes was going to even try to suck Street into something way over his head, he'd roll over on him and never give it a thought. No one was going to interfere with his life. It may not be much of a life by most people's definition, but it was his.

Just then, Street remembered the reason he was out there in the first place. It might save him several hours hanging around on the corner, or a four city-block hike on foot. "Any reports of a John Doe found in any hotels around here tonight?"

"One of the girls spill to you about it?"

Street's heart sank. *So, Kim was right.*

"No, just talk on the street and I like to be in the know. That way I can keep my eyes and ears open."

Shotgun picked up the radio and made a call to dispatch. While waiting for a call back, the three made small talk about the disappointing Lions' and Red Wings' seasons and pinned their hopes on the Tigers. When the return call came in, Shotgun took it and turned back to Street.

"Bingo, but no John Doe. Seems we got ourselves a disgruntled constituent type running around town. The body bag is the temporary home of Congressman Dunn."

"Who the hell is that?" the driver asked. Street was very curious, himself, but didn't want to look too curious.

"Don't you guys watch CNN?" Shotgun said. "Dunn had just thrown his support behind Senator Madsen as presidential candidate. When Dunn talks, people listen. He's the Merrill Lynch of politics."

"But Madsen bought it a couple of days ago," Street said.

"Exactly," Shotgun answered. "Right after that, Dunn was approached to be Madsen's replacement candidate. Same ideologies, same platform, even bigger persona. He was the party's first choice but had originally turned it down saying he wasn't sure the timing was right. Then, when Madsen turned up dead, he reconsidered. Probably figured the timing must be right or Madsen wouldn't have been a threat. Everyone thought Madsen was gaining ground, but Dunn was going to hit the ground running. If you ask me, someone sure wanted them both out of the way."

The driver laughed. "This will give the conspiracy freaks something else to blog about."

All that Street could think about was Kim being into something way over her head, way over all of their heads. His mind raced in several directions. *Now what?* he thought to himself.

"Well, now that you know, keep your ears open though it's highly unlikely that any of the hookers you know were involved with men of that caliber. I'm curious about you asking if there was a body..." As their radio interrupted with a code familiar to Street, he quickly backed away from the patrol car as they engaged lights and sirens, thankful for their diversion.

Standing alone in the cold, Street pulled the collar of his coat up tighter around his neck. He didn't like the sudden turn his life had taken. Who was Kim and what was she getting them involved in? Standing alone on the corner, he felt a chill that wasn't due to the temperature.

He wondered where Lacy had gone off to and what was up with the dead "johns". Was there a deeper connection than the obvious? Snugging the collar of his lightweight jacket up around his neck to keep the damp out, he decided to report back to the others what he had found out and then stop by to check on Grandma Mae. It was getting late and she'd be wondering where he was.

9

Street's hassling by the cops turned out to be the break Lacy needed. Her instincts were always right on, something she prided herself on. Though he kept his cool, she sensed that Street was hiding something. Why else would he seem relieved that the cops might interrupt their conversation? He should have been dismayed by that possibility.

On the street, it's always wise to keep your eyes on your surroundings but she couldn't ignore that he had, several times, glanced across the street at The Library. Lacy hoped that Street had unwittingly given her a direction to pursue. When Street walked in, he was surprised to see Lacy perched on a barstool, making chitchat with the barmaid. She seemed almost flirtatious, something that the young barmaid was definitely picking up on but wasn't sure what to do with.

"Don't let me interrupt anything," Street said, composing himself and taking the stool next to her. He wanted to know more about Lacy and thought he might never get a better opportunity.

"Nothing to interrupt, yet," Lacy said softly, winking at the barmaid. Then, turning her full attention to Street, she poured on the tough. She had tired of the cat and mouse game.

"If you know Kim, or know of her, get the word out on the street that all she needs to do is get with Mick and he'll explain the reactions she been having. Just some drug interactions. Nothing to be afraid of if she takes care of business. She'll understand everything once she talks to Mick." Lacy thought that sticking as close to the truth as possible would be best.

"Like I said, never heard of her. And besides, you sure ain't no home-visit nurse." Street answered as coolly as he could, keeping his eyes straight ahead.

Just then, Jay opened the back room door and stepped through.

Pulling the door almost closed behind him, he nervously glanced around the bar. He'd been off the floor for too long already and needed to make his presence known. It was a locals' hangout, but even some of the regulars could get out of hand with the barmaids once in a while. Jay's bulk and no-nonsense attitude provided the much-needed equilibrium.

He was surprised to see Street sitting at the counter and motioned to get his attention. After casting a curious glance at Lacy, Jay crooked his head toward the back room. The subtlety did not escape Street. While Lacy turned her attention back on the barmaid, he slid off the stool and followed Jay into the back office.

Kim was still on the cot, shaking uncontrollably. Apparently, she'd had another episode. Angie was visibly upset and wasn't even trying to hide it. Jay was at a loss for what to do as he took his seat on the cot next to Kim.

"I still say we need to call 911," Jay said. "Either she's tripping on something or she's having a breakdown. Not a good scenario either way. We can't let anything happen to her." Jay seemed genuinely concerned.

Before Angie could voice her agreement, Street surprised them with the information he had. "I got the news you can use. It's drug induced and there's a second stiff all right, just like Kim said. Another political type."

Jay cut in. "How do you know? You weren't gone that long." Then quickly asked, "Got a name?"

"Dunn."

"Jesus H. Christ!" Jay said, shocked.

Angie looked from one to the other, eyebrows raised in question.

"He's been likened to the second coming of the Lord," Jay answered the unasked question. "But again, talk is cheap. He made a lot of enemies with his straight up talk, but it's always easier to talk the talk than it is to walk the walk."

"It's the way the game's played," Street responded and then backtracked to introduce Lacy into the mix. He relayed the conversation between them but left out the unessential stuff. They weren't there to listen to his sexual fantasies. No one could believe that Kim was on drugs and wondered what Lacy's connection was.

"You mean she's in this bar?" Jay asked. "Nothing exciting ever happens here. My life is nothing more than spans of boredom interrupted by occasional bursts of monotony. Now I'm in the middle of a full-blown conspiracy!"

"She was sitting next to me," Street said, as Jay headed to the door to take a look for himself. He was confident that Lacy would still be in the same spot, sticking close to the barmaid.

Opening the door a crack, Jay peered out and found Lacy talking on her cell phone. He stood there until Lacy caught sight of the opened door and looked in his direction. They made eye contact for only a brief few seconds, and as Jay closed the door behind him he was convinced that he had never before encountered such a cold, ruthless woman.

"A real piece of work, huh?" Street noticed the unsettled look on Jay's face as Jay rejoined the group.

"I definitely wouldn't want to get on her bad side," Jay agreed.

"I've seen her from every angle and she doesn't have a bad side. But seriously, I know what you mean. Even her ass exudes attitude," Street replied before turning to Kim. "Listen up. You need to tell us everything you know about Mick and whatever drugs you're on. None of it has to make sense. We can sort it all out later."

Kim sat in silence, unsure of what to do. With every passing second Street was growing more impatient. "You ever hear the expression 'take away close'?" he asked her. Even before she could answer, he started explaining. "It means that we all put an offer on the table to help you. But, since you're hesitating to take us up on that offer, we're all getting real close to taking that offer off the table and to close the deal. You'll be on your own. No skin off our collective asses. Either start talking or we start walking." Kim still hesitated. Street got up and headed for the door. It was his version of tough love.

"Don't go. Please." Prepared for this reversal he knew would come, Street slowly turned and returned to the group. Overcome by fear and desperation, Kim started from the beginning—a beginning mainly recalled through flashbacks. In spite of what Lacy had said, Kim denied drug use. Whatever else she remembered she freely conveyed, though nothing made sense. When she finished, everyone was at a loss for words. She could see their apprehension to believe her and sat there waiting for someone to make the next move.

"Your phone," Street finally said with hand extended, palm up.

Without challenging him, Kim reached into her purse and pulled it out. He snatched it from her before she could change her mind and flipped it open, running through her list of contacts. It was a very small list. It didn't take long to find Mick's name. First name only, no last. He knew he was taking a chance, but it was the only chance they had.

"Call Mick," Street told Kim in a no nonsense tone, handing the phone back to her.

"And say what?" Jay interrupted, true to form. "Kim, here. And I want to know why you've messed with my head and turned me into a whoring political assassin?"

"Good point," Angie said. "That might scare him off."

"I'm way ahead of you," Street explained. "Lacy implied that Mick suspects something's up. Kim must've done or said something that spooked him so he put Lacy on the case to get word to Kim to contact him. Therefore, he's expecting her call. Once she makes the call, he'll probably start talking. Until he does we have nothing more to go on. Therefore, the next move is Kim's."

"Makes perfect sense," Angie finally agreed. "Go on, Kim. You have everything to gain and nothing to lose at this point. And remember, no matter what, we're on your side." Angie's sincerity was the reassurance Kim needed, though neither Street nor Jay voiced the same sentiment.

"And put it on speaker," Street ordered. "I don't want no 'he said, she said'."

10

Kim's hands were shaking as she speed-dialed Mick and engaged the speakerphone. The call was answered almost before it started ringing. Mick had certainly been anxious to get her call. Angie, Street, and Jay huddled in closer to Kim and stayed as quiet as they could, barely daring to breathe.

"Where are you?" Mick asked, in feigned conversational tone.

"I stopped at a bar to have a drink."

"Are you feeling okay?"

"Any reason I shouldn't be?" she asked.

"No. No reason I can think of."

Mick did his best to hide his edginess, but Kim was exhibiting a feistiness that he hadn't expected. Something was definitely wrong. And based on what little Lacy had found out from the barmaid, he had to agree with Lacy that Kim was in the back room of The Library and she wasn't alone.

"Sounds like you're on speaker." Mick baited her, positive that she had an audience.

"My phone's acting up. Speaker's the only way I can hear you."

Kim's truthfulness, even a partial truthfulness, about using the speakerphone surprised him. He had expected her to deny it. Maybe he was worried for nothing, after all. But what was all the secrecy in the back room about? Kim seemed to be under the thin protection of her newfound friends who were shielding her from something perceived as a threat.

Mick decided to play it safe and tell Kim just enough to satisfy her curiosity. He'd include enough truth to throw Kim and everyone else off of one track and onto another. Off of suspecting unjustifiable wrongs and onto acknowledging wrongs justified by the greater good. A ploy as old as mankind used by the power hungry to keep the ignorant, complacent masses in line. A ploy that a growing number of savvy, newly-awakened citizens were beginning to recognize for what it was—an occasional unfortunate circumstance pounced on by politicians to promote their own agendas and encroach further into regulating the lives of others. *If it will save just one person....*

Or, even worse, tragedies concocted by government agencies in order to come up with the solutions to appear savior-like. Make the problem, wait for the reaction, provide a solution. The solution always included further inroads into curbing individual freedoms.

When Mick finally spoke, he said with a sigh of resignation. "Listen carefully, Kim. I'm not going to insult you with a bunch of bullshit. I know you're having second thoughts about your assignment, but whatever misgivings you're having are strictly from the drugs you agreed to take to block your past in case you were ever caught. It was for your protection as well as the Bureau's. But for some unforeseen reason, I suspect you're having an unexpected reaction that's causing you to lose focus on the objective."

"Bureau? Objective?" Kim was confused and wanted him to get to the point, to spell it out for everyone's benefit, especially hers.

"You're the tool that will keep this country on the path to greatness." Mick had thrown out the bait and then went silent. Kim and the others exchanged surprised and outraged looks among themselves.

Mick thought about how much easier everything was before the flashbacks started. Now, if only he could word it properly with just the right amount of spin, he could get Kim back under control. And, if her friends were listening as he suspected they were, then they would be on board just long enough to let their guard down until any threat from them could be eliminated without drawing too much attention.

Street signaled Kim to respond.

"How so?" Kim finally asked, not sure she really wanted to know.

Mick had no choice but to play his hand. "Listen carefully to what I have to say Kim, and don't try to judge it or to make too much sense out of it. It's a hell of a lot to take in. Just listen and trust me. For now, I can only tell you that you're a government special agent and that you accepted an assignment to help secure the political foundation of this country. You volunteered to eliminate a few men who have, or had, the potential to undermine the American way of life by promising people things they really couldn't deliver. They were causing a lot of unrest—possibly even a civil war-type revolution, if you will. Think of the potential ramifications."

Angie, Street, and Jay could not believe what they were hearing. Kim was a government agent on a special assignment to murder politicians? Mick was not a pimp? Who was Lacy? Kim looked even more confused than she had looked earlier, and to everyone's surprise she shot back her own questions. The very questions they were asking themselves.

"Exactly what's your position in all of this, Mick?"

"I'm obviously also with the Bureau. I'm your direct supervisor. Let's leave it at that for now because it's too complicated to explain over the phone in just a few minutes."

"And Lacy?" Kim pushed on. There was no point acting ignorant of Lacy's existence.

"Let's call Lacy a free-lance operative at this time. She's no longer an official member of the Bureau. She is, however, crucial to the success of the mission."

"Are you telling me that I actually agreed to prostitute myself, with you acting as my pimp, and kill politicians on command?"

"I have your witnessed handwritten and video agreement to participate in this mission," Mick broke in. "It's in a very safe place, for everyone's protection."

Mick was lying through his teeth. "If it makes you feel a little more righteous, though, it wasn't an assignment that you readily agreed to without a lot of thought. Actually, it took a considerable amount of persuasion coupled with irrefutable proof that these men had the ability to disrupt the direction of this country."

"Why don't I remember any of this? And what if I choose to withdraw from this assignment?"

"You don't remember because the drug that you agreed to take, CRP-24, enables you to have a very selective memory. And as far as withdrawing from the assignment? So that there's absolutely no misunderstanding on your part the answer to that is, 'Not a chance'. You're in it to win it. You withdraw when I say you withdraw. The security of this country is at stake and I won't allow anyone's bleeding heart to jeopardize that." The emphasis was emphatic and not lost on Kim, or anyone else for that matter.

The gravity of the situation had really sunk in and the four sat huddled together in shocked silence.

"So, where do we go from here Mick?" Kim finally summoned the courage to ask.

"Just lay low for a day or two. The flashbacks may be bothersome but just ignore them. I'll be in contact about the identity and location of your next, and probably last, assignment and after that we'll talk about the antidote and some debriefing to re-enter your former identity. When that happens you won't remember any of this and it will be like your life never skipped a beat. You have my word that you'll suffer no repercussions. Deal?"

"Are you saying that I'm going to get away with murder?"

"It's done all the time. It's all about who you know and how well you play the game. Remember that. Hell. You'll probably get a medal," Mick laughed with confidence.

"I'll be waiting for your call." Kim couldn't wait to put an end to the call, to the lunacy.

"And Kim?" Mick cut in before she could hang up. "Remember this. The future of this country, and all Americans, is in your hands." With that said for everyone's benefit, the call ended.

"Hot damn!" Jay uttered under his breath.

Angie was at a loss for words. Street was not. "You did real good, Kim. Real good. You almost had me convinced that you were down with the plan. And as for Mick, he bought it, hook, line, and sinker."

"Going along with Mick would be the easiest thing to do," Kim said quietly, more to herself than to her companions, "but I just want my life back, whatever it might be. And I don't believe for a minute that I'm going to be assimilated back into my former identity like none of this ever happened. I know way too much. I need to get back control of my life. But even if I knew what to do I'm not sure I have the guts to do it."

Jay spoke up. "For some reason, you've been hand-picked to be the pawn in the manipulation of our government's politics. This country is in a sad state of affairs but no agency, not even a government agency, has the right to manipulate it to their own ends regardless of how they sugar-coat it as being in the best interest for America. Americans should decide what's best for Americans!" His emotional conviction was moving.

Kim was surprised by Jay's sudden outburst. "But as you always say, 'you can't fight city hall'."

"And I stand by that. You can't. You'd have to have a hell of a public backing and no one really cares what's going on behind close doors as long as their lives aren't being noticeably affected."

"But they are," Angie said. "If we're given a handpicked group to pick from at election time, which is what this boils down to, then our voices aren't really being counted or represented."

"You do have a marvelous grasp of the obvious Angie, and remember that Jay said 'noticeably affected'," Street cut in. He had a way of getting to the heart of the matter.

"The problem is that most people don't know or don't care that things are being manipulated. Sure, we do now, but we didn't know or care before today, until we found out we were personally affected by it. Then too, most changes occur, or should I say are designed to occur, so gradually that they go unnoticed by most people until someone finally catches on and speaks up about it. But by then, everybody's gotten adjusted to a new way of doing things so they don't care that there's more red tape to get their driver's license, to get on a plane, to acquire and maintain personal protection, or that the paycheck they deposited at the bank so they could pay their bills suddenly has a hold on it for days on end. Geez, you can't even access your own money till you have permission from the banksters."

"What do you know about payroll checks?" Jay asked sarcastically.

"Grandma Mae told me about it. I had to loan her some cash for a couple of days so she could pay her bills on time until her retirement money was made available to her. It was some new banking policy a while back. Don't any of you think for a minute I don't know what's going on. But let's get back to the two dead politicians and what they had in common.

"Madsen and Dunn not only saw the stranglehold being put on our liberties, they were also pointing out all of the deception going along with it. And because they were gaining popularity they had to be put down. The powers-that-be aren't about to let anyone interfere. Everyone needs to keep in mind that Mick said that he has another assignment for Kim. We need to figure out who that might be and where Mick and Lacy are."

Jay cut in, "I have to admit I'm as intrigued as the rest of you, but why should we get involved? It's not going to accomplish anything except bring a lot of heat on us, and for what? We can't fight city hall and we sure as hell can't solve the country's problems."

Angie spoke up. "It's sort of like eating an elephant—we'll have to do it one bite at a time. First, let's just concentrate on solving Kim's personal problem for right now and the rest can follow. She wants her life back, to know who she is, to stop the horrible flashbacks. But she's going to need our help. Street, can we count on you?"

"Definitely," Street agreed. "While it's true that my life ain't much, I like to think it's my own. The thought of being used as a pawn in anybody's game just pisses me off. Who knows? It could be me next. Doing something, anything, beats sitting on my ass and letting it all happen."

"Jay?" Kim asked with a look of hesitant expectation.

"Hell. Why not? It won't do any good but at least it's more excitement than I've had for a while. I'll dig around online and see who lines up politically with our two recently deceased presidential candidates. It just might give us a clue who your next 'hit' is."

Street, still intrigued with the seductively mysterious Lacy, claimed his own task. "I'll stay on Lacy's tail," *oops, Freudian slip,* "I mean trail, and see what I can turn up. Kim, you just go about your business as usual. Don't bring any attention to yourself. Mick has to think he's still in control. Angie, stay close to her. If she has any flashbacks, get as many details as possible. They could be important pieces of the puzzle."

With everyone more or less in agreement, they parted company with each wondering if they were doing the right thing. But no one had more misgivings than Kim. To vindicate her actions she longed to take Mick's word that she was acting in the best interest of the country. But she couldn't shake the feeling that she was being used for the worst kind of evil imaginable and that, either way, she would never own her own soul again. Now at the crossroad, it came down to going along with the plan or fighting it, but neither approach felt completely right. Putting blind trust in Mick was out of the question. Then again, why should she trust her newfound friends? She would have to learn to trust her own instincts, like she used to. But it was not going to be easy.

11

Alone in the back room, Kim and Angie sat in silence, lost in their own thoughts. Kim wondered what more she should reveal, and Angie wondered what she should ask. Plans were in motion to help Kim, but no one really had the big picture. No one really knew what they were getting themselves involved with, however good their intentions were. They were all just flying by the seats of their pants.

Many years on the streets had honed Angie's astute perceptions of others and she had a good feeling about Kim. She felt sure that Kim was a good person caught up in an unthinkable situation that she couldn't handle by herself. Once Angie had that good feeling about someone she always went with her gut instincts and would move heaven and earth to help them. With Jay and Street out of the way, she felt there was a possibility that she could get Kim talking about the more personal aspects of her flashbacks that she might not want to share with them.

"How about some girl talk?" Angie asked gently.

"About?"

"Up to you." Angie was not going to pressure.

"I don't know that the three of you should be involved." Kim's words were without much conviction so Angie took advantage of that fact.

"Too late for that," Angie laughed. "We're in this up to our proverbial asses."

A long uncomfortable silence ensued. Angie was the model of patience as she settled herself into a half reclining position against the wall. Her body language conveyed that she wasn't going anywhere, anytime soon.

Kim tossed around different scenarios from her flashbacks trying to make some sense of them and to see what clues she could glean from them that would give additional credence to Mick's declarations.

"A penny for your thoughts," Angie prodded gently.

Kim looked up at her for a long moment. She wasn't sure if she should trust anyone, herself included. She had always been so confident in herself when her parents were alive. They encouraged her independent thinking and praised her for it. Then in one brief instant they were gone, taking with them the cherished spirit they had fostered and nurtured. It wasn't their fault and they certainly wouldn't have wanted it that way. It was just that her parents were rare and Kim soon found out that not many couples would be happy to parent a newly-orphaned young teenager. Even fewer, someone as fiercely outspoken and self-reliant as she was.

Kim had exhausted several foster families when an elderly aunt and uncle finally came to her rescue, but by then she had learned to stifle her spirit just to get by. When she could finally be herself without fearing rejection, she had constrained herself so long that the habit was quite ingrained.

"Two heads are better than one," Angie added, hating clichés but wanting to capitalize on any weakening of Kim's resolve.

Several more minutes of interminable silence. Then Kim sighed and started speaking.

"The people that I trusted in the past have put me in a very bad spot. Maybe I have nothing to lose by trusting people I hardly know."

"Well, from where I'm sitting, that certainly is a logical conclusion." Angie settled back and closed her eyes, waiting for Kim to make the next move. It didn't take long.

"I remember being attacked," Kim spoke very quietly, as if to herself. Angie sat up slowly and leaned in toward Kim. Kim's forehead and upper lip glistened with perspiration indicating a good measure of duress from the memory.

"I was in a warehouse. A freezing-cold, dirty, abandoned warehouse. Don't ask me how I got there because I have no idea. At first he was just shoving me around. Calling me names. I was passive so I wouldn't get him angrier, but that seemed to heighten his disgust and the shoving escalated into slapping. When I didn't respond to that it made him even madder. The next thing I knew he was punching me and trying to strangle me. I tried to get away from him but I couldn't. The more terrified I was the more he enjoyed it. I screamed over and over but there was no one to hear it. He was filthy and big. He shoved a small plastic vial of bitter crystals into my mouth and told me to swallow them down. I remember gagging and trying to spit them out but my mouth was so dry that there was no spit. He laughed and said that he had an excellent chaser in his pants if I needed some help getting it down. I managed to swallow most of them, praying the whole time that someone would find me or that he would either finish me off or that the crystals would. Just when I thought he was going to leave me there to die he grabbed me by my hair and pulled me to my knees, and unzipped his pants…"

Tears were streaming down Kim's face and her hands were shaking. Angie's eyes were ready to spill the tears that were welling there.

"By that time, my mind was starting to do really crazy things. Everything I looked at was grossly distorted and bleeding the most vivid colors," Kim continued. "I remember trying to reach up to see if my nose was as broken as it looked and felt but my elbow wouldn't work. Even through the bitterness of the crystals I could taste blood. He laughed like it was all just a big joke as he tried to stuff himself into my mouth." Kim started sobbing uncontrollably and Angie put her arm around Kim and pulled her in close.

"The stench." Kim's expression said it all. "The foulness of him made me sick to my stomach. I decided my best chance for any kind of revenge was to throw up all over him, so I did. He raised his hand like he was going to hit me then stopped, saying it was going to be hard enough to explain my broken nose to the boss. He picked up the hoodie that he had ripped off of me, wiped himself off, and threw it in my face. He told me I was a two-bit whore and to never forget it."

Kim was exhausted, but relieved to finally share her ordeal.

"My God," Angie said as they both sat there sobbing. "Someone is definitely out to make you a pawn in some kind of sick plot. That whole episode must have been to indoctrinate you into a false lifestyle and identity. After hearing that, I'm more convinced than ever and even more determined to help you get to the bottom of this."

"That's how it's looking to me too. I'm not really a hooker, I'm just supposed to think I am."

"Hooker or not, none of that matters. It's just another way to make money. Beats standing in the welfare lines."

"I'm not passing judgment, Angie," Kim said between sobs that were becoming less frequent. "But we're not just talking hooker, we're talking assassin as well. One of my flashbacks jives with Mick claiming that I'm a government agent. Why would a hooker have memories of being at a shooting range, doing some pretty serious target shooting? And it was no neighborhood shooting range, either. Lots of suits around, and I was one of them. I had on a nice dressed-for-success two piece, navy blue pants and blazer. The kind of outfit a hooker wouldn't make two bucks wearing."

"Hell. You wouldn't even get picked up looking like that. That would not look like good-time clothes to any guy I know." They both laughed at the thought.

"They're the kind of clothes that are government protocol and just one more piece of evidence that Mick could be telling the truth, at least up to a point," Kim said in a more serious tone, unsure whether she should be encouraged or disgusted at the direction this was taking.

Angie wanted to be sure that she understood what she thought she was hearing. "Are you saying what I think you're saying? That you're a government employee being used as a pawn by your own employer against your own country?"

At the basest level, they both knew it was a question not requiring an answer. They sat there in silence trying to digest what appeared to be the harsh reality.

"You're being used by our government against our government," Angie repeated, incredulously.

"Someone has stolen my life to suit their own needs," Kim said. "If there's any truth at all in what Mick is telling me, and based on my flashbacks I have no reason at this point to think otherwise, then I obviously have the skills and training to at least put up one hell of a good fight to get my life back."

"I don't want to rain on your parade Kim, but this isn't just about you. It appears to be a whole lot bigger than that."

"Agreed. But I have to at least try. If I succeed, then everything else could follow. It will be like pushing over that first domino."

"And if it doesn't go as easy as you think it will?" Angie softly gave voice to the unthinkable.

"Then nothing on this earth will ever be a concern to me again." The finality of Kim's statement was sobering.

12

As soon as Street had stepped out of the back room of the bar, he ordered another beer and hung out as nonchalantly as he could. He was waiting for Lacy to leave. With Jay back on duty, the young barmaid who had been the object of Lacy's attention busied herself with the rest of the customers, a task she was thankful for. If truth be known, Lacy was making her uncomfortable. It was one thing to flirt a little for monetary gain, regardless of where the gain would come from. It was another thing to actually have to come through with unspoken promises.

There was a coldness about Lacy that made the barmaid pretty sure that "no" would not be an answer that would be tolerated by Lacy. If put in a compromising situation, youth and inexperience would not overcome age and treachery, and Lacy certainly seemed uncompromising. The barmaid did her best to avoid eye contact as Lacy moved toward the door. *Win some now, win some later,* Lacy thought. She was, after all, being paid for business, not pleasure.

Lacy stepped out onto the sidewalk and paused, making a pretense of looking both ways as if wondering what direction to take. At the same time, through the big glass window to her right, she noticed that Street was sliding off the barstool and laying some cash on the bar.

Her car was parked one block down and one block over so she started in that direction, slow enough to allow Street to follow or to be sure he wasn't. He was. She would soon know if it was a coincidence or not. Ducking into an all-night coffee shop to get a coffee-to-go that she didn't really want, she soon emerged and noticed that he was definitely following her. *What an amateur,* she laughed to herself. *I hope those skinny legs can do zero to sixty in under five seconds.*

Quietly following her at a safe distance, Street stopped short of the well-lit parking lot she had catty-cornered over to. It would figure that a classy broad like her would have the kind of ride that wouldn't be left in the street under a broken streetlight. He played a game of trying to pick out her car and had it narrowed down to three.

Knowing that she would not have her back to him for long as she got into her car, he sidestepped behind a large bush and squatted down as best he could, while keeping her in sight. The little memory games he played while selling pot on the street were going to pay off tonight. It could get boring hanging out on the streets so he amused himself by learning every make and model for every mode of transportation be it car, motorcycle, bus, or bicycle.

Those government jobs pay better than I thought, he smirked, as she opened her car door.

He recognized it as the new Lexus he had drooled over at the Detroit Auto Show. Now, if he could just get a look at the plate.

I ain't Irish but I'm sure lucky tonight, Street smiled as the parking lot lights shone on the back license plate as the car rolled forward. As his eyes did their best to focus on the letters and numbers, she suddenly gunned the engine and sped out of the lot and out of sight. She took some comfort in the fact that, even if he got her plate info, it was not registered under her name, but under that of a trust.

"Damn it!" Street muttered to himself. He was only able to get a partial plate, but he pulled out his phone and placed a call.

"Donnelly. Street, here. I know you're off duty but I need a favor. Can you call into dispatch and run a partial plate for me?

"I can't say, yet. But it could prove interesting and when I get a handle on the situation you'll be the first to know. Just something I'm checking out.

"No, I won't try to take the law into my own hands. Everyone knows I ain't the activist type.

"Awesome. RYF 5.

"That's it. That's all I got. I told you it was a partial.

"Red Lexus LFA," Street added, knowing that with a partial plate, more info would be needed.

Donnelly let out a long, low whistle indicating that he was impressed.

"No. I didn't move up into the high rent district. But now you can understand my curiosity. Why would such a fine piece of machinery be in this neighborhood to begin with. It may be nothing. Then again, you sent word that Mercedes was seen doing business across state line and to keep my ear to the ground. Not many nine-to-five jobs in these parts can pay for a four hundred thousand dollar car. Just doing what you asked, Donnelly.

"Should I get back with you, like, next week?" Street asked impatiently.

Ignoring the sarcasm, Donnelly told Street to hang tight and wait for a call back. Within minutes, Donnelly had the information.

"Chantilly Trust? What the hell kind of name is that?" Street's agitation was evident.

"What the hell's a trust? What about an address?" he asked Donnelly.

As briefly as he could, the cop explained the premise of trusts and how they're used to protect assets and identities, which in this case was certainly working. But, even if he had been able to pull up the requested information, Donnelly would have been leery of giving it to Street. He had grown fond of Street over the past several years and didn't want to see him involved in something over his head that could get him hurt, physically or legally.

"Who ever owns the trust has taken the steps for anonymity which could prove to be innocent enough, or not. I'll dig around and see what I can come up with. If I can somehow connect a name and address with the trust, me and Branson will swing by and check it out. That's the best I can do."

Seeing that he had run into a brick wall, Street acquiesced. "Good enough. Later."

Suddenly remembering Grandma Mae, he flipped open his phone and hit speed dial. "Grandma Mae, I didn't forget about you, just got hung up a little longer than I thought. I'm on my way."

Street knew that even though she hadn't made it to the phone, she would be listening for his message. After five years he still wasn't used to answering to anyone. Even as a kid on the streets, he came and went as he pleased and there was no one to care that he did until Grandma Mae found him. He liked the freedom he had and, though sometimes having someone like Grandma Mae counting on him proved to be difficult in his line of work, he had come to like the feeling of being needed. It was a good feeling that there was someone out there who would worry if he didn't come home at night.

He made it the few blocks over to her house in twenty minutes even with his stop at the convenience store. She indulged herself one night a week with a pint of French Vanilla ice cream that Street picked up at the all-night market. She always insisted on sharing it with him but he never liked French Vanilla—something he kept to himself. The weekly routine was that he scoop it out into what sounded like two bowls, and then he would sit across the table from her like always as she unknowingly enjoyed the entire pint by herself.

Taking the front porch in three easy strides, he knocked their secret knock and then let himself into her house. Announcing himself, he threw the ice cream into the nearly empty freezer. Even from across the room he saw the smile on her face.

"What'd you have for dinner, Grandma Mae?" Street bent over to hug the woman and she held onto him for a few seconds, patting him on the back. She liked the human contact.

"Meals-on-wheels is such a blessing, too bad their stew isn't," she chuckled. "In my day, I could throw together a pot of stew like nobody's business. The secret to the flavor is sherry, and the cheaper the sherry the better the flavor."

"Maybe you need to get down to that senior center and show 'em how to do it," Street told her as he helped her out of the chair. He took her hand and guided her into the kitchen. She took her seat, patiently waiting on the ice cream.

"Hard to believe I'm going to be eighty-eight come Sunday," she announced. It was more for conversation than revelation, as Street would never forget her birthday, as she had never forgotten his. "Never thought I'd live this long. Never wanted to after my husband and son died. But here I am, still ticking along sixty years later. Failing eyesight, but otherwise fine. I must have a purpose yet unfulfilled."

"At eighty-eight the purpose better reveal itself soon," Street said in a teasing way.

"I suppose it had better," she said with an odd mix of spunkiness and melancholy.

Street understood her melancholy, but it always made him sad. "Can't life be a purpose unto itself?" he asked, setting both bowls down on the table and placing the spoon in her hand.

"That would certainly simplify things for you now, wouldn't it? But I have to believe that life is the means to an end, not the end in itself. We all have the possibility to do something great in life, we just have to listen for it and answer the call."

She went silent as she slowly enjoyed the ice cream. Reaching across the table he slid the pad of paper and pencil in front of himself. Hearing it, she started her short litany of what she needed from the market, as well as some household chores that needed doing. She knew that in the morning, after breakfast, Street would do his best to accomplish everything before he left for work.

"It was surely a blessed day, the day you found me, Street."

"Actually, as I recall, it was you who found me," he playfully argued.

Five years earlier, he had jumped the little picket fence out front trying to avoid a serious thrashing from the bigger guys in the neighborhood. He wasn't fast enough. Hearing the ruckus, Grandma Mae came out the front door brandishing her cane and wailing the backsides of the three bullies.

"Let's just say we found each other and let it go at that," she said, remembering the day like it was yesterday.

"Fair enough, Grandma Mae."

"It's still chilly out there. You warm enough? You could sleep in the spare room you know." Grandma Mae wished she had a dollar for every time she said that to Street and for every time he gave her the same answer.

"Now, what would your church ladies think about that?" They would both laugh at the thought. "Actually, my little apartment is plenty warm. Also, I can keep a better eye on things from over the garage. You know, it's easier to see the big picture—the yard, the garage, the house from a distance. Besides, everyone knows I'm there so no one's gonna mess with nothing here."

"Well, I sure can't argue with that kind of logic. It's always easier to see what you're not standing in the middle of."

Announcing that she was tired, Street offered to help Grandma Mae to her room. As usual, she declined. She knew her way around her little house and, with a little caution, managed by herself quite nicely. He would never intrude on her independence, nor would she have allowed it.

After a hug, Street took a few minutes to tidy up and make sure the house was secure. He lingered at her bedroom door just long enough to make sure she was sleeping. He paused there longer than normal and was overcome by a sense of sadness as he watched her shallow, but steady, breathing. At eighty-eight years old, how much longer could he expect to have her with him? After what he had been privy to earlier that evening, once she had passed on, would he ever be able to place his trust in another person ever again?

The chill in the air had found its way into her tiny bedroom, so Street walked quietly to the end of her bed and opened up the spare afghan that lay there more for fashion than function. Having settled it over her, he picked up the list from the kitchen table and locked up behind himself as he stepped onto the small back porch.

His eyes strained to adjust to the dimness between the porch and the garage. *Add brighter porch lights to the list,* he thought. When his eyes had adjusted to the diminished light, he let them roam around the perimeter of the property. He must just be unnerved from the day's events. What he thought was his eyes adjusting to the darkness and playing tricks on him couldn't possibly be a shadow stealthily moving around the corner of the yard. No. There had to be a logical explanation. There always was.

Again, he thought he caught something out of the corner of his eye. He berated himself for getting spooked so easily. It was probably just a shadow cast by some cloud cover moving across the moon. He forced himself to steady his breathing while listening intently for any sounds coming from that direction. He briefly considered going back into the house but decided against giving into his uneasiness.

Satisfied that he was alone, Street quickly closed the gap between the house and garage. He made it up the stairs to his small apartment. Once there, he inserted the key, turned it, and opened the door in one smooth motion. Inside, he made no move to turn on the lights. He wanted to be as discreet as possible. Instead, he walked around the studio-type apartment, window to window, and cautiously peered out. His eyes followed the fence line and then focused on the back of the house. No movement. Everything checked out okay. He noticed that he was barely breathing. *Jeez. What the hell's wrong with me?* he thought. *I'm acting afraid of my own shadow. And no one even knows I exist, let alone that I have a clue as to what's up with Kim. Well, no one except Lacy,* he reasoned, suddenly feeling worse for the thought. *Lacy,* he thought, *now that's one stone-cold bitch.*

13

In spite of the security guard downstairs, Kim had double-checked the locks on the door and windows of her apartment when she had arrived back home earlier. She put on some comfortable clothes and rummaged in the fridge for something to eat and then carried a plate of food over to the sofa and sat down. She half-heartedly ate her sandwich while she browsed through a magazine, trying to focus on anything other than what had been occupying the past few hours.

The phone startled her back to reality. Maybe it was Mick calling to set up her next assignment. She let it ring and ring. She had enough to think about. All went silent and she waited for the voicemail. Nothing. The ringing started again and her curiosity got the best of her. She reached for the phone, but then hesitated. It wasn't Mick after all. The caller ID indicated it was Rod. Her hands were trembling. Now alone, her earlier bravado had waned considerably. She bordered on being disgusted with herself.

Through an act of sheer willpower she forced herself to pick up the phone, unsure whether she should be happy or sad. She and Rod Windthorpe had definitely connected and it was the kind of connection that one hopes for but rarely finds.

For some unexplainable reason the selective memory Mick had programmed her with didn't seem to apply to Rod. This happy realization could be used to her benefit but, if used for her benefit, could it be to Rod's detriment? Decision time. Maybe she should just eliminate all contact with Rod. It would be unfair to knowingly put him in harm's way.

Finally, "Hi there."

"Hey there, yourself. I'm going to be in town on some business tomorrow and was hoping we could get together for dinner."

Kim clutched the phone tightly, wondering what to do. His voice was so confident, so sure. How could she involve him in a situation there was no future in? They had met by happenstance at a coffee shop one morning when he was in town for a business meeting. He shared some information about himself and she downplayed her career as nothing more than a customer service rep for a chain of businesses. She wondered what would happen if he ever found out that she was not who he thought she was. That she was someone inherently evil and instrumental in the deaths of two men, maybe more. Maybe Dunn and Madsen were just the tip of the iceberg. Kim shuddered at the thought.

"An early lunch would actually be better for me, if that's okay," she finally responded. She had no idea when Mick would call but knew that when he did the plan would involve an evening assignment.

"Perfectly okay. I'll call you when I land and we'll figure it out from there. If you're sure you're up to it," he added. "You seem a little off."

"I'm fine, just a long day. We'll talk tomorrow."

Kim tried to sound like everything was alright, but that's precisely what was bothering him. She was trying too hard. He suspected Kim was hiding something. He had built his fortune on hunches and he was certain that she had a story to tell.

Kim settled back on the couch with a feeling of comfort from knowing that she would see Rod tomorrow. She picked up the remote, turned on the TV, and soon found herself staring at side-by-side pictures of the two dead politicians who seemed to be staring accusingly back at her. She nervously fumbled for the "off" button and cut off the reporter in mid sentence. She'd had enough reality for one day. She slipped into bed and tried to sleep, but it was useless.

Kim spent the night wrestling with a collage of disturbing scenarios interrupting her restless sleep and woke up feeling as if she hadn't slept at all. Reaching over to the nightstand, she picked up her phone to check for messages. None. She noticed that it was later than she thought and was surprised that she hadn't heard from anyone, especially Mick.

Then she remembered that Rod would be coming into town in a few hours. That motivated her to crawl out from under the covers. The toss-and-turn night had really taken its toll. Dull skin, puffy eyes, and hair going in ten directions greeted her in the mirror. She had her work cut out for her so she quickly put on a pot of coffee.

The intense grooming session paid off and in short order she was ready for anything. With time on her hands, she sat back with a fresh cup of coffee and forced herself to rethink her dilemma.

She was aware that her thoughts and memories were now becoming clearer, as if she was slowly coming out of her drugged brain-fog. But, try as she might, she could not stretch her mind backward far enough to see with absolute certainty where the beginning of her mess started. No matter how she looked at it, the warehouse attack seemed to be the rude and brutal indoctrination into her new identity, but she knew it had to have begun prior to that. At some point in time, Kim had to have given her spoken or unspoken consent to the mess her life had become.

Her brief flashback of herself at the target range gave some measure of credibility to Mick's implication that she was a government agent, but Kim was unwilling to buy into the idea that she willingly signed on for this assignment. She wasn't about to just take his word for it. She couldn't imagine that she would ever have agreed to be brutalized in such a manner, or that it would have been necessary to temporarily become someone else in order to act in the best interest of the country if the cause was truly just. And regardless of how noble the cause as explained by Mick, murdering people in cold blood was not setting well with Kim. Somehow, she had to find out the truth for herself.

The ringing of the phone broke into her thoughts. Seeing it was Rod, she was relieved and answered quickly. Even her most upbeat tone of voice didn't fool him and he could tell that she was still preoccupied. He decided to not press the issue at this point, opting instead to wait until they were together. If she wanted to end their relationship then he would rather postpone the inevitable hoping that with a face to face encounter he'd be able to change her mind. He had flown his private plane and was waiting at the small airfield on the outskirts of town.

Traffic was light, so she made the drive in twenty minutes. She slid over to the passenger seat as he came toward her, preferring that he do the driving. Rod slid in behind the wheel and was as amazed as always by her very plain, simple, unadorned beauty. She was the perfect example of the "less is more" axiom. But today there was a sadness in her eyes that was unmistakable. He leaned toward her and gave her a quick kiss.

"Where would you like to go for lunch?" he asked, choosing to temporarily ignore her obvious uneasiness.

"Someplace quiet," Kim answered, then unexpectedly, "I really need to talk to you about something."

"Am I getting my walking papers?" he teased.

"You may want them after hearing what I have to say."

Whatever was bothering her would soon be revealed. He suggested take-out from Panda Express and the solitude and privacy of a small, local park. Getting her nod of approval, he put the car in reverse and started for the highway.

14

Her usual playfulness was subdued as they made their way through lunch. Almost mindlessly she reached for a fortune cookie and broke it open, more for something to do than any desire to read the fortune inside or to eat the cookie.

"You don't actually believe in those things, do you?" Rod asked, hoping to open the door for the more serious conversation she had alluded to earlier.

"Why not? This little slip of paper probably holds more insight into my future than I have at the moment. Too bad they can't give a glimpse of the past."

Rod reached across the table and held her hand tightly between his own. Looking into her eyes he could see the pain. He would do anything to see it replaced with the lightheartedness he had seen over the past couple of months.

"You're probably wondering why I've called this meeting," Kim finally attempted a clumsy start.

Now with a deadly serious tone, Rod responded. "There's nothing you could tell me that would change the way I feel about you, Kim."

"Nothing?" she asked.

"Nothing," he said with finality. "You're obviously struggling with something, but why go it alone? You'll feel better when you get it off your chest."

"Wow. Where did you say you earned your psychology degree?"

"From the College of Hard Knocks."

Kim pulled her hand away and pushed the windblown hair from her face. Leaning forward, she took his hand. "Even though you're not a local, you may have read or heard about the two politicians that were found dead here over the past week."

"Who hasn't? That kind of news is of national interest," he replied, surprised that such events would impact her in anything more than a casual way. "Seems they were caught in some compromising situations…" Rod stopped short of finishing the sentence as it dawned on him that Kim might somehow be involved.

"Talk to me, Kim," he said softly. "Like I said earlier, nothing can change my feelings about you. And fortune cookies don't hold the answers to your future. You do."

"Right now I'm more interested in my past. Without that, I have no future."

"The past is just that, the past, over and done with."

"Great philosophy from someone who has a past that he can actually look back on. My past is coming through in sketchy little unpleasant flashbacks that all lead to the same conclusion."

Rod was intrigued with the unexpected direction the conversation had taken. Intrigued and confused. "Which is?"

"I don't know who I am, I'm definitely not who I'm supposed to think I am, and worst of all, it seems that I'm responsible for the deaths of the two presidential candidates." Kim had blurted this out so fast that it was almost as if she was afraid that if she hesitated she would never say it.

"And you think this because?" The inflection in Rod's voice was clear that he was waiting for some supporting evidence. She didn't make him wait long. Kim poured her heart and soul out to Rod. She left nothing out, from her brutal assault to her sexual encounters with the two dead men and then her suspicions that she was a government agent.

Rod sat across from her, incredulous at what he was hearing, yet believing her nonetheless.

He had been so engrossed in her story that he had become completely unaware of their surroundings for a few minutes. He was surprised at himself as he always made it a point to be aware of everything going on around him. He quickly scanned the small park. The elderly man who'd been walking the dog by the pond when they first sat down was nowhere to be seen. Except for a car that had somehow managed to drive in unnoticed and park next to Kim's, the parking lot was empty. His eyes roamed over the park once again. He saw no one.

"Looking for someone?" Kim asked.

"Yes. I don't see anyone in the park, yet that car belongs to somebody, a very wealthy somebody."

Kim followed his gaze. "Well, you certainly do have a marvelous grasp of the obvious on both counts."

Her phone began vibrating on the table and she reached for it as Rod continued to look around, bewildered and somewhat unsettled. She recognized the number as Street's and excused herself as she answered.

Kim's face turned ashen as she listened to what Street was saying. Even as she heard the words, her mind had difficulty comprehending the meaning. The food she had eaten earlier threatened to reappear as Street gave her the details as he had understood them from Angie.

Apparently, Angie had not been able to get through to Jay on his cell phone. Hoping that he was an early riser, Angie decided to go to the bar to find out if he had been able to get online, as he had promised, to find any clue as to who Kim's next assignment could possibly be—who would be most politically aligned philosophically with Dunn and Madsen. With everyone understanding the urgency of the situation, she was sure that Jay would have wasted no time in doing some research.

According to Street, when Angie arrived at The Library, the front door stood slightly ajar. Odd. Angie had a fleeting sense of dread. Ignoring her instinct, she pressed on and pushed the door open wide enough to slip through.

Greeting her was silence. Dead silence. She thought about turning back and calling the cops but then scolded herself for letting her imagination get the best of her. The daybreak sunlight was scant as it shone across the plank flooring of open expanse from the front door to the bar.

In the scant rays of sunlight the broken glass shards lit up like crystals. Looking around, tables and chairs were overturned, and glasses and bottles were strewn everywhere. Someone had put up one hell of a struggle. Angie stood frozen to the spot. Jay must have been robbed.

The low, guttural moan brought her back on task. It was coming from behind the bar. She moved quickly, but cautiously, toward the barely human sound expecting to find Jay, but nothing could have prepared her for the scene that confronted her.

The young barmaid was naked and spread out on the floor like a battered rag doll. All three major orifices were bruised and bloody. The variety of bottles strewn around her left no doubt as to what the assaults were perpetrated with. Angie called 911 as quickly as she could and knelt beside the girl, who by some miracle was still alive. She fought back her fear and the waves of nausea as she held the girl's hand tightly, assuring her that help was on the way while she listened intently for any sounds that would mean they weren't alone. She took off her coat and started to spread it over the girl and that's when she saw the bloody, jagged edges of a longneck beer bottle protruding from the girl's vagina. She turned aside and gave way to the nausea.

Angie wondered where Jay was. She knew that he would never have allowed this to happen. Not if he was alive. The barmaid was weak and barely conscious, but Angie knew that her best chance to get some information would be lost if she didn't act quickly. She gently and compassionately pressed the girl for some answers.

"I told her 'No'" was all the girl kept saying, weakly and between sobs. It didn't make sense to Angie until Street filled her in on Lacy's attentive behavior toward the girl and his suspicions that Lacy was involved.

"And Jay?" Kim was almost afraid to ask.

Street hesitated briefly. "Unfortunately, he didn't fare as well as Marie."

According to the police and their initial reconstruction of the crime scene, Jay had went out the back door to take the trash to the dumpster while Marie was restocking, but he didn't get far. He had been ambushed.

The police didn't allow Angie into the alley, even though she offered to make the identification. They told her that even his own mother would not be able to identify him. It looked as if someone had used his head for a prolonged martial arts practice session. Even identification through dental records would be iffy. That determination would be made once enough teeth could be found to identify. Of course DNA had come a long way…

Rod was still intently scanning the park, trying to find the owner of the car. Even though he was picking up bits and pieces of the one-sided phone conversation he had no idea what Kim was dealing with. As curious as he was about that, he was more curious about the parked car. Just as he had decided to walk toward the car to see if anyone was in it, Kim began crying. He sat next to her and pull her close.

"Lacy?" Kim asked Street, finding it hard to believe that a woman could be so vicious.

"You two haven't met but, believe me, she's definitely got the coldness and the muscle for it," Street replied, remembering the soft curves over her well-muscled, Amazonian frame. "And Angie said that the police noticed that the trail of fading, bloody shoe prints leading from the alley, through the back room, and into the bar looked like a female's stiletto-type shoes. Marie implied that she was attacked by a woman and I did notice that Lacy had on black thigh-high boots with stiletto heels and very pointed toes."

He was disgusted with himself for even thinking that he had found those boots, paired up with black lace, to be highly erotic just last evening. With Lacy wearing them, they had become the murderous weapons of Jay's brutal destruction.

"But, what's the motive?" Kim choked on the words.

Street was quietly serious as he pondered some possibilities. "We already know that her and Mick are in cahoots. My best guess would be that she somehow figured out that you were the center of attention when we were all together in the back room and was trying to get out of Jay what he knew about your situation, which means that I'm also a target."

A cold chill went down his spine as he thought about the uneasiness he had felt the night before when he left Grandma Mae's house. Maybe he had not been alone after all. But, earlier, he had watched Lacy drive out of the parking lot and into the night, unaware that he was even there. He then replayed the scenario over and over again in his mind and fear and self-loathing set in.

He had been so sure he had not been noticed as she had driven off that it never occurred to him that he was grossly underestimating her. Someone with her training could have easily spotted that she was being tailed by an amateur and then doubled back. She would then be the pursuer instead of the pursued. She probably noticed him even as she was getting her coffee. Hell, she probably laughed to herself as she waited in front of the bar while he put his money on the counter so he could tail her. Street felt even sicker than he already was. He silently cursed himself. If Street's hunch was right, there was a good possibility that Lacy now knew where he lived, which also put Grandma Mae in harms' way.

"Do you think Jay told her what she wanted to know?" Kim felt selfish even asking it.

"It really don't matter either way. Jay would've only confirmed what she already suspected and to people like this, just the thought of looking over their shoulders all the time will make them take drastic measures. Jay was a dead man either way." He didn't share his thoughts that he and Kim and Angie were probably next on the list.

"But why the barmaid?"

"For the hell of it." Street's tone was suddenly sharper and filled with anger. "I'm no criminal profiler, but I think Lacy looked at Marie as a sporting event or reward after she did Jay, and when her advances were met with resistance she retaliated by hurting the girl with phallus-type instruments. Logically, there's no other explanation as Marie had no information for Lacy and Lacy had to know that."

"Now what?" Kim asked, leaning against Rod while he scanned the park again. She was at a loss for what to do next. Her earlier resolve had faded with the latest news and the guilt she was feeling that Jay and Marie had paid such a horrible price because of her.

"We got no choice but to step up our game," Street said.

Kim wasn't sure she was hearing right. "Step up our game?" she repeated. "These people are playing for keeps, Street. Do you want to get us all killed?"

"Hell no! But the best defense is offense. If you think for one second that this is all just gonna go away if we pretend like it never happened, think again. We're obviously onto something big and they know we know. They're gonna have to get rid of anyone who might be a threat. We'll never be safe. No one we know will ever be safe. Our lives, as we knew them, are over."

Kim looked at Rod, sorry he was now involved. His eyes were still roaming over the park, searching for the driver of the mystery car. How was she going to explain the new turn of events to him? How much could he be expected to understand?

Kim knew that Street was right. She was a pawn in a very deadly game. She did not own her own life. Now the game had extended to others with no end in sight, and whoever was in control was not going to give up and go away until all witnesses were eliminated and they got what they wanted. There really was no choice to be made other than to get highly proactive on their own behalf.

With new resolve, Kim asked, "What's the next step?"

"First, I'm gonna move Grandma Mae in with one of her friends over on the next block, just to play it safe. Then, I'm gonna pick up where Jay left off and do some online investigating of who's who in the world of politics. We need to have an idea of who your next target might be before Mick calls you with the assignment on his typically short notice. If we can somehow get in contact with a possible target ahead of time, we can figure out how to fuck up the plan before you actually have to do the deed because at that point you either do the deed, or you're dead."

"I'm dead either way."

"We all might be, but it's about buying ourselves enough time to maybe figure our way out of this mush-fuck."

"What about Angie?" Kim asked. "She's not safe right now, either."

"When Lacy approached me on the street corner and asked me if I knew you, she followed her instincts that I was hiding your whereabouts at The Library. It's no coincidence that she walked over and hung out there. My bad. She must have caught me all nervous and glancing over to the bar hoping you didn't walk out while she was with me. Later, she must have seen Jay motion me into the back room." Street paused, then went on. "She has a description of you but she never actually saw Angie." He let that sink in a minute before continuing. "As far as we know, Lacy has no idea that Angie even exists."

Kim quickly read between the lines and understood the implications. Not only was Angie in no immediate danger, but Angie and Lacy could be face to face and, armed with a description of Lacy, only Angie would be the wiser.

"I think I know where you're going with this, Street, but I'm not risking Angie's life in a face-to-face encounter with that bitch. It's bad enough as it is. Besides, my memory seems to be improving. Maybe given enough time, my mind will produce the answers we need."

"First of all, time ain't on our side. Things are moving way too fast and drug reactions are unpredictable. As far as Angie goes, it's too late. That is one stubborn girl. She's not going to be counted out because she knows that to be safe she would have to walk away from us like we never existed, but even then there's no guarantee that Mick and Lacy would never make the connection between all of us. And, Angie happens to like her life like it is. Was. Hell, we all did, but those days are gone. I know the girl and she'd never agree to live the rest of her life looking over her shoulder. End of story. Let me finish Jay's job to dig around online for your next "hit" and I'll let you know what I come up with. Besides, I got a plan to formulate. Call me the minute you hear from Mick, or if you remember something useful."

As Kim put her phone down prepared to update Rod on the turn of events, she noticed that something had caught his attention. She followed his gaze to the small bright reflection moving slowly along the top edge of the partially opened, tinted rear window of the mystery car.

"That's odd," he said, almost to himself. Then, with sudden clarity of understanding, he flung Kim to the ground as the small bright reflection exploded in a burst of gunpowder. Rod could feel the draught of air as the bullet whizzed by where Kim's head was, just seconds ago. He dove to the ground between Kim and the parking lot, shielding her with his body.

They both tensed, bracing for the impact of the next round. Instead, they heard the car's engine start and the tires screech. Judging by the Doppler effect, Rod knew the car was racing away from them. He rolled over quickly to catch a glimpse of the driver but all he could see was a small, red blur as it turned out of the park and onto the main road. In seconds it had disappeared, becoming an anonymous part of the busy highway. Kim and Rod held each other tightly.

"Unlikely that this was random and I sure wasn't the target. This has something to do with that phone call you just got. Let me help you," Rod said.

"I don't know that you can. I don't know that anyone can. I only know that I will have no life, and nothing to offer anyone in the future, if I don't unravel the past and free myself from this nightmare. The others, well, they're already involved and there's no rewinding any of that. But you're not, and that's the way it's going to stay."

"That's not exactly true. This shooting incident involves me. I could have been killed and now they know you have someone else in your life. But I have a lot of contacts, not to mention money. There must be something I can do."

"Assuming you're faceless and nameless to the shooter, maybe we can keep you that way. You can do me the most good by going home. I couldn't deal with you getting hurt, or worse. I promise I'll call you if there's anything you can do from your end and I'll most certainly call you when I'm free."

In spite of his insistence on knowing what was going on and what the call was about, she stuck to her guns. He finally relented.

He slid his own phone across to her. "Use this to call me. No one knows who I am so the phone records can't be accessed to trace the calls. These people are obviously highly connected and they'll stop at nothing. I can do the most to help you and your friends from behind the scenes if they don't know I exist. I'll just pick up another phone this afternoon and text the number to you on my old phone. Just promise me that you'll stay in contact."

"I promise."

Kim could find nothing to argue about in Rod's plan so they drove in silence to the small airport while staying vigilant of everything around them. Not a word passed between them as they held each other briefly, and then parted company. Neither knew what to say or if they would ever see each other again.

15

Mick slowly wheeled his car onto the short stretch of dirt road while making frequent checks in his rear view mirror. Up ahead, he could see the old two-lane covered bridge. Though it had been boarded up after the new highway and bridge had been completed a decade earlier, those who really wanted privacy always found a way in. He would have preferred to meet Lacy under cover of dark, but she insisted they meet now.

He pulled up cautiously behind her empty car and parked, wondering where she was. Not having her in plain sight was unsettling for Mick. He always found the covered bridge to be unnerving after dark, but daytime wasn't setting much better with him. You never knew who you might meet there and the only way out was the way you came in.

Young lovers were always a safe and welcomed sight, though rare, as the bridge had become a haven for unsavory activity. The road in and out was such a pot-holed mess that even the shift cops who were supposed to patrol it generally didn't, though claimed they did.

Only after the occasional body was found there were the patrols to the bridge increased, and then only until the public outcry died down, which didn't take long. The general public had a short memory for distasteful inconveniences. In general, John Q and Jane Public did not want to face reality.

Mick made a mental note to suggest to the city council that the entrance to the old road be blocked permanently for the safety of the citizens who never thought of suggesting it themselves. It had been ingrained in the public's mind that things like this should be left to others who would surely have their best interest at heart. Mick smiled at that comforting thought.

Lacy opened the passenger door and quickly slid in beside him.

Mick was startled, but didn't show it. He berated himself for his unawareness of his surroundings. It was that type of unawareness that had caused the quick end of the pharmaceutical guru's life. Had the chemist been more aware, he may have had a fighting chance against Lacy for a precious, measured short time more.

Lacy looked seductive in black lace and stiletto boots and Mick felt a fast growing need to relieve his sexual tension. "A little overdressed for before five o'clock," he commented, assuming she had dressed with him in mind.

"Actually, I'm still dressed from last night's business."

She wasn't quite sure how she was going to break the news of last night's events to Mick, and all of the recent activity had her excited and looking for an outlet. As she situated herself in the front seat in the most suggestive way, she could see that she had Mick's full attention. Hiking up her short skirt even higher, she reached over to unbuckle Mick's belt and then saw that he had already taken care of that, and his zipper.

"I like it better when you make me beg for it," she said, as she brought up one leg to slowly peel off the thigh-high leather of her right boot. The crimson stains splattered all over her boots glared boldly at Mick, who recognized immediately what they were. He recoiled instantly, more from anger than revulsion.

"What the fuck have you done!" he screamed.

"I did what you told me!" she screamed back.

"Bullfuckingshit! I never told you to hurt her!"

"I never touched your precious whoring 'hit' bitch!"

Hearing this, Mick calmed down considerably. Kim had not been hurt. But someone had been, and now everyone would be on the alert.

"You fucking cunt!" he screamed again at this realization.

He lunged toward Lacy who had let her guard down slightly, but only for an instant. Lacy knew she needed to get him out of the car and into the open. Her martial arts skills were second to none but could not be deployed in such small confines. Mick knew this as well and shot the heel of his right shoe up and out as she reached for the door handle. She screamed in pain as the heel made contact with her hand but she continued grasping the handle. He shoved the heel of his shoe harder against her hand and began grinding it in a strong semi-circular motion. She raised her left leg, poised to use the blood-stained stiletto heel on Mick to her best advantage, and whether face or crotch made no difference to her.

"Cops," she said, glancing out the back window. She watched the approaching cruiser weaving its way slowly to the left and right of the most vicious potholes. She lowered her leg and Mick withdrew slightly.

"Must be rookies," she said, more to herself than to Mick. "The regulars never patrol here, they just say they do. They won't know what hit 'em." The excited gleam in Lacy's eyes was unmistakable as she started straightening herself up, ignoring the damage to the back of her hand.

Mick, however, was thinking more logically. He pulled Lacy toward himself, half surprised that she didn't put up a fight. She followed his lead so that by the time the cruiser had pulled up behind them they looked like any other amorous couple in search of some afternoon delight. Hopefully, the cops would buy their act and move on. If Lacy had to step out of the car, her bloodstained boots would be hard for even a rookie to miss.

Mick discreetly loosened his shirt even more and then fumbled out of the car, feigning embarrassment. One cop approached Mick while the other ran the computerized check on the plate, all the while watching everyone closely. Ignoring orders from the cop that he get back in the car while they ran the plate, Mick stood there and pleaded his case that they were just getting some kicks behind their spouses's backs. Immoral maybe, but not really illegal, he pleaded.

The two cops were unyielding so Mick had no choice but to pull out the heavy artillery. "Say, isn't your boss Kevin Cavanaugh?" he asked. "Kevin and I go way back. Went to the academy together. I'm godfather to his only child, Adrienne. Brunette, green eyes, twenty years old, just got engaged to Dan Hewitt, son of District Attorney Marsha Hewitt. I'm sure if we can get him on the phone he'll straighten this whole mess out. Kevin can be real rough but I'm pretty sure I can get him to see that you were just doing your job." After a calculated pause, he continued. "I mean, it's not like you two were down here hoping to score some…"

Bingo. Mick had hit a nerve. The driver put on an air of bravado as he told Mick to get his nuts off and move on. Mick watched the cops back up and turn around and then cautiously drive off down the pitted road before he got back into his car.

"Nice bluff," Lacy spoke up.

"No bluff. All true. It's always good to have friends in high places."

"I mean the part about them looking to score," she said.

"I'm told that I'd have a better than fifty/fifty chance to hit a home run with that line. Even if the cops aren't using or dealing the thought of even being suspected makes them nervous."

"Where were we?" she said, totally sexed up and sliding toward him.

"My heel was grinding your hand to pulp, and you were trying to decide whether that stiletto would look better lodged between my eyes or my balls."

No longer in the mood, Mick roughly pushed her away. As she raised her left hand to slap his face, he grabbed her wrist and put on enough pressure to snap it in two, but then stopped short.

"Now that I have your undivided attention," Mick said, "tell me everything that happened since the last time I talked to you, and I mean everything. Don't leave anything out."

As she recounted the events, Lacy told him about Marie but downplayed it. She knew that he would hear it on the news, anyways, so disclosing it was a must, but the brutality of it could be passed off as media sensationalism. Even if he got really nosy and made a contact with the trauma center, he would never be able to get any information. Lacy was confidant that the government-issued HIPPA regulation would not only protect Marie, the victim, but in this case herself, the perpetrator, as well. *What a great system*, she thought.

Mick knew her tastes were not mainstream and not only condoned her unusual appetites, but generally helped to whet them. But she also knew that Mick had his boundaries of acceptable behavior, and what she did to Marie would be judged harshly by him, and punished severely.

Mick felt unsteady. Lacy was a loose cannon. It had been made very clear from the start—no collateral damage. "So," Mick went on, "the bottom line is that all of that energy expended only to find out nothing of any value. Do you really think I care where that fucking little street hustler lives, and with whom?"

"My mission was to find out if Kim is on to us, to the plan…"

"What don't you get?" Mick asked with deliberate coldness. "I called you specifically after I talked to Kim while she was at the bar. I told you that I had to give up some info to her. I told you she had me on speaker and that I played well to the audience. Just enough truth to believe, just enough lies to deceive. And all with the National Anthem playing softly in the background. At that point you were merely supposed to get rid of the useless bar owner, manager, whatever the hell he was, as planned. With everyone thinking that Jay was a warning, it would serve as a scare tactic for the rest of them to keep them in line. But, of course, that wasn't enough action for you."

"Sarcasm certainly becomes you, Mick, but you're relying too heavily on the efficacy of CRP-24 and on Kim telling the truth. She's already demonstrating an unexpected chemical breakdown of the compound. She may suspect more than she's letting on and the ones who would know would be the ones who hang with her. I turned back on Street and followed him because he may know something useful and I need to be able to put my finger on him, or someone he cares about, for leverage. And, there may be someone else who may know."

That had Mick's attention. Lacy told him about staking out Kim's apartment after she had doubled back on Street to see where he lived. She'd watched Kim's place for a couple of hours thinking Kim might be spooked enough to hightail it out of town. When she was confident that wasn't the case, she went back to The Library at about two-fifteen a.m. as planned.

Standing in the alley, she had watched the bar manager-owner boot up the computer through the security-barred window of the back room, but before he could do anything more the barmaid, Marie, was bringing in bag after bag of trash and setting it by the back door.

He and Marie exchanged a couple of brief comments and then he started hauling out the trash. As planned, the element of surprise was in Lacy's favor. Without one question asked or one answer given, she struck the first blow. It was over in minutes. Lacy was anxious to get inside and see if Marie had had a change of heart but, of course, she didn't admit that to Mick, preferring instead to let on that Marie had seen her and could identify her.

Afterwards, pumped up with adrenalin, Lacy drove the few blocks back to Kim's and waited patiently for Kim to make her next move. Hours later, Lacy followed her to the airport and then the park. She left out the part about her near miss of Kim's head. Mick would never buy the fact that Lacy's real target was Rod and that it would have served two purposes. One, to put even more fear into Kim and two, to reduce the number of potential witnesses to what was going on.

"All work and no play. You must be tired," Mick said, feigning sympathy. "The guy was probably a 'john'," he added.

"Definitely not." Lacy was adamant. "This one's special. Any woman could pick up on that."

"That certainly disqualifies you," he said.

"I'm in no mood to engage in a battle of wits with an unarmed man," Lacy said, deftly fielding the intended insult. "Anything new I should know about?" she suddenly asked.

"Only that the most well-known revolutionary conservative of our time has resurfaced and stupidly announced a press conference. Insiders say that he's going to announce his bid for a White House run. I was hoping that he would be too afraid to roll out his political platform in public right now and that, in time, the current growing unrest in this country would fade to black. But, unfortunately, he's moving forward."

"Isn't it possible that the recent deaths are just fueling the flames of the grassroots revolution? Even though the deaths look innocent enough, two in a week look suspicious. A third will cinch it in most peoples' minds and probably gain a lot of converts to the cause of the martyrs."

"Enough! A third could effectively let people know that there's a force greater than themselves at work here! That, in itself, will make most of them turn away from their precious cause. The reality of the unknown will be too frightening for them to face."

"What if you're underestimating their numbers and their resolve? Then what?"

"Simple. Then we put Plan B into effect."

"Plan B?"

"As planned, everyone's come to rely heavily on their government to take care of them—to spoon-feed them. Anyone who relies on the government for any kind of assistance which, by design, is most everyone nowadays, will fear things being taken away in retaliation. 'How will we survive?' they'll cry. 'What will we do? Who will take care of me when I'm sick?' When push comes to shove they'll be too afraid to speak up and fight back for fear of what they might lose."

"What about the rest who aren't tethered to government assistance programs? Granted, they're the lesser of the population these days but they're also the most independent."

"I believe the majority of them were happy to donate money and talk the talk when they felt that their own necks were safe enough, when they had the comfort of operating anonymously within the collective. But when they see their leader gone, along with the magnitude of the retaliatory efforts against those who proudly and bravely take up the banner, it will drive the rest of them to their knees and have them scurrying back to their mouse holes."

"What kind of retaliation?" Lacy asked.

"As an example for all, the dissidents who decide to bravely and stupidly carry the torch forward will immediately start losing what little they have left of their personal freedoms, not to mention their scant remaining personal assets. Since we control the media, news will go nation-wide, hell, worldwide. They'll be portrayed as threats to the new and improved American Dream. They will no longer be able to move freely about, at will. Their every move will be monitored. Their 'Federally insured' accounts will be frozen. They won't be able to purchase what they please, when they please. Friends and family will turn away from them, fearing reprisals for the mere association to them."

"And if you're underestimating the situation?"

"Then the people will live in fear of mass punishments. What punishments, you ask? The price of oil can suddenly and unexplainably start rising even more uncontrollably than it has. Gas prices will rise to new, obscene highs which will effect the production and price of virtually everything in the world. All of that will certainly take their minds off of whatever else might be going on. And, thanks to the media coverage, it won't take many dissidents being publicly singled out as examples to put an end to the upstarts once and for all."

Mick wondered briefly if he had said too much, but it was too late now. He thought it best to get back to the subject of Kim's next 'hit'.

"As soon as we can see how Kim can best be used to get close to him, we'll put the wheels in motion. If I decide that Kim's recent unpredictable behavior makes her too risky, then your special talents will be utilized," Mick said.

"At my discretion?" Lacy's meaning was unmistakable. Mick ignored her.

"And his name is?" she asked.

"I practically drew you a road map just now. If you have to ask then you don't deserve to know."

Mick knew that Lacy's interest was definitely piqued. He also knew that, in spite of all of her faults, Lacy knew how to get the job done. He just had to find a way to keep her under control until the mission was accomplished. After that, Lacy would be too much of a liability to keep around. Her actions last night could have serious adverse effects on the outcome–an outcome with much at stake.

The sun was starting to set and Mick was anxious to be on his way. Once again, he shunned Lacy's advances and pushed her away. She got out of his car in a disappointed huff and stared at him coldly as he backed into a small clearing and drove off down the dirt road. He could not get rid of the nagging thought that he had told her too much.

16

After watching Rod skillfully pilot his Aero Commander into the air, Kim felt a good measure of bravado leaving with it. She looked around nervously, almost expecting to see the red Lexus looming in the distance, watching, waiting. Fear and doubt crept over her.

Someone had followed them to the park and tried to kill her. That someone had to have followed her from her apartment. She remembered the uneasiness she felt when she got home last night, as if she wasn't alone. Kim shuddered at the thought.

She was thankful that her breakthrough flashbacks were becoming more frequent, but far less intense. Kim thought it ironic that the flashbacks were now far less disturbing than her current reality. There was an odd measure of comfort in discovering what the past held, no matter how horrible, as opposed to not knowing anything about an uncertain future.

Kim looked around again and decided that she was relatively safe sitting in the parking lot of the small airport so she pulled out her phone to call Angie. She couldn't imagine what Angie must have gone through last night. She started to speed dial and then remembered Rod's phone was in her purse. She transferred Angie's and Street's numbers into his phone, turned the ring tone up on hers so that she would hear it when Mick called, and then slid her phone back into her purse.

Angie answered immediately. She was just leaving the police station where she was asked to file a report about what had happened at The Library. Kim was full of questions and wanted to know everything, but Angie thought it best to wait until her, Kim, and Street could meet somewhere together. But, where? The Library was out of the question, not only for now, but also in the future. The thought of hanging out in the place where two people had been so horribly brutalized was out of the question.

"There's a small church at Blair and Dragoon," Angie said. "The doors are always open this time of day, though not many people go in. Most of the time there's just a two-person cleaning crew. Unless we're being followed, no one will think to look for us there."

"And, if we're being followed?" Kim asked.

"Well, I guess we'll either know it or we won't. Either way, we don't have a choice unless we want to just curl up in a corner somewhere."

Angie paused long enough to give Kim time to back out. When all she got back was silence she said, "I'll let Street know to meet us there in an hour." Kim explained her change of phones and Angie said she'd pass it along to Street.

Traffic was heavy and it took over thirty minutes for the short ride back into town. Kim constantly looked around for anyone following her and the mental and physical distraction caused the near hit of an oncoming car. By the time she pulled into the church parking lot her nerves were frayed. Longing for the safety of the church, she took one last look around to make sure she hadn't been followed and then started to get out of her car.

The loud BANG! sent her flying for cover at the side of her car though she didn't know which direction it was coming from. Another loud BANG! She crouched down as close to the ground as she could get and braced herself for the pain that would follow the next gunshot. She hoped it wouldn't hurt for too long.

Seconds later, an old pick-up truck drove into the lot and pulled into a space near the church entrance, just on the other side of where Kim had taken cover. Another loud Bang! and with a puff of black smoke shooting out of the exhaust the old truck shook a little, then stalled out. An elderly couple emerged from the truck and started pulling mops and buckets from the rusted out truck bed, completely oblivious to the excitement they had caused.

Embarrassed, but breathing easier, Kim stood up. She took a few seconds to pull herself together and then walked up the steps and into the old church. The smell of incense was faint and the glow from the votive candles was subdued. Kim found both to be comforting. Looking around, she noticed she was alone. Since she was the first to arrive, she took a seat on the aisle in a middle row. It would afford her a better vantage point to watch each of the church's entryways.

Hearing the big wooden main door quietly close, she looked in that direction. A woman wearing an obnoxious large, green plaid coat and bright floral headscarf was shuffling toward her. The woman's head was bowed respectfully as she came up the aisle. She stopped at Kim's pew and genuflected. *An entire church and she's going to sit on top of me.* Kim briefly considered moving but her hesitation gave the woman the chance to slip into the pew next to her. *Maybe it isn't an innocent elderly woman, after all.* Kim was frozen to her spot as the newcomer scooted closer to her and slowly pulled the scarf away from her face.

"Wow. Do you have a kinky client lined up, or what?" Kim asked, relieved.

"Or what, and we'll leave it at that," Angie said, trying to smile.

"Street's under the impression that no one knows you exist, so why the disguise?"

"Because he's been known to be wrong a time or two. Just don't tell him I said that."

With the gravity of the situation settling over them like a wet blanket, Street's quick arrival was a welcome interruption. He came in through the annex and looked around the small church before confidently joining Kim and Angie. The quiet of the church was short-lived as the cleaning crew busied itself in the small wings off of the main church. With the distant noise as the backdrop, the trio got down to business with Street leading the way.

"The phone swap was quick thinking on Rod's part," Street acknowledged, looking at Kim, "but are you sure he can be trusted?"

"As much as anyone, I suppose, and more than most. He could have taken a bullet for me today."

"Good enough. Is he gonna be a part of the action?"

"He wants to," Kim answered, "but I can't have that. This is my battle and it's bad enough that it's now become yours. It cost Jay his life and Marie will never be the same again. I can't in good conscience involve anyone else."

"Street and I get that this is more personal for you but we all know how this is shaping up and it's not pretty for anyone, not just yourself," Angie said.

"Listen up, ladies. No time to rehash. I still have to pick up my inventory and then hit the street. Life goes on and I've been busy all day. I moved Grandma Mae in with one of her friends for a few days. And let me tell you it did not go down easy. I had to tell her I was gonna do some painting and the fumes would be hard on her."

"You lied to her?" Angie was shocked.

"So it wouldn't be a lie, I actually started painting the front hallway. I can't have her thinking harsh about me or catching on that something ain't right. I don't want her worrying.

"As it turns out, her friend's granddaughter is a nurse at the trauma center so I used my powers of persuasion to find out that Marie is going to be okay physically. A surgeon was called in to do some repair work and apparently it could have been a whole lot worse. Right now she's highly medicated and in such a state of shock that she's blocked out the worst of it. When she's ready to talk, they'll have a shrink drop by."

Kim was worried about Marie's ongoing safety. "How about police protection? It's odd that Lacy would not have finished Marie off since she can make the link between Lacy and Jay's murder."

"She has police protection round the clock." Angie offered what information she had learned earlier at the police station. "So right now, we don't have to worry about keeping anybody alive and healthy, but us."

Street glanced around to make sure they were still alone before continuing, then huddled closer in. "Not exactly true, Angie. I found a possibility, no, more like a probability for Kim's next 'hit'. His name's David Gallagher. He's called a press conference for tomorrow afternoon and strong speculation is that it's to announce his candidacy for president."

"David Gallagher," Angie repeated. "The name doesn't sound familiar."

"Neither one of us has exactly been interested in politics. Besides, we're too young to know much, if anything, about him," Street told her. "He's in his seventies and in a wheelchair, but there ain't nothing wrong with his mind."

Kim was confused. "How can he be any kind of threat?"

"He's a retired congressman who is the 'man' himself. He mentors politicians of like minds in the ways of constitutional, conservative government and the dangers of veering off its course. He's the father of the current grassroots movement to restore freedom to our people and get this country back on the right track. From what I read, everything he warned about and was ridiculed for decades ago has actually come true. And those predictions have gained him an increasingly growing and faithful following."

Angie cut in. "What chance does he have, being old and in a wheelchair?"

"I wondered about that too, but checking out the political blogs, the grassroots activists are all abuzz. Even the political pundits are reeling from the mere thought of what the press conference could mean. Even without the Internet he was gaining a lot of support years ago, so much that an attempt was made on his life. Most thought, and still think, it was an inside job, if you get my meaning. He ended up in the wheelchair but instead of dampening the spirit of his loyal band of followers, it just fanned the flames of unrest even higher and helped to enlist even more to the cause. I'm ashamed to say that I had no clue this was all going on till now."

"That makes two of us," Angie said.

"It's amazing how making a martyr of someone fans the flames of revolution," Kim said, while shrugging off a brief flashback of herself at the firing range. As she was getting a better foothold on her past, the flashbacks were less intense and far less disturbing. Angie and Street cast knowing looks at each other as they noticed the fleeting concern on Kim's face and then her determination to concentrate on the task at hand.

"That, and the power of the world wide web," Angie added. "The Internet can increase a movement exponentially. But how can we be certain that Gallagher is Kim's next target? I mean, with all due respect, the guy's old and handicapped. How will Kim fit into that scene?"

"We can't be certain till Mick makes a move. It's his game. And I agree that the situation isn't typical, but don't either of you forget what Mick said—that first and foremost Kim's a trained agent. Mick will simply have to change up the modus operandi and use her in any way that suits him."

"Makes sense," Kim agreed. "As far as he knows, I'm still under the influence of CRP-24. Assuming I have no memory of the past, he knows I won't question any changes."

Angie noticed that the cleaning couple were moving their supplies into the main church. She started pulling the scarf more forward around her face, lowering her head at the same time. As she suggested that they move into one of the annexes, the cleaning woman spotted Angie, dropped the bucket to the floor, and started in their direction.

"Angela? Is that you? How's your momma? I heard she's been sick."

"She's doing fine, Mrs. Murdock, just fine. I'll tell her you were asking about her."

"And your daddy? Haven't seen him at church lately."

"He's been working a lot. I'll be sure to tell him you were asking."

"Well, I can see you're in a hurry. I'll see you at services."

"Okay Mrs. Murdock," Angie said as she nodded for Kim and Street to follow her. The surprised and confused looks the two were exchanging between themselves did not go unnoticed by Angie, who offered neither apology nor explanation of her church attendance in spite of her career choice. The trio exited the pew but didn't get far when Mrs. Murdock turned and started toward them again.

"You know, that scarf would look beautiful with my new coat. Is it new? I'd like to pick one up for myself."

"No need for you to do that Mrs. Murdock," Angie said as she removed it from her head and placed it around the older woman's shoulders. "As it turns out, as you can see, it doesn't go with anything I have and it would look lovely on you."

Amidst half-hearted protests from the cleaning woman, Angie insisted the old woman keep the scarf and then gracefully extricated herself from the situation. With Street and Kim right behind her, they moved their meeting to a small vestibule and stood by the service door.

"Where's Gallagher's press conference going to be?" Kim asked.

"He lives in D.C. so he's more accessible to mentor his agents-of-change, so the press conference is at some place called The Press Club. That way he won't have to travel too far from home, wheelchair and all. If Mick tells you your next assignment is in D.C. then we can be pretty sure Gallagher's our man. There's nothing for you to do but contact Mick and find out what you can. We'll work up a plan then, when we know exactly what we have to work with."

"But, that's not how it's done," Kim objected. "He always calls me. If I call him it might look strange."

Street was losing patience. "Because of what happened to Jay and

Marie last night, the rules have changed."

"I'm not so sure we can pull this off by ourselves," Kim said, her former resolve again showing signs of weakening. "Maybe we should contact the authorities."

"How do we know which authorities can be trusted Kim?" Angie had taken serious note of Street's inference about Gallagher's previous attempted hit being an inside job. She knew what he meant. And then there's Mick. Wasn't he Kim's boss?

"Well put," said Street. "Blind trust put all of us in this position to begin with. But in the end, Kim, it's really your show. We're just the supporting cast."

"You know what's right, and not just for yourself." Angie picked up where Street had left off. "If you don't do this thing, you'll never be able to live with it–with the fact that you could've made the difference but didn't even try. If you try, if we all try and fail, well, at least we can take some measure of comfort in the fact that we did try." That being said and with all in agreement, the three slipped out the service door, preparing to go their separate ways.

At the same time, proudly wearing her new floral headscarf, Mrs. Murdock decided to get her husband's high blood pressure medication from the truck. She pushed through the heavy front entrance door and was stopped abruptly in her tracks. She went no further.

For one brief instant Mrs. Murdock felt the intensely hot pain of metal screaming through her skull and brain, and then skull again. Bloody bits of gray matter shot everywhere in sprays and globs and chunks. She went down quietly in a crumpled heap. Before her brain could register the pain response that would elicit the agonizing scream that should have followed, it was over. Her body lodged grotesquely between the old wooden door and the doorframe.

While Kim, Angie, and Street parted company at the side of the church, and Mr. Murdock whistled a happy tune while he mopped the floor, Mrs. Murdock's eyes stared vacantly into the church as her blood pooled up beneath her and slowly trickled its way down the crumbling church steps.

Completely devoid of emotion, Lacy noticed with mild curiosity that the bright floral scarf, though badly damaged, had somehow managed to stay in place on what was left of the shattered head. She then pushed her handgun, with silencer still attached, under her sweater on the front seat. Completely unnoticed, Lacy slowly drove away from the church and disappeared in the traffic.

17

Street had been pacing the corner for over an hour when Donnelly pulled up to the curb and stopped. He was alone. Street took a quick look around and then leaned on the open window ledge.

"Where's Branson?" Street asked.

"You his shift captain?" Donnelly answered the question with a question.

"Just a concerned citizen." Street went silent and waited for Donnelly to speak his mind. It didn't take long.

"I called in a lot of favors, city wide, to get some info on The Chantilly Trust. Nothing. Seems like the owner of your Lexus is getting what he or she wants–privacy. The registration mailing address of the trust is to a P.O. box so we struck out there. Damned near impossible to stake out a box."

"All I know about the driver is that her name's Lacy," Street offered. "At least that's what she said. I was hoping to put her as the legal owner and then score an address."

"Hell, why didn't you say her name was Lacy?"

"Did I forget to mention that?" Street acted surprised. "I didn't really figure the car was hers, anyway. Too pricey. Figured the registration would bounce back to her boss, boyfriend, whatever."

"Oh, I see," said Donnelly. "You didn't really want to see who was new to Mr. Roger's neighborhood. You just wanted to see if she was a kept woman before you put a move on her."

"Something like that." With the way things were stacking up, Street decided to keep the situation tight between himself, Angie, and Kim and not mention that what he was really fishing for was an address on Mick.

Then Donnelly started humming a tune, adding words as he remembered them. "Chantilly lace and a pretty face…"

"Don't bother with American Idol, my man," Street told Donnelly. "Too karaoke. You are definitely not going to Hollywood."

Ignoring Street, Donnelly said, "I'm not even sure if Chantilly Lace is the name of the song, but it went something like that. It was a big hit when I was a kid. Always on the radio and American Bandstand. Probably not on Soul Train, though. My mom used to sing it while she did the housework."

The look on Street's face told Donnelly that Street was making the connection. "You're getting there Street. Chantilly's a fancy lace material like for wedding gowns and veils and such. Chantilly Trust. Chantilly lace. Lacy. The car most probably belongs to her, but no guarantees. And it certainly doesn't mean she doesn't have a man out there willing to ruin your day."

With nothing else to be gained from Donnelly, Street wanted to be on his way. Though there were more pressing things to deal with he had bills to pay and a supplier to keep happy. He had some goods to sell and the cruiser would keep customers from waiting around too long. They got spooked easily, even though everyone knew Street was on decent terms with the local law enforcement.

"I'll keep that in mind, Donnelly."

As he backed away from the car, the cop spoke up again.

"By the way, listen up for any talk on the street for info about who could have taken the back of an elderly woman's head off as she was coming out of that little church over on Blair and Dragoon."

Street stopped dead in his tracks, unsure of what he had just heard. "Say what?"

"The old couple that cleans the church over on Blair and Dragoon. The Murdocks. Mrs. Murdock went to their truck to get the mister's medication and when she didn't come back he went looking for her. He found her in the front doorway of the church, the front of her head blown out through the back, ten ways to Sunday."

Street's knees threatened to buckle under him. He felt nauseous and faint. Donnelly's voice was just some distant patter making noise in his ears. Fighting the nausea he asked the question, fearing the answer. "Was she by any chance wearing a flowery looking head scarf?"

"How'd you know that?" Donnelly asked. "Hey, are you okay? You don't look too good. How'd you know she was wearing a floral scarf?"

"She's a friend of Grandma Mae's," Street lied as he focused his attention on getting his legs under him. "Better she hear it from me than somebody else. Later."

Leaving Donnelly and a few bewildered but patient customers behind, he hustled down the street and around the corner. He ducked into the sheltered doorway of an abandoned restaurant and frantically glanced around in search of the red car.

He had to get word to Angie but wasn't sure how to break it to her that her friend, Mrs. Murdock, had taken a bullet that was most certainly meant for her. He called Kim instead. Street clumsily blurted out the news. Kim was speechless for a few seconds and Street wondered if the call had been dropped.

"There's a slim chance that it was just a random shooting," she finally said.

"What are the odds of that?" Street asked. Silence, as Street looked up and down the street.

"Not good," Kim finally admitted. "We both know that bullet had Angie's name on it. Poor Mrs. Murdock. And Mr. Murdock! What must he be going through, finding her like that?" Kim was seriously distressed by the news and could barely talk between sobs. "This is all my fault."

"Hey! Back it up a little. Don't be owning someone else's guilt. The only difference between you and Mrs. Murdock is that she's a dead victim and you're a live one, as are the rest of us I might add. I feel bad about it too, but we need to focus on what it all means."

"What it all means is that we're all fucked!" Kim shot back. "We're all targets. Even Angie, who we figured no one knew about, is on the hit list. Mick must know that we're on to everything and told Lacy to get rid of us. Maybe we need to go to the police. No! The FBI!"

"No way. Our only chance to come out of this alive is to keep it on the down low. I don't know how they found out about Angie, but let's use Mrs. Murdock to our advantage."

"For God's sake, Street! What the hell's wrong with you? The poor woman's gone!"

"Exactly," he said as calmly as he could, nervously glancing around the darkened street. "Let's not let her death be in vain. If she's

anything like Grandma Mae, she'd want some good to come from it."
Kim's silence encouraged him to go on.

"We have to assume that Angie was the intended target and Lacy
was the shooter, at least until we find out otherwise. So, let's assume
that Mick ordered the 'hit' and figures Angie's dead. Now, with Jay
and Angie gone and Marie too traumatized to talk, both Lacy and Mick
think you and I are the only ones that know something's up. But they
probably figure we'll be too scared to do anything about it."

"Don't count on that to keep us safe, Street. These are ruthless
people. Don't think for a minute that we're not next," Kim said.

"What do you mean 'we'? For now, as far as they know, I'm the
only unnecessary loose end. Mick still may need you, for awhile."
Street paused to let his meaning sink in.

In the short silence that followed, Kim went over all of the little
memory scenarios that were coming together in her mind like the last
pieces of a puzzle. She could tell that whatever drug she had been
under the influence of was wearing off. Putting the last piece in place
no longer seemed as frightening or impossible as it did just days
before. When she finally spoke, Street noticed a new resolve.

"You know, I've been sitting here waiting for Mick to call, yet
hoping he wouldn't. Hoping it would all just magically go away. But
those politicians are dead and Jay and Mrs. Murdock are gone. Marie
has been assaulted and that should have been Angie back at the
church." Kim stopped to catch her breath. "I've let myself be
victimized by being passive so I have no one but myself to blame for
the spot I'm in. For the spot we're all in."

"Self-pity doesn't become you Kim," Street said. "You can't take
responsibility for us or for the rest of the whole damned country. They
think Angie's already dead so she may come out of this alive if she
lays low, but you and I are dead meat."

"It's bound to be all over the news about Mrs. Murdock," Kim
argued.

"Most likely, but highly unlikely that Mick and Lacy waste their
time watching the news. It's obvious that they have more important
things to do. Like I was saying, it's just a matter of time before they
find us. Mick can't afford to leave any loose ends around. But I can't
stand by and just let that happen because there's no one but me to take
care of Grandma Mae."

"Do you have a plan?" she said.

"The man always has a plan."

Street leaned forward a bit and checked out the street and sidewalk in both directions. Assured that he was alone, Street told her what he'd been playing out in his mind. Kim listened carefully.

"Sounds good except for the part about waiting for Mick to call me. The best defense is offense, with a little bit of surprise thrown into the mix. I'm going to initiate the contact and see if we can't get the ball rolling on our timetable for a change. I'll let you know the minute I know if we're right about Gallagher being the next target. If I am, we book the next available flights, but separately."

"You go, girl," he said, relieved at her change in assertiveness.

"And by the way, you're there for backup only, Street. I know how to handle myself."

"Believe me, I have no plan to be a dead man."

Before heading for the safety of his little apartment to wait to hear back from Kim, Street decided to take a minute to call Angie. He wanted to assure himself that she was okay and to assure her that they would all make it out of this alive. Just as he started to dial, he noticed Chantilly Trust slowly rounding the corner heading in his direction. The street was deserted so Lacy took her time, going much slower than the posted speed. He could only guess that she was carefully and methodically looking for himself or Kim.

He was barely breathing as she slowly approached. When she was within fifty feet he panicked. The glare from his phone's LED screen announced his whereabouts in the small, dark space. He flipped the phone closed and tucked himself, as tightly as possible, into the corner of the doorway.

Directly in front of the doorway, the car slowed down even more, then came to a dead stop. He tensed. Seconds ticked slowly by. He patiently waited for the inevitable. He had to force himself to breathe. He closed his eyes, anticipating the impact of metal on skull. He was glad Mrs. Murdock didn't know what hit her as the waiting was sheer torture. He hoped it wouldn't hurt too much, or too long. He wondered who would help Grandma Mae. The seconds ticked by like minutes in the deserted stretch of neighborhood. Then, unbelievably, Lacy accelerated and drove slowly out of sight.

18

Mick Jensen had wrapped up some routine business at the Bureau and decided he needed a drink. His earlier encounter with Lacy had really unnerved him. Still feeling the impact, he ran a few errands and then stopped by a little neighborhood sports bar not far from his office. A few hours later he was still there. Having found out that his phone conference with his boss had been delayed due to an unexpected family emergency, he was really in no rush to go back. Not ordinarily a people-person, Mick suddenly preferred the distraction of others so he wouldn't think about the seriousness of everything that was at stake. He needed a break.

The flat screen TVs were mounted on every wall in the bar and, as expected, there were a variety of sporting events being televised. Every once in a while an ardent fan in the bar let out a whoop and a holler to mixed reactions from the rest of the audience and then quiet would settle in, once again.

With his back to the wall, Mick sat at a small table in the corner so he could keep an eye on everything as he drank his martini. He wasn't looking for interaction and offered none. When the conversation shifted from sports to politics, however, that caught his attention.

"Moving the caucus up to the day of the big game is really going to impact the turnout," one said to the other. "But, that may be part of the plan. Politics is so goddamned crooked."

"What the hell's a caucus?" asked the other guy.

"Your kidding, right?" the first guy asked.

"Hell no. But it doesn't sound good. And if it has a bad impact on the turnout for the game, well that's downright un-american."

"I meant a bad turnout for the caucus, you idiot. It's like an election primary."

"Don't know nothing about that either, and don't care to know.

Caucuses, primaries, I leave all that stuff to people smarter than me."

"Which is most everyone," the first guy muttered under his breath. Undeterred, he then tried to get the attention of the crowd in the bar, but no one was interested in talking politics.

Mick noticed with a satisfied grin that the topic of conversation centered around stats, contracts, free agency status, point spreads, and handicaps. Everything you could hope to know about sports and little else. He eased back into the corner and closed his eyes. He felt like he could finally relax, until his phone rang.

The call brought him back to reality. It was Kim, but why was she calling him? She had specific instructions to wait for his call. That's the way the game was played. He decided to play it cool.

"Kim?" In spite of the relaxing benefits of the martini, he had to force himself to sound more casual than he felt.

"Hey Mick. You said you had an assignment for me. I was just wondering if we could get moving on it."

"What's the rush?"

"No rush, really. It's just that I feel like I'm getting sick. Sore throat. Nothing serious but you never know where it'll lead and I may not be on top of my game in a day or two."

She had never taken the initiative to call him before. She had always done what she was told to do, but if she was getting sick then it made sense to Mick.

"How are you feeling otherwise?" he asked, testing the waters. Though she sounded normal, he was dying to know what was going on with her memory

"Great! Why would you ask such a thing?" Kim asked.

"No reason, really."

"So, who am I hooking up with, and where?"

"Actually, I haven't firmed up the plans yet, but I can tell you that you'll need to be prepared to pack a bag for a couple of days."

"A couple of days? Sounds intriguing. Usually it's just a couple of hours."

"You'll be flying out of state. That's all you need to know right now. As soon as I hear something I'll make the arrangements and call you back with your flight and hotel information. No need to rent a car. The airport shuttle can take you where you need to go and then back to the airport when the job's done."

"How about a hint?" she coaxed.

"No hints. It's a surprise."

"Well then, a woman needs to know what kind of clothes to pack."

Mick laughed hard. "Really, Kim, that's a good one."

She masked her irritation. "Well, I'm not going to be butt-naked to and from the airport am I?"

Still chuckling, Mick conceded the point. "Dress for snow. A cold front moved in."

Bingo, thought Kim. No guarantees, but it was unusually cold in D.C. the last day or so. All the news stations were carrying public interest segments on the plight of D.C.'s homeless during the unexpected frigid temperatures that the shelters weren't prepared to deal with. And all of this going on under the noses of Washington's elite, whose only concern was raising millions upon millions of dollars to buy print space and air time in hopes of getting re-elected to the privileged life of excessive salaries, lifetime cadillac health insurance plans, and just as lucrative retirement pensions. Yes, Street had probably pegged this one right. Gallagher was the likely target.

"I'm waiting for word on the details, then I'll let you know. Why don't you go ahead and pack? Then you'll be ready at a moment's notice."

"Okay, Mick. I'll throw a few things together right now. By the way, how come you haven't sent any clients my way lately?"

"I'm not sure I understand." Mick wasn't sure how to respond.

"It just seems like I haven't had any action lately. Maybe they just haven't been memorable." Kim decided to stop there. Pushing the point might just have the opposite effect and raise suspicion instead of diminishing it. She needed him to think that her and her memories were no threat.

"Whatever. Not important. I'm going to go pack. A couple of days will more than make-up for my losses. Call me as soon as you can."

Mick was confused but didn't dwell on the fact that the CRP-24 seemed to have kicked in again. What a stroke of luck! He made a mental note to have the new chemist go over the research and efficacy reports to see if the erratic results could be pinpointed to a cause and eliminated before they had to use it again.

19

So she wouldn't worry, Street put in an appearance with Grandma Mae and then carefully looked up and down the neighborhood as he left her friend's house. Seeing no one, he bounded down the front porch steps two at a time, eager to close the distance to the safety of his apartment as fast as he could.

As usual, it was cloudy, and the scant bit of light erratically filtering through the clouds from the moon didn't give him the kind of light he would have preferred, given the circumstances. But, on the other hand, Street knew that only having a scant bit of light tonight would afford him at least some measure of cover.

Most of the street lights had been repeatedly broken out over the years by the neighborhood lay-a-bouts who had nothing better to do with their time, and the city soon tired of replacing them. Detroit was no different than every other city in that much of the tax revenue went to support the wages and perks of the public servants. There wasn't much left for needed routine maintenance. Street was so preoccupied with the idea of installing sensor lights around the property that the phone startled him. He was jumpy. He slowed down and took cover beside a huge, old maple tree.

"What's up?" he spoke quietly into the phone and then listened carefully as Kim told him about her earlier call to Mick.

"We're not waiting around for that bastard to call!" Street whispered loudly into the phone. "We're each gonna book a flight tonight, and separately in case our charge cards are ever checked out. There's gotta be two empty seats with all the carriers making this their hub and the economy so damned bad. I don't have it all figured out yet, but somehow we need to get word to Gallagher and get him to take us seriously. If we can't do that, then he's a dead man."

"Hey! No pressure here! And remember, I'm not actually going to do this 'hit'."

"You won't have to. Once Mick's on to the fact that his plan's all fucked up, he'll put his prize pit bull on it. There's too much at stake for him to just walk away from it, and once Lacy sinks her teeth into something she just don't let go." He wisely kept his earlier close encounter with Lacy to himself. He saw no reason to freak Kim out any more than necessary since tensions were already on overload.

"What are we gonna do with Angie?" Kim asked.

"I'm on it. I already called her and word of Mrs. Murdock's murder had already spread throughout the congregation. She already figured that it was no random homicide. Angie figures that Lacy must've somehow found out where she lived and followed her from her house to the church. That's scary stuff. Now I just have to convince her to hole up with Grandma M..."

Street stopped in mid sentence and shuffled around the tree, away from the street and out of sight. The scattered traffic had been moving along nicely, a steady stream of headlights coming at him from both directions and tail lights going away from him. Little cause for concern until the headlights of an approaching car slowed down to a crawl. Street watched as the headlights snugged up to the curb and then inched their way along, stopping every fifty feet or so before crawling forward again. Ignoring Kim's frantic questioning about what was going on, he stepped even further around the tree. He was barely breathing. How in the hell did Lacy know where he was?

He could hear his heart pounding in his ears. The car's headlights angled in on the tree as it suddenly came to a dead stop, ignition off. He couldn't afford to let her out of his sight as he tried to figure out what to do. He braved a cautious look around the massive old tree trunk, being careful to not put himself out front any more than necessary to establish a line of sight with his adversary. What he saw caused him to chuckle nervously, overcome by relief. Pizza delivery!

"I'm right here. Calm down," he finally said to Kim. "Geez! We need to keep our shit together. I mean, I'm jumping out of my skin over a damned double cheese and pepperoni stuffed-crust pizza!"

"You practically gave me a heart attack, Street," Kim scolded.

"As I was saying, I'll try to get Angie to hide out till this is over. If something happens to us then she'll have a decision to make. Either keep quiet about everything and hope they never find out it wasn't her who took the bullet; go so deep into hiding that even God wouldn't know where to find her; or find a way to blow the whistle on the whole damned operation and let the authorities give her a brand new identity."

"Not much in the way of choices," Kim said.

"Just let me handle her. Book your ticket and we'll meet at Dulles International Airport at 8 a.m. There has to be at least one Starbucks at the airport. We'll be in phone contact and go from there."

Cutting through the alleyway, Street wasted no time hopping a neighbor's fence and sprinting quietly across the back yard. Two houses to go and he'd be home. But, from a distance, he saw the glint of something shiny as it moved around the outside of Grandma Mae's house. Focusing intently, he could make out someone maneuvering their way around the small frame house, ducking in and out of the scattered bushes. There was no mistaking that body. Lacy!

Just minutes earlier she had knocked on Street's apartment door, eager to put a bullet in his face and out the back of his skull, but no one had answered. Now, moving like a jungle cat, she stealthily went from window to window but saw no sign of anyone. She wondered where they were as she made her way back to her car, boldly parked out front, and sped off.

Street watched her every move, amazed at her brazenness. When he was confident that she was not coming back, he slipped up to his apartment. Safely inside, he allowed himself to think the unthinkable. If it hadn't been for the glare from the moon glinting off the silencer of her gun, he would have never seen her. He would have taken the steps up to his apartment two at a time, as usual, loudly announcing his arrival in the dead silence of the night. He was convinced that he wouldn't have made it to the door.

He didn't dare turn any lights on. Instead, he used the scant moonlight to book his flight. He threw a few things in a small backpack and then remembered that he would have to check his bag in through security in order to take his switchblade. Wanting to get the hell out of there before Lacy decided to come back, he threw the backpack into a small suitcase and quietly opened the door. Hoping she hadn't returned, he crept down the stairs and disappeared up the alley. With every step he half-expected to feel a bullet tear though his body with deadly velocity.

Following Street's orders, Kim had immediately booked her flight. She packed a few things and wished that she had a handgun, the same handgun that seemed so familiar to her in her flashbacks. Preferring to kill the extra time at the airport instead of nervously pacing around her apartment, she then called a cab, leaving her own car behind as a decoy to give the appearance of being at home. She met the cab at the side service entrance, well away from the front door. She looked about nervously as they sped toward Metro Airport.

20

The conference call that Mick was expecting finally came in, catching him deep in thought. He was the wind beneath the wings of the most powerful man in the country. No. Not the president. The most powerful man in the country was definitely not the president. Mick thought smugly that that made himself the second most powerful man in the country. If something unfortunate happened to his boss then he was ready to step in and assume the role.

"Is your mother going to be okay?" Mick listened politely as his boss responded to the inquiry about the family emergency. Truth be told, Mick didn't really care. He cared only about one thing–himself.

Mick was thankful that he had been in the right place at the right time. When his boss had approached him with the plan a decade earlier, he'd had his share of misgivings. The boss was barely thirty at the time but he had been promoted through the ranks rapidly due to his intelligence and critical thinking. He really knew how to analyze a situation and find the weaknesses. Most importantly, he knew how to take advantage of those weaknesses. The boss sensed that what Mick craved was power and to be able to make a name for himself, a name Mick's dad would both envy and be proud of. The boss knew Mick wouldn't be hard to convince, and in short order Mick was sure he had been singled out to orchestrate destiny.

"Actually, I have Kim on standby," Mick spoke into the phone. "She seems completely back under control so I think it's safe to go ahead and use her, for the last time.

"No, not in the usual way," Mick responded to his boss's concern. "That would be damned near impossible with Gallagher's physical limitations, not to mention his moral ones. The man's too good to be true. The other two had well-known weaknesses for well-built blonds and were easy to exploit, but Gallagher's above reproach. And because of Kim's recent antics, she has become completely dispensable so I'm thinking to have her take him out sometime during his press conference, for the entire world to see. Besides, it should look different than the others just to throw people off."

Mick continued on, explaining the plan. "She'll go in to The Press Club as a private-hire security agent after being delivered her phony ID and untraceable weapon through one of our contacts in D.C. When she gets a good shot, she'll take it. In the ensuing confusion, one of the official security team will do their sworn duty and take her out. I had already made arrangements for Kim's two remaining confidants to be eliminated, and that job's already half done. After that, the only people who will know exactly what's going on will be me and you, and neither one of us is going to talk."

His boss was not easily convinced of the plan's viability and argued the point with Mick. Mick hid his frustration and calmly said, "It sounds that simple because it is that simple. Sometimes the simplest ideas are the ones that work best. Not unlike your idea to find the dirt on the owners of key media corporations and their top political journalists. If I remember correctly, what you couldn't find you invented. It's like having them on the payroll without the expenditure. They're thrilled to say what they're told to say, and all designed to sway public opinion with no paper trail back to us."

The boss finally voiced agreement with the plan, so Mick continued. "With the help of the media and with the revolutionaries out of the way, our guy Hennessey is in an excellent position to take the primaries. As an added bonus, he's already putting it in the public's head that the Internet in this country should be curtailed as a national threat. Just like his predecessors, he's very susceptible to the power of suggestion. In time, the next logical step would be its elimination as the evil it is. All we have to do is have the media put out some phony statistics that will scare the hell out of John Q and Jane Public so that by the time Internet restrictions are being legislated the citizens will actually breathe a sigh of relief and be clamoring for more."

Mick listened as his boss offered a suggestion, then said, "You're right. Starting a steady stream of statistics after the elimination of key websites, all showing a decline in violence and an improvement in family values and education scores will have the public clamoring for even more restrictions and there will be nothing that the grassroots revolutionaries will be able to do to stop it. With the loss of key politicians preaching a return to constitutional government and personal freedoms, and the Internet ban that will stop the dissemination of information, the political revolution in this country will come to a screeching halt. Without the instant spread of information, the body of the movement will suddenly have no legs."

After Mick and his boss ended their conversation, Mick felt revitalized. The only thing missing was the desired notoriety. Secretly, he longed to have his name in lights. But he had to dumb down about the project and his role in it for now. At least as long as the boss was alive.

Mick then placed his call to Kim, thinking she was killing time in her apartment and unaware she was already through airport security. She ducked into a quiet spot so he wouldn't pick up any telltale background noise, and tried to sound nonchalant.

"Sitting at home, thumbing though Vanity Fair, waiting for your call," she responded dutifully.

After Mick detailed the plans he went a step further, believing she was back under control of the mind-altering drug. "This will be your last assignment, Kim. You've done a tremendous service for your country and we won't ask for any more sacrifice from you. David Gallagher has an agenda that puts every American in harm's way. His platform may look and sound good, but it will destroy everything. If steps aren't taken to shut him up, the unrest will grow. The potential for a civil war in this country will increase. America as we know it will be in shambles. We will be set back two hundred years, or more."

Yes. Right back where we started. Back to the Constitution and a chance for America to start over and stay on track. Kim placed her finger over the speaker in case the airport intercom would come on. She was nervous and wanted to get off the phone as soon as possible. She couldn't believe what she was hearing. She also knew that Mick was telling her the truth about this being her last job. He wasn't stupid. He would never leave any loose ends. *Street better come up with one hell of a good plan.*

Kim went to her boarding gate and found a seat as removed from the rest of the passengers as possible. She felt physically sick. How would they even get close enough to Gallagher to explain anything, let alone convince him they were telling the truth? If Gallagher went on with his press conference, Mick must have a backup in place for the 'hit'. He would never leave something this important to chance, especially since he knew the effects of CRP-24 were showing signs of instability.

Kim never noticed the passenger taking the seat next to her. It was the scent that caught her attention. She thought about Angie, thankful that her friend was alive and safe. "First time to D.C?" the stranger asked.

Angie peered at Kim from under the brim of her cap. "Don't think you were going to leave me behind. Being as I'm supposed to be dead, no one will be looking for me. I'm just going to hide in plain sight."

Kim was glad to see her. "Street said you were going to stay with Grandma Mae."

"That's right. Street said it. Not me. When he said what was going down, I booked a flight. Pure coincidence we're on the same one," she said. "These new security rules sure make things difficult. Can't ask who's on the flight. Can't bring what you want."

"Except for being made to feel like I'm guilty of being a potential threat until proven otherwise, I didn't find it too bad," Kim said, sarcastically.

"That's because you're not packing what I'm packing," Angie said, reaching into her carry-on. After a little digging she brought out two small, clear glass bottles and held them up for Kim to see.

"Gin or Vodka?" Kim asked, thinking that either one would go down pretty smooth right now.

"Vitriol. In the new TSA allowable three ounce size."

"Russian?" Kim assumed.

"No, American made. Good old H_2SO_4. You may know it as sulfuric acid."

Before Kim could speak, Angie continued on. "I know it's not very dramatic, but this stuff will melt the rust off of steel. Imagine what it would do to flesh. It may not cause a fatality, but it'll make someone wish it did. It's the best I could do and, who knows? It might come in handy."

"How did you find out about this stuff?" Kim asked in amazement. "And, where did you get it?"

"I'd like to be able to say that I really paid attention in chemistry class, but the fact of the matter is that I like to read fiction and it's been used with much success in more than a few stories. Don't ask me how I got it, it's not important."

"You don't happen to have a handgun in that bag, do you? The acid is so, well, personal. I don't plan on getting that close to an assailant."

"That's not something anyone plans, Kim," Angie's tone was suddenly more serious. "Jay and Marie sure didn't plan on it either."

That conversation brought the reality back to the forefront. Kim reached out and took one of the bottles from Angie and, holding it in front of her, tipped it on its side.

"It can be diluted with water to thin it out," Angie jumped in to explain. "That's why there's room in each bottle. The only chance you might have is to get close enough to fling the liquid at someone."

The second Angie spoke the words, the gravity of Kim's situation revisited them like a New Year's Day hangover. For the rest of the flight the two retreated into silence and as far away from reality as they could get.

21

Rod's long flight to Palm Springs afforded him plenty of time to think things through, yet he was still confused. What was going on with Kim? He promised her he would stay on the sidelines and let her handle things her way, but it was one promise he had no intention of keeping.

Once at home, his first priority was to cancel his late afternoon business appointment even though it had taken three months to get the man to the bargaining table. There were bigger things at stake than corporate takeovers. Sitting in front of his Mac, Rod started typing everything he could remember about what Kim had told him. When he was done, he sized the "sticky note" and slid it to the upper right corner of the screen so it would be handy if he remembered something else.

Sifting through online newspapers would be much too tedious so he googled the most likely combination, "political deaths". No good. Hundreds of thousands of possibilities. Everything from natural causes, to suicide, to homicide, and spanning dozens of centuries. Rod was surprised to find that political assassination was just as prevalent in ancient times as it was today.

He knew his way around the Mac but had never been one to sit and idly search out information, which now put him at a disadvantage as to how to proceed. His interest was business and financials, things that were more concrete and easy to find.

He then typed "political murders". Still too many. Millions, in fact. He got up and walked over to the bar. Rod poured a couple of fingers of Dewars into a glass and walked over to the window overlooking the pool. Between sips of scotch, he kept mulling things over. How did Kim get herself involved in this mess and, more importantly, would she be able to get herself out of it?

Include the name of the city! That should narrow it down.

Encouraged, he hurried back to his desk and retyped. Then, in a last minute brainstorm he added the current year. To be even more specific he selected "search tools" and then mouse-clicked "past week" and then sat back, satisfied with what instantly appeared on the screen. "President eulogizes Madsen and Dunn" was the very first entry. Madsen and Dunn. Madsen and Dunn. Entry after entry.

Sipping on the Dewars, he opened up one after the other and then chased down link after link, and before he knew it he had killed two hours. Most links led to Gallagher and it was no stretch to piece it all together. Gallagher had to be the next "hit". It all made sense. Rod berated himself harshly. *Jesus! I should have seen this one coming a mile off.* He vowed to pay closer attention to what was going on, politically, in the future.

Before Rod started focusing heavily on his most recent business dealings over the past year or so, he had become intrigued with a new, refreshing political philosophy and now it all started coming back to him. Gallagher was the "father" of the new revolution. A presidential bid by him would hardly go as unnoticed as it had decades earlier. He googled "Gallagher" and the news of the press conference scheduled the next day at The Press Club was at the top of the list. Every political pundit had grabbed that ball and ran with it. Everyone was speculating on what it meant, and what it would mean for the future. And the speculation was worldwide as what went on in America would affect international events.

He picked up his phone and called Kim, but no answer. He called her on her personal phone, again no answer. He'd never been to her apartment, but knew it by name. He looked up the listing on line and called.

"Security. Sean speaking."

"Sean. I'm calling from out of state. I've not been able to reach Kim Haven."

"I didn't catch your name."

I didn't give it. "I'm Kim's attorney," he lied. "She called earlier about a consultation but I haven't been able to get through."

"We're not allowed to give out info on the residents. Privacy issues. You know. Same as a hospital."

"As an attorney, I can tell you that simply telling me that you've seen her and that she's okay will not violate that regulation," Rod bluffed, then waited.

Looking at the front entryway Sean's attitude took a sudden turn. "I went out for a smoke and she was getting into a cab. She had a small suitcase. Gotta go." Rod knew that Kim was on her way to D.C.

Sean did not wait for Rod to hang up. The vision he saw coming through the door was what wet dreams were made of. At twenty-five Sean had scored more than his share of action, both free and bought, and this piece was worth all of that put together and then some. His hand went immediately to his crotch and he quickly stroked the building erection through his pants. She was no vision. She was real. She leaned forward on the counter putting her large breasts within easy reach. Sean was mesmerized. The black lace enhanced her assets.

"I'm looking for Kim."

Trying to sound cool, Sean replied, "She's a popular girl tonight. You a friend, or a client?" Sean had his suspicions about Kim's line of work and just the thought of his visitor being a client got him even more excited.

"Who else wants to know?" Lacy asked, ignoring the implication. Sean watched the manicured fingers slowly stroke her nipples through the sheer black lace.

"Her attorney. From out of state."

"What did you tell him?"

As if hypnotized, Sean answered obediently. "That she got in a cab a couple hours ago, with a small suitcase." Right now, Sean would have walked over a mile of red hot pahoehoe lava for sixty seconds with this woman.

"How will I ever repay you?" she asked.

Sean's imagination was reeling. His erection was rock hard. Lacy made a suggestion. "Maybe there's a quiet place we could use for a few minutes."

"We've got a back office," Sean stammered excitedly, as he nodded toward the dimly lit adjoining room. "But it probably won't take that long," he laughed nervously.

"I'll guarantee it," she said, following after him. Glancing around to make sure they were alone, she reached into her purse and wrapped her fingers around the silenced handgun.

22

Convinced that his deduction was correct about Gallagher, Rod immediately called to have his plane pre-flighted for a trip to Washington D.C. but was told it would take several hours. Impatient, he booked a last minute flight on a commercial carrier and didn't even bother packing a bag. He'd get whatever he needed, when he needed it. Except for leaving his secretary a rather vague message, no one knew that he was gone or where he was headed. No one, except Lacy. She was good at connecting the dots, with a little help from a very cooperative Sean.

"I told you never to come here," Mick said sternly as he pulled a surprised Lacy out of the hallway and into his office. He had been locking up to go home when he saw her coming toward his office on the video monitors on his desk. He nervously glanced at the surveillance monitors stationed in the hallway. He would have to destroy the evidence as soon as possible.

"You're assuming I came to see you," Lacy responded, smugly.

"Who else would you be coming to see? Your ass was canned by the boss himself, in case you forgot."

"Is 'canned' the new lingo for…"

"Shut the fuck up! You're disgusting! Like the boss would ever debase himself with the likes of you!"

Lacy's seething anger was evident. It was all she could do to restrain herself from slapping his face. "Don't even think about it," he said, reading her mind, "or that steady influx of funds into your little offshore account won't be so damned reliable anymore."

Lacy laughed hysterically. "Really. That's funny, Mick. The way the government and the Federal Reserve have devalued our currency, Monopoly money has more value. From now on, pay me in gold or silver."

"You just don't get it, do you?" Mick shot back in a tone implying that he was talking to a moron. "Devaluing the dollar is part of the plan. In magician terms it's called diversion. Keep the people worried about the value of their dollar and its diminishing purchasing power. Keep them worried about having to work until they're dead. That way they won't have the time or the energy to even think about delving into what's going on right under their noses. And every time our benevolent president announces a plan to help them, even a little, they're so grateful for that little bit of handout that it takes the focus off of the big chunks they're giving up to get that meager handout."

"Well, if it's all that easy then why are you so worried about a few politicians more or less, or the grassroots movement?" Lacy challenged.

"In a word, Internet. Hell, there's even people from other countries voicing support for the grassroots movement going on here. They're hoping that it will influence what's going on in their own pathetic countries. Check out all the networking sites. England, Australia, Canada, Russia! This isn't Vegas, baby! What happens here doesn't stay here!

"The world has always had its independent thinkers," he continued. "But the ideas were more isolated, less imminently threatening. Instant worldwide communication has changed that. Now everyone is *Tweeting*. A virtual revolution can be instigated on a benign sounding site called *Twitter*. So right now, it's a game of staying one step ahead." Suddenly remembering that he didn't know why Lacy was there, he turned to face her. "By the way, what are you doing here?"

She took a few seconds to decide how much to tell him. "It looks like Kim left town."

"I know. I sent her on an assignment."

"When?"

"About thirty minutes ago."

Lacy couldn't wait to throw him the curve ball. "According to my source, she got in a cab a good two and a half hours ago and had a small suitcase with her."

"Which cab company?" Mick asked, feigning control, but clearly agitated. "And is your source reliable?"

Lacy thought back to how quickly Sean's memory had improved when she had asked him the same question. "Citywide Cab. And the barrel of a gun resting between a guy's balls sure improves his memory."

"And your source?" Mick's intent was clear.

"Let's just say that he no longer cares that him and his testicles parted company."

Mick barely heard her answer. He was frantically dialing information for a phone listing for the cab company. He wondered what the odds were that Kim decided to lay low and checked into a local hotel while she waited for his call. Pushing his Bureau weight around he had his answer within minutes. The cab had been dispatched directly to the airport. He called TSA and in no time pulled some strings for the needed information. Kim was, at that very moment, on a flight to D.C!

Lacy had witnessed Mick's rage in the past, but tonight's was the topper. After the most vile rage, he threw his phone across the room. "Get your sick ass to the airport! I don't care if you have to fuck your way onto that plane with the entire flight crew, just make sure you're on a flight to D.C. tonight and call me when you get there. I'll let you know what to do then!"

Mick rudely shoved Lacy to the door, and then into the hallway. He didn't even bother to close the door as he raced across the room to pick up the phone. His hands were trembling as he speed-dialed and waited impatiently for his call to be answered. "Boss," he spoke into the phone, "we've got a problem. Kim's already on her way to D.C.

"No, I didn't send her, she went on her own.

"What do you *think* this means?" Mick's voice rose shrilly. "She's acting like a rogue agent. I didn't want to bother you with this before but she's had some minor reaction issues to CRP-24. Just a little unpredictability is all."

Mick instantly felt stupid for making such a ridiculous statement. There was no room for any unpredictability in a mission of this scope and magnitude. How foolish.

"I'm *on* it. I just sent Lacy," Mick responded, hoping for a chance to explain.

"Yes, Lacy. But I can explain." Mick suddenly doubted that any explanation as to Lacy's involvement would appease the boss.

"Yes sir. You can be assured that Lacy will see to it that the mission is accomplished. I had no choice. I'll take responsibility for the decision and then we'll eliminate her too.

"And, stay close to your big screen tomorrow," Mick offered in appeasement. You won't want to miss Gallagher's press conference. It will be reality TV at its finest."

With the call behind him, but feeling only slightly more in control, Mick pulled his flask from his desk and swallowed a few quick mouthfuls. He put his head back and tried to relax but, even with the alcohol, relaxation escaped him. There was too much to think about.

Mick's mind was reeling. Kim lied to him. She acted like she was at home and hadn't even packed yet while, in reality, she was already at the airport. That could only mean that she knew more than she was letting on. Kim was playing him for the fool. She must have figured it out and was on her way to warn Gallagher. There was no other explanation. The chemist had promised that the drug would work flawlessly. Mick was angry. If the chemist was still alive Mick thought he'd actually enjoy watching Lacy slowly kill him.

The entire plan was in jeopardy. His career. The political agenda for the country. His own agenda. Everything hinged on the success of the mission. He had handpicked Kim himself and would be held responsible. What the hell had happened to her passive nature? Where the hell did she get her backbone and her own mind?

23

Though Kim and Angie had worked it out with other passengers to trade seat assignments in order to sit together, they sat in silence. Neither was interested in small talk and what they really wanted to talk about was not for anyone else's ears. They tried to sleep, but couldn't. The business that lay ahead had their minds running in a dozen directions. In her own mind, Kim went over her plan again and again.

She had no choice but to meet the contact person Mick had told her about earlier. The contact would have her phony ID and a gun. Not doing so would raise suspicion. Besides, she would need the ID to be able to get anywhere close to Gallagher and the gun would give her much more confidence than that small vial of acid.

Next, she would have to convince Gallagher and his people that she was telling the truth. After that, they'd all have to go into hiding until they figured out the best way to handle things. She really didn't have a plan in the event that he didn't believe his life was in danger, or didn't care that it was. Failure to convince him was just not an option.

Angie sat next to Kim, thankful to be alive. She believed that her path crossed with Kim's for a higher purpose. In some perverse way, she believed that Mrs. Murdock's death was also for that higher purpose. If everything was as it appeared to be, then she had been spared to perform a future function. She let a calmness settle over her, confident that the purpose would be revealed at the right time. She stole a glance at Kim and hoped she would have the opportunity to find out more about her.

Once Kim and Angie landed at Dulles, they searched out the Starbucks. Street had managed an earlier flight and had already picked up his bag from the carousel. From there he had ducked into a restroom, unzipped his suitcase, and pulled out his switchblade. He slipped it into a thin slice of space between his right boot and his outer leg, leaving the tip of the handle peeking out of the top. He then lowered his jeans back over the boot. *David up against Goliath, and this switchblade is my slingshot.*

He thought about calling Grandma Mae from the restroom but realized the ceramic tile floor and walls would magnify the intercom announcements and he didn't want to arouse her suspicion. Her sight was failing, not her hearing. As he was roaming around trying to find a suitable place to make his call, his phone rang. It was Kim.

"Hey, there's nothing suspicious about hanging out at Starbucks with some friends, even at the airport. Just tell her you're seeing off a good friend." Kim told him when he had voiced his concern that Grandma Mae might catch on where he was and wonder why. "Just make your call from here. We'll get you a coffee."

Friends? We? Nothing got by Street.

"Please don't tell me Angie's with you!" Already knowing the answer, he went on. "That girl must like tempting fate," he said.

"It's her decision, her fate to tempt, Street. I'll order you a grande, you're going to need it."

The three sat at the small table and Street placed his call. When he was through, both girls saw him in a new light. Kim couldn't resist. "Wow. Beneath that tough street facade beats the heart of a kind, caring individual."

"Keep that to yourself," he said. "Can't have my image being ruined."

"Is Grandma Mae on your mom's side or your dad's side?" Angie asked, suddenly realizing how little she knew about him.

"Neither. She's no blood at all. She's just a near blind, eighty-eight year old woman with no family left. None except me, that is," he answered, sipping his coffee.

Kim was intrigued. "Then how did you two get together?"

"As Grandma Mae likes to say, 'God works in mysterious ways'."

"Amen to that," Angie said.

"A while back, she saved my ass from a serious thrashing and let's just say that I'm returning the kindness. Anything I can do to make what time she has left easier, then I'm happy to do it."

Angie was curious. "Does she know anything at all about what's going on?"

"No. I just told her that there's a situation that needs my attention.

She never pries. She just says 'Always remember that right makes might, Street. Each of us has a destiny to fulfill.'" The impact of Grandma Mae's words settled over them as they sat pondering a very uncertain future.

Seconds later, Kim looked at her watch and pulled her scribbled directions out of her jacket pocket. According to Mick, the park she was to meet her contact in to pick up the ID and the gun was about twenty minutes from the airport and on the way to The Press Club. Gallagher's press conference was scheduled for noon. That didn't leave much time to be able to get to him and convince him that his life was in jeopardy. Even a hot, sharp knife would have trouble cutting the tension at their table. The time had come. Street was the first to speak. "What's the plan, Kim?"

"Other than meet my contact at the bronze statue by the fountain in the park, I don't have much of a pla…"

"Then I do," Street interrupted emphatically. "It took some fast talking, but Donnelly texted me with Gallagher's home address." He looked at Kim. "You'll get a cab. Angie and I will get the one right behind you and follow you to the park. You'll have the cabbie wait for you and then take the cab out of the park, turning right. Have him drop you off somewhere up the road."

"Where up the road?" Angie asked.

"Don't matter where. We're gonna be right behind her so we'll pull over and pick her up. From there, we'll head over to Gallagher's house. I think our best chance to convince him is in private. We need to get to him before he gets to The Press Club. The security for the conference will be beefed up and there'll be way too much commotion for him to give us the time of day once he's there."

"What did you have to promise Donnelly for the address?" Angie was savvy enough to know how it all worked on the street. "You don't get something for nothing."

"Looks like my supplier went to the dark side. They've had him under surveillance and what Donnelly told me was pretty convincing. I'm going to have to roll over on him."

"Sorry, Street," Kim said. "You must be disappointed."

"Yeah, but life's full of them," he said. "A good reason to not take anything for granted, or at face value. I would have bet my life that he would have never put my life or freedom in jeopardy."

"Didn't he promise you that he'd never get involved with the hard stuff?" Angie was surprised.

"A promise is just a comfort to a fool," Street replied, thinking back to how many people had let him down. "Don't ever forget it."

"And if we can't make a contact with Gallagher at his home?" Kim wanted to be clear about the plan.

"Then we'll go to plan B," Street answered, "but don't ask me what it is because I haven't got it all figured out yet. Ready to roll?"

As the three got up to leave, Kim handed each of them a small, folded piece of paper. "If something happens to me, the only other person who might miss me would be Rod Windthorpe."

"Nothing's going to happen to you. Remember, Grandma Mae says 'Right makes might'," Street said as they walked to the passenger pick-up area.

24

In typical airport fashion, the cabs were lined up and in no time two swooped out of the pack, jockeying competitively to pick them up. The three split up quickly and Kim took the first cab while Street and Angie piled into the second. Kim gave the cabbie her destination and then nervously cast a glance out of the back of the cab window, making sure that Street and Angie were following her out of the airport grounds. They were close behind.

Everyone rode in silence as the cabs wended their way through town. Suddenly, Kim found herself making a right turn into an old cemetery. She panicked. What was going on? Looking back, she saw the second cab pull slowly up to the curb and stop, just outside the entrance. Something must be wrong.

Even from a distance, the panic-stricken look on Kim's face was evident. Thinking fast, Street used both thumbs and texted Kim. When the incoming text message alert chimed she pulled out her phone. "Stay cool. Memorial Park is cemetery. Plan ok."

The cemetery was small but well-maintained and the bronze statue rose up like a beacon in the midst of all the small tombstones. There was a blanket of snow on everything, but not enough to obscure the fact that the only floral displays were red. She thought it odd, but very striking.

"Where to?" asked the driver, slowing down to a respectful crawl.

"That bronze statue up ahead."

"I'm D.C. born and bred," the cabbie volunteered as he drove toward the statue. "Not much goes on in this town that I don't know about. Take this here cemetery. This started out as the private family cemetery of the Jenkins family back in the late nineteenth century. It's an interesting place. Lots of history and drama. And, there's requirements to be buried here.

First, you have to be dead." The cabbie laughed as if he had never told this story before. "Second, you probably noticed the red flowers. Only red flowers can be placed here. Two reasons," he went on as if he'd been asked. "It was Old Mrs. Jenkins favorite color and," he paused for dramatic effect before he went on, "it symbolizes blood. The first nine family members to be buried here all died violent deaths, either at someone else's hand, or their own. That's right, Miss. Everyone buried here was either murdered or committed suicide. Since it already had somewhat of a theme going for itself, the family decided to open it up for other burials of homicides or suicides. Kind of like letting the spirits of violence spend eternity with their own kind."

"Interesting," Kim said, not knowing what else to say and somewhat disturbed by the story. They were slowly approaching the statue, but she saw no one else. She looked at her watch. They were right on time. She looked behind her to make sure that Angie and Street were still there. They had pulled up a little so that they were all in full view of each other.

"Well, that's not actually the interesting part," the cabbie continued, clearly relishing the build-up for the grand finale. "This has become a 'killing field' so to speak. Every once in a while, the caretaker or a family member will stumble upon someone who's been murdered or committed suicide right here in this cemetery."

"Creepy," Kim said. She had been so intent on the story that the man coming out from behind the statue caught the corner of her eye and scared her. *I better start paying attention or I'll get us all killed.* She waited until he pulled a black baseball cap from his jacket pocket, put it on, and spun it backwards.

"Wait here," Kim told the cabbie.

"Hey, I'm not participating in nothing illegal here, am I? I don't want no trouble. I got a family to take care of."

"I assure you, you're not. I have to catch a turnaround flight and I'm just here to pick up some antique jewelry items that were purchased by my boss from someone on the outskirts of town. I suggested Fed-Ex or UPS but he's not a very trusting soul. Can't say I blame him. Besides, meeting here sure beats a drive across town in bad traffic."

"Sounds good to me," the cabbie said as he turned the radio on and settled back in his seat. Through half-closed eyes he watched Kim walk toward the man, who took her by the arm and guided her behind the statue.

"You fit the description, only better," he said, focusing much too long on her legs.

"The package?" Kim held out her hand, eager to get the hell out of this place. He pulled it from beneath his coat and placed it in her hand. The weight of the gun caught her off guard. It had been a while since she had held one.

"It's always a surprise how much one of those little things weighs," said the contact. "And, it's completely untraceable. The photo ID is so perfect that even your own mother would believe it."

"I assume the gun's loaded?" Kim asked.

"Fully. Ever use one?"

At first, Kim wasn't sure what to say. Then finally, "No". Outside of her few friends, Kim trusted no one and with good reason. Any other answer would imply that she remembered her past and could throw up a red flag if this guy had been told to watch for any. "You'd better go over a few things with me."

He slipped the gun out of the bag and placed it in her hand. He watched her intently. Was he watching for her to hold it correctly? For a sign that she recognized the comforting feel of it in her grasp? She clutched it clumsily, almost dropping it.

"Amateur!" he muttered under his breath.

"Look. I only have to get close enough to get a good shot. I have my orders, you have yours. Show me quickly how to handle this thing or this'll be the last job Mick throws your way. On top of that, he may decide to make this your permanent home!" As if to emphasize her point, Kim gestured around to the grave sites with an outstretched hand.

Kim was amazed at how quickly her contact got busy with the task at hand. As the lesson progressed, she felt a sense of familiarity with the handgun. A familiarity she did her best to keep hidden. When she felt that he was satisfied that she was nothing more than a fast learning amateur, she put the weapon in her purse, thanked him, and started toward the cab. He called out after her.

"Hey! Best of luck to you!" Maybe she was being too sensitive, but he seemed to emphasize the word "luck".

With Kim safely back in the cab, the driver followed the narrow asphalt road around the cemetery back to the entrance. Following Kim's instructions, he turned right onto the main road and didn't seem to notice that the second cab waited a few seconds then fell in behind them. About a mile up, Kim told him to pull into the next parking lot and stop.

In the meantime, curious about the ID, she pulled it out of the brown bag just enough to check out the quality. It was excellent. Her fingers were shaking as she pushed the ID back into the bag and pulled some cash from her pocket. She couldn't stop shaking as she paid him and got out of the cab. How frighteningly easy it was to assume another identity. The ID looked so authentic that it even had her wondering if it was real or fake. Would she ever know who she really was?

"Hey, Miss, are you okay?" the cab driver said, noticing she was upset. "Don't worry about me. I just mind my own business. I don't see anything. I don't hear anything. If everyone would just mind their own business we'd all be a lot better off."

"I'm fine, thank you," she said. "But, everybody minding their own business is part of the reason for the current mess this country's in!" Her cabbie pulled away quickly. He didn't want to get involved in any political discussions. When the second cab pulled up, the door swung open and Kim slid in beside Street.

"Where to?" asked the second cab driver, who didn't seem the least bit curious about what was going on. As a starting point, Street gave him the closest main intersection to where they needed to go. The driver let out a long, low whistle. "Hope you're not in a hurry. The traffic on the highway's really backed up."

"Accident?" asked Angie.

"No," the driver explained. "If you don't follow politics then you probably never heard of David Gallagher. All the hubbub this morning is about his press conference at noon. He's expected to announce his run for the White House. The live broadcast and print media are converging on his residence trying to get a story, even before he gets to The Press Club.

On top of that, his supporters are coming out in hordes as a show of support as well as to act as his personal security detail on the way to the Club. I don't think that even Gallagher himself expected this kind of reaction. In the past, the media has always trivialized the man and his ideas. But this is big news. It'll improve their ratings, especially if there's another attempt on his life. He barely survived the last shooting. I'm afraid he won't survive the next one."

"You seem pretty sure about that," Street said.

"Look. Gallagher can turn everything in this country around and that's what the corrupt elite is afraid of. It's not in the best interest of the powers-that-be to allow his message to spread anymore that is already has."

"You sound like a supporter," Kim observed, now even more hopeful that they could get to him in time.

"One hundred percent, dyed in the wool. I've been a part of the movement for years. I do it for my kids, my grandkids. But I have to admit that I wouldn't mind living long enough to see honest people running this country. By the way, you might want to rethink your destination until later on, after the traffic has thinned out in that area. Maybe go directly to The Press Club instead."

"Yeah, maybe." Kim seemed lost in her own thoughts. What seemed like such a good idea last night now seemed like an insurmountable task. Seeing the hesitation, Angie nudged Kim hard hoping to get her back on track. For a few long seconds Kim sat there, staring out the side window as if in a trance. Angie leaned in close and spoke softly, but intently. "Reclaim your life, Kim, and the rest will fall into place. If not now, then when? If not by you, then by who?"

Kim's mind played out a myriad of alternate scenarios, even more frightening than the task at hand. With newfound determination, she pulled out her counterfeit ID and flashed it across the seat. The driver took a quick glance and Kim spoke up. "We're part of Gallagher's official security escort. Not getting to his house is not an option."

"You sure don't look like no official security people I've ever seen."

"That's what makes us so damned efficient," Street jumped in. "Nobody suspects that the three of us are the best damned security team in the country. Believe me, nobody wants to keep him safer than we do."

Angie added, "For us, it's not just a matter of life and death. It's far more important than that."

"To Gallagher's, and quickly," Kim ordered with new determination, hanging the ID around her neck.

The driver glanced in his rearview mirror. "Hell, why didn't you say so?" he asked as he picked up the pace, changing lanes to make his way over to the fast lane. They made it across town in record time.

25

The cabbie dropped the three off as close to Gallagher's home as they could get, given that the streets had transformed themselves into parking lots. He offered to wait, but Street shoved some cash into his hand and told him to take off. The driver handed him his cell phone number, "just in case", and tried to find a place he could turn around in.

The three moved back and forth between parked cars and vans with video and audio equipment mounted to the roofs. They made their way quickly and found themselves confronted by a huge crowd outside the massive security gate that blocked the entrance to the long private drive.

There was no need for a human guard at the gate. The video monitors were well-placed to scan the front of the property. Where the line of sight ended from those monitors, the cameras mounted on each corner of the wrought iron fencing surrounding the property took over. No one could come or go anywhere without being seen and recorded.

The house sat back a good distance from the street. It was not as large as the exterior trappings would imply but it, too, was equipped with monitors. The wheelchair ramp to the front door left no doubt that they were at the right place.

The early arrivers were zealously guarding their posts at the gate, with the latecomers relegated to spilling over into the street. The chatter was incessant and provided an annoying background drone as Kim, Angie, and Street spoke up enough to be heard by each other, but not overheard by those around them.

"How the hell are we gonna get in?" Street asked.

"I thought you were the man with the plan," Angie said.

"No one said nothing about trying to break into no fucking fortress."

"Wait a minute!" Kim said sternly. "Mick set me up as Gallagher's security. They have to be expecting me." She dug around her purse and pulled out her phone. Wrong phone. She found the other phone and started to call Mick, then realized the futility of trying to have a conversation in this din. She started texting Mick when Angie stopped her. "How are you going to explain being at the house this early when you were supposed to be at The Press Club later on?"

That stopped Kim dead in her tracks. *How could I have been so stupid?* "Now what? Any ideas?" she looked to Angie and Street.

The crowd seemed to be diverting their attention toward a small service gate off of the main gate. Kim followed their attention and saw two large men muscling their way through the throngs of people. The two were headed in their direction. The men were besieged by questions from reporters and fans alike and, while polite, claimed that all questions would be answered at the press conference.

Street was the first to suspect that they were the object of the mens' mission. To confirm his hunch he pulled Kim, with Angie in tow, and started weaving in and out of the crowd, ignoring the girls' questioning looks. The two men kept their sights trained on the three of them at all times, so as to not lose them in the crowd. With Street confident that his hunch was right, he stopped.

"Here's the plan. See those two big guys coming our way? I'll bet you that if we stand here they're going to invite us in."

Angie was surprised. "Based on?"

"Our good looks, finesse, and charm," he answered.

"Well, that certainly covers me and Kim. But what's going to buy your ticket to the show?"

Within seconds the two men elbowed Street and Angie out of the way as if they didn't exist, and flanked Kim. Amidst Kim's protests, they practically lifted her off her feet and half-carried, half-dragged her through the crowd, then through the gate, soon disappearing from view. Kim's last sight of her friends were of them signaling her to keep quiet about the two of them. She was, after all, supposed to be alone. And indeed, at this moment, she felt very alone.

Away from the noise of the crowd, Kim feigned a feistiness she didn't feel and demanded to know what was going on. Ignoring her, they escorted her into the house through a small side entrance doorway that led into an oversized country kitchen rife with the aroma of fresh brewed coffee and the morning's breakfast. They put her down and she looked around, amazed at what she saw.

It was definitely a kitchen, but so much more. It looked like a command center. Charts and graphs lined each wall. Desks were scattered about, laden with phones, books, and files. Filing cabinets were utilized wherever they happened to have been set down in whatever free space could be found.

Looking beyond the kitchen into the great room, she could see that it also served a duel function with the massive fieldstone face of the fireplace acting as the foundation for a huge organizational chart. Like the kitchen, charts lined each wall and desks were scattered about. Large bookcases held giant tomes, certainly not the type of books for leisure reading.

"Special security, huh?" one of the men said, looking her over. "You don't look like much to me. In the way of security, I mean," he added, making sure his meaning was not misconstrued.

"That's precisely what makes me so damned good," she said, mimicking Street. "No one expects much so they're not prepared."

"Makes sense," said the second guy. "Kind of like getting sucker-punched."

"Exactly," Kim agreed. "How did you know who I was?" This little detail was really eating at her. It felt like a set-up. Nothing made sense to Kim. Gallagher did not know she existed and the arrangement was for her to go to The Press Club, not the house.

"Your boss called and explained that the Bureau was sending you out as a back-up to our own security, that no one would be expecting you in the crowd and that would be an added bonus."

"My boss? And how did you know to look for me just now?"

"Look. A call came in about twenty minutes ago. We were just told to bring you in, that's all."

Kim's heart was racing. No one should have known she was there. No one! She had to act fast. She had no idea what was going on, but nothing was making any sense. It was now or never!

"I need to talk to Mr. Gallagher! His life is in danger!"

"His wheelchair is a daily reminder, Miss. That's why you're here."

"No! I mean there's an actual plot to kill him at the press conference! If I can just explain it to him, stop him from going! My friends and I can explain everything. My boss is in on it and is setting me up to take the fall. He doesn't know that I've figured it all out. There are a lot of people that don't want Mr. Gallagher to run for the White House."

"There are even more people who do," one of the men said.

"I'm telling you the truth. Let me meet with Mr. Gallagher. I'll explain everything. I know he'll believe me. My boss, Mick Jensen, had Madsen and Dunn killed as well. He had me drugged to do his dirty work but the drugs are wearing off and I'm figuring it all out. He sent me here to kill Gallagher at the press conference and then he's going to have me killed as well. Please! Just a few minutes of Mr. Gallagher's time. He has to go into hiding until this is settled. Please believe me!"

"Actually, he's not even here. For convenience and security, he stayed last night in a hotel near the press conference. And Mr. Jensen called and explained that he had just found out that the agent that he had dispatched here to protect Mr. Gallagher was actually a rogue agent with her own agenda."

"What? That's a complete lie. Mick is the one with an agenda to run the country from behind the scenes! By eliminating anyone that might work against his agenda! Think about it, for god's sake! Don't you find it odd that Dunn and Madsen turned up dead this week?"

The two men looked at each other with mild amusement. They were told that after Kim's real motives had been discovered, that her gun had been loaded with blanks so she posed no real threat. They were just supposed to humor her until Mick could get another agent there to take her into custody. A cell phone interrupted. After the short conversation, the man turned to her and said, "There's an agent Lacy on her way to escort you back to headquarters."

The two men never knew what hit them. Her leg flew up and her foot caught the jaw of one of them, sending him backwards over a desk. As the second man rushed her, her foot slammed into his kneecap. He collapsed to the floor in pain. She had no desire to hurt innocent people no matter how misguided they were. She opted to make a run for it.

Bolting out of the door, she caught the attention of the audience gathered at the gate as she ran across the expanse of yard. The wrought iron fence was too high for her to climb over and Gallagher's men had locked the gate behind them, earlier. She had to find a way out.

Angie and Street were at a loss for what to do but hoped that, for whatever reason, Kim had been ushered into exactly where she needed to be and would be able to convince Gallagher of the plot against him. Then the commotion in the street caught their attention. A very seductive looking woman was getting out of an airport limousine and all eyes were on her. Lacy!

They couldn't let themselves be seen by her. They started off in the opposite direction, pushing their way through the crowd and staying as close to the fence as possible. That's when they saw Kim dashing across the yard toward the side fence. She looked frantic. They pushed through the throngs of people and tried to catch her attention. It was useless. Kim was focused on finding a way out. Once Angie and Street broke free of the crowd, they sped around the corner of the fence and Kim caught sight of them.

"Get me out of here! Hurry!" she screamed as she ran along the fence, hoping to find some type of opening that she could squeeze through.

Street and Angie kept up with her, staying beside her with the fence between them. She was running from something and had no time to explain. They felt helpless until Street spied the dumpster at the far corner of the property. It was positioned about six feet from the fence, under a huge, dead pine tree. From the looks of the equipment and trash receptacles lying around, the tree was going to be cut down and loaded into the dumpster.

"Kim!" Street shouted, pointing to the dumpster. "Use a trash can and see if you can get to the top of the dumpster!"

"Then what?" she screamed. "That's too far across and a ten foot drop!"

Looking ahead, Angie saw a noticeable elevation in terrain about ten feet beyond the dumpster on their side of the fence.

"Jump to the right of the dumpster! We'll help break it!" Angie yelled.

"My fall? Or my leg?" Kim shouted as she tried to make light of the situation.

Lacy was unaware of what was going on at the far side of the property. As she had found no one at the gate to escort her in, as promised, she pulled the handgun from her pocket and to the surprise of her audience, fired two rounds into the gate lock and let herself in. She was anxious to get her hands on Kim. Mick had given her strict instructions, but he knew she wasn't one to do as she was told. Not wanting an audience, she turned to the crowd and in her most threatening manner warned everyone to stay where they were. Her coldness impacted the crowd and no one dared disobey.

All eyes were on Lacy as she strutted up the driveway and disappeared into the house. What she found there sickened her. She hated weakness. The two men were barely injured and yet they were lying there in pain.

"Where's the agent?" she demanded.

"She's gone," the one moaned as he held his knee. She landed a heavy kick to his knee and he screamed. She looked at the other guy and he cringed in terror. She raised her gun and took aim between his eyes. She held her aim for a long second and then turned and walked out of the door. "Such weakness is not worth the energy or the bullet," she said out loud as she picked up her pursuit of Kim.

She stopped at the side of the house and looked to the front gate. The crowds' attention was now focused on the other side of the property. Following their lead, she rounded the corner of the house and saw the trio at the far corner of the lot. Lacy recognized Kim and Street but who was... "Angie!" she gasped in disbelief.

Kim had already dragged and hefted a large, dead tree branch that had been lying nearby and had it propped up against the dumpster. Pumped with adrenalin and with frantic coaxing by Street and Angie, she had even managed to hoist it to the top of the dumpster and was now trying to slide it forward to act as a bridge to the top of the fence– her only way out. She pulled her handbag over her head and tossed it over the fence to Angie.

Lacy smiled to herself and raised her gun. *I can hit all three before the dimwits can even think of scattering in different directions. They'll stick together. It's part of the herd mentality.* She savored every second.

Which one should be first? she mused. *Kim's the most important, but the other two are already on the other side of the fence and could get away. Street and Angie first. I'll save the best for last and give her a few seconds to reflect on the pain and suffering she's caused.*

She steadied her stance and swung the gun in a slow arc toward

Street. Then to Angie. Back to Street. Just above the left eye. *No.* She lowered the sight to the center of his neck. Might as well take his head clean off. Street had been watching in horror and the instant him and Lacy had made eye contact he shoved Angie hard to the ground to his left and he dove to the far right.

The silenced shot created a "whoosh" as it flew into the airspace where Street's neck had been just a split second earlier. Kim quickly cast a backward glance in time to see Lacy swing the gun in her direction and take aim. Kim gave the tree branch one last mighty shove and it met its mark on the other end.

She crouched on all fours and started across as fast as she could. Street and Angie were both hugging the ground and screaming at her to hurry while keeping Lacy in their sights. No one saw the car coming. They only heard the horn and its relentless wailing growing louder, the closer it came. Once it registered with Street and Angie, they rolled out of the way and made room for the cab as it careened into place next to the fence and stopped on the high ground.

Wordlessly, the driver jumped out and swung open the back door. Angie and Street dove into the back seat just as Kim took a long, diagonal leap from the end of the tree branch and landed on the roof of the cab, followed closely by a bullet. The hot metal met its target, tearing through her jacket and grazing the fleshy part of her arm, creating an intense, wet burning sensation. She rolled quickly to the hood of the car and then fell to the ground. Bullets were pelting the cab, in search of a human target. The cab driver pulled Kim to her feet and shoved her, head first, into the front seat and fell in beside her.

The metal on metal was deafening as Lacy fired round after round into the cab, hoping to score a hit. The driver floored the gas pedal and sent sod flying everywhere as he spun out crazily onto the road. He sideswiped an oncoming car and cut off another in his attempt to put distance between them and the shooter.

Lacy swore under her breath and ran for the airport limousine still parked out front. Pushing through the crowd, she put the barrel of her gun to the limo driver's neck. "Decision time. Leave and live, or sit and die. Either way works for me."

Something in her eyes told the limo driver that she was not one to make idle threats. Five seconds later he stood by and helplessly, but thankfully, watched Lacy drive off. The cabbie had driven a safe distance away in record time and, seeing no one following them, said, "To The Press Club, I assume?"

"Yeah," Street replied, still trying to catch his breath. "Thank God you stuck around."

"Just wanted to catch a glimpse of Gallagher, maybe get a picture. I didn't count on all this, though."

Kim tried to ignore the patch of red widening on the sleeve of her jacket, while assuring her friends that it was just a flesh wound.

"Why are you helping us?" she asked. "How do you know we're not the bad guys?"

"I don't know anything for a fact–I always follow my gut. Sort of like my gut feeling when I first started following Mr. Gallagher, and that all proved to be good. Sometimes your instinct knows before your mind can sort it all out. By the way, my name's Jonathon. And back there? You weren't on the meter," Jonathon said, reaching over to trigger the start button. "But you are now. I don't make the rules, I just follow them. At least until I can change them," he laughed. "And so we don't waste any time, I'll drive, you talk."

Back at Gallagher's house, while the one injured man stared in disbelief at his swollen knee, the other had called 911 and then dialed Mr. Gallagher.

"Mr. Gallagher. Mr. Jensen was right that his agent might figure out where you live and come here. We had her but she got away. And she did try to plead her case saying that your life was in danger but not from her, just like Jensen said she would. When she found out that another agent was coming to pick her up, she freaked and ran.

"Actually, sir, I'd be more worried about the second agent. The two of us are lucky to be alive. 911 is on the way, but I'll explain when I see you. Be careful. Something very strange is going on. The one agent is blonde and from what I could see out the window, she may have taken a bullet in her upper arm. But the real rogue agent in my opinion is the other one, the one with black hair. Her name is Lacy. She's ruthless. But I wouldn't trust either one, for right now."

Mick had been nervously pacing for hours. After taking Lacy's phone call as she left Gallagher's house in the commandeered limo, Mick sucked it up and finally made the call to his boss. After the short, expected tirade at the turn of events, Mick assured his boss that Lacy was on her way to The Press Club where she would finish off both Gallagher and Kim, and with any luck throw Street and Angie in for good measure. After that, Lacy would be the last loose end they would have to deal with. That is, if she made it out alive. Then, they turned their attention to their next prospective presidential candidate.

"Are you sure that Michael Hennessy knows what's expected of him?" Mick asked. "And, the consequences of betraying us?"

Mick laughed nervously. "It's utterly amazing what men, or women for that matter, will do to be Commander-in-Chief. They will give up their very souls for the second highest office in the land." Along with his boss, Mick laughed at the very thought of how easy it was to purchase loyalty.

"Second highest office," the boss laughed, "that's funny."

"And, we don't even have to purchase their loyalty with our own money," Mick continued. They laughed again. "Through the voluntary compliance scam, better known as the IRS, the citizens of this great nation pay out money earned by their own blood, sweat, and tears for the privilege of being betrayed by the very person they're paying to represent their own best interests. Amazing." More laughter.

But, Mick's bravado dwindled after the call ended. His boss made no pretense about holding him responsible for the current dilemma. And, why shouldn't he? Mick had spearheaded the implementation of the plan and had guaranteed its success. Eager to make his mark, he had trusted the chemist and had relied heavily on the efficacy reports for CRP-24, but they had let him down. And he had been sure that he could keep Lacy's involvement a secret, but that had become impossible. Little to nothing was going as planned. Mick should have had contingency plans in place, but he didn't. It never occurred to him that him or his plan would fail. He knew that he'd better come up with something fast.

Tucked safely away in a hotel suite near The Press Club, Gallagher and his campaign team stared in disbelief at the breaking news story on the flat screen. Every station in town was pre-empting scheduled shows to report on the events unfolding at Gallagher's house. Some coverage was better than others due to better positioning at the gate, driveway, and surrounding fence. But, every station managed to capture video of Lacy taking aim and firing at Kim, Street, and Angie as they escaped in a cab. As usual, the media were all speculating on what it all meant. As usual, they were all clueless. They had yet to be told by the owners of their stations just how, and what, to think and say about it.

Surrounded by his campaign team, Gallagher paused briefly and then finally spoke up. "Ladies and gentlemen. The fact that we've had to take precautionary steps to sequester ourselves like this speaks to the strength of our message and the fear it's invoking. What we've just seen is further proof that the powers-that-be will take drastic measures."

"With all due respect, sir," his young campaign manager interrupted, "this campaign and its supporters are the real powers-that-be."

A cheer went up and the small group gathered around applauded the sentiment. Gallagher smiled and acquiesced. "I stand corrected, young man, and it's because of all of you, and countless others like you, that we will someday emerge as the powerful voice that we are. However, after watching the news, I'm afraid things are worse than I thought. Please make the decision to stay or go based on your own personal risk assessment and obligations. No one will think less of you and there is much to be done behind the scenes where it will be safer."

In a show of solidarity, one staffer after the other looked to the campaign manager and asked for their assignments as if Gallagher had never uttered those words. "The youth of today is what gives me such hope for tomorrow. It's what's made being confined to this wheelchair endurable. Let's get on with it, then," he said.

26

Due to a good tail wind, Rod landed in D.C. well ahead of schedule and hailed a cab. Generally, most cabbies would volunteer newsy bits of information picked up from passengers and other cabbies throughout the day as a way of making small talk to pass the time. But Rod's airport cabbie was more entrepreneurial than most. When Rod casually inquired about Gallagher, the cabbie sensed there was more than a casual interest and the only thing he was going to give away for free was the bait that would lure Rod in.

"I believe the gentleman you're asking about was spotted by my brother-in-law going into one of the older hotels by The Press Club just yesterday. He's a cabbie for another outfit and was waiting to pick up a fare back to the airport and couldn't help but notice, considering the wheelchair and specialized van. Not to mention the entourage."

He stole a look at Rod's face in his rear view mirror to get a read on his passenger's reaction, but Rod didn't seem too impressed. The conversation might not be profitable after all.

"And you're sure it was Gallagher?" Rod asked half-heartedly, feigning only a casual interest.

"Of course, I really can't be sure unless I call my bro-in-law. I don't pay no attention to politics. What's the use? It don't matter what I want. Politicians are in it to win it for themselves. Anyway, my sister's husband's not as generous as me about giving away info. They got seven kids if you get my meaning. Three of them in braces. One's got asthma. It's not cheap, you know."

Rod handed the cabbie three hundred dollars and the cabbie was clearly unimpressed. "Don't mean to be insulting but three hundred doesn't go far these days, what with its current state of devaluation and all. Now, if you had an ounce of gold you could spare..."

Rod pulled off another three hundred to add to the bribe.

"Gold's hit another all-time high, over eighteen hundred dollars an ounce. Just a decade ago it was three hundred. Six hundred dollars is not quite one-third of an ounce, what with the premium and all. My bro-in-law won't appreciate being bothered on his day off for less than an ounce," the cabbie remarked.

"Six hundred's my last offer. It'll get him seventeen ounces of silver. Rate of return is as good or better than gold and he should diversify anyway. On the other hand, I'm sure there's a cabbie around that doesn't have kids with crooked teeth or breathing problems."

The cabbie closed his hand around the money before Rod could change his mind. "Seems to me I remember my bro-in-law talking about the gold-silver ratio lately and mentioning The Mayflower Hotel over on Essex and 23rd."

"Get me there," Rod said. As the cab sped off, he tried repeatedly to reach Kim. But, she couldn't hear the phone ringing over the noise of the traffic and the chatter of her companions. Rod had no idea where Kim was or how she was going to approach Gallagher, but he wasn't about to let that stop him from doing his part. He texted Kim that he was in town and on his way to The Mayflower to contact Gallagher and keep him from going to the press conference.

Rod did not move in political circles but was very successful and well-connected in his own right. And, he didn't get where he was by being passive. He was determined to get to Gallagher. When the cabbie dropped him in front of the massive stone entrance to the old hotel, Rod ignored the cabbie's announcement of the fare owed, simply telling him not to wait. The tone in Rod's voice brooked no argument and the cabbie begrudgingly pulled away.

Rod hustled into the well-appointed lobby and was immediately swept into the excitement of everyone watching the eye-witness news video as it played out on the screen. He watched in horror as Lacy took aim at Kim as Kim leaped into the air and landed clumsily on the roof of the cab. There was no sound of a gunshot. Maybe Lacy had held back. The videographer zoomed in on Lacy and revealed that the gun had a silencer attached. He felt sick as Lacy squeezed off another round as Kim rolled to the hood of the cab, and then fell to the ground. With Kim out of sight of the cameras, seconds past as Rod anxiously wondered if she was alright. When Kim finally struggled to her feet and into the front seat of the cab, there was no mistaking the growing red stain on her right jacket sleeve.

Thinking fast, Rod asked to see the hotel concierge. For years, he had good-naturedly suffered being told that he looked like Matt Jamieson, one of the nation's top broadcast journalists. He decided to see just how good the resemblance really was. When the concierge approached, he immediately mistook Rod for Jamieson and asked for his autograph. Signing a hotel business card in the most illegible way, Rod went along with the ruse. He never identified himself as Matt Jamieson and was never asked for any identification.

"I'm afraid Mr. Gallagher was expecting me twenty minutes ago, but my flight was late getting in from New York," Rod said with a delicate wave of the wrist. "If you just give me his room number..."

"It's hotel policy to respect the privacy of our patrons, Mr. Jamieson," the concierge said as he pulled out a cell phone. "I'll just let Mr. Gallagher know you've arrived."

"No need to waste any more of your time."

"I can assure you, it's no waste of time," he said, as he turned his back on Rod. He spoke quietly to someone on the other end and then turned to face Rod.

"Mr. Jamieson. How embarrassing. It would seem that Mr. Gallagher's campaign manager knows nothing of your interview..." The statement trailed off like a question, hoping for the right answer. Rod quickly obliged.

"My new intern will be looking for another job tomorrow morning. She assured me that everything was arranged. I was skeptical about using her but she's the station manager's cousin so you can imagine the spot I was in," Rod said, again with a delicate wave of the wrist.

"Yes. Yes," the concierge commiserated quickly. "I have the same problems here. But, it's not love, but paperwork and nepotism that makes the world go 'round. Very touchy situation for people in our positions. Very touchy. I'll take you up and see if we can't work this out for you."

Rod fell in step with the concierge as they walked to the elevator. With the hotel's privacy rights so easily ignored he made a mental note to never stay there in the future, and wondered if Gallagher and his security team had seen the news coverage of the earlier events at his house. If they had, the task of convincing everyone that Gallagher's life was in danger would be much simpler than he anticipated.

On the eighth floor, the concierge escorted Rod off the elevator and down the wide expanse of hallway to a suite of rooms with an oversized entrance door, perfect for the bulky, motorized wheelchair. The plush carpet added to the luxurious quietness of the hotel, one of its key features. The carpet was so plush and quiet that neither Rod nor the concierge heard the approaching footsteps from an adjoining hallway until it was too late.

Lacy landed several fast blows to the concierge and he crumbled wordlessly to the floor. Rod reacted swiftly to the assault and swung his leg. He connected with her arm but missed his intended target–her elbow joint. She never noticed. The feral gleam in her eyes told him that she would cut him no slack and would enjoy every minute.

Though she rarely made mistakes, Lacy realized she had under-estimated Rod and wondered if she should have taken him out first, while the element of surprise was on her side. But then, she wouldn't have been able to enjoy herself. While martial arts was one of Rod's passions, a hobby he pursued avidly, it was an all-consuming obsession to Lacy.

Like an animal on the hunt, she stalked and baited him, landing blow after blow until he was staggering backward down the hallway. There were a few seconds of excruciating pain, then an adrenaline rush that made it possible to ignore the pain while looking for any opportunity to land a lethal blow. He rebounded and they volleyed blows back and forth until the door to Gallagher's suite opened a crack as someone tried to see what the commotion was all about. "Lock the door!" Rod screamed, breathlessly.

That momentary diversion was a costly one for Rod. Lacy landed a kick to Rod's torso that sent him sprawling backwards, knocking over a heavy, wrought-iron plant stand. With Rod on his back, Lacy rushed forward to take advantage of the situation to finish him off. With newfound strength, Rod reached overhead behind him and grabbed the legs of the plant stand and swung the stand like it was a Louisville Slugger. The twisted iron connected with her left leg and she buckled to the floor. For a moment she was stunned, but just for a moment.

"You're mine," she hissed as she looked at him hatefully, "after I do your girlfriend. I wouldn't want you to miss that." To Rod's amazement she effortlessly righted herself and, with only the slightest of limp, disappeared quickly down the hallway and into the stairwell.

Thankful to be alive, he decided not to follow her. Rod knew that Lacy was capable of delivering on her promises.

With the commotion over, Gallagher's door opened and his team descended on Rod. They got him to his feet and helped him into the hotel suite, quickly closing and locking the door behind them. He looked around the living area of the suite which had been turned into a small campaign headquarters and wondered where David Gallagher was. Just then, the small group parted way and Rod found himself face to face with Mr. Gallagher.

"My staff thought it best for me to go into the bedroom as it appears from an earlier news story that someone may want me dead." Rod appreciated the man's blunt honesty. He also could not have asked for a better introduction. The severity of the situation had landed right at their door, to be witnessed first-hand. It wouldn't take much explaining after all.

"Mr. Gallagher, my name is Rod Windthorpe," he began. "This whole thing sounds crazy and plays out like a really bad B movie, but believe me when I say that everything I'm about to tell you is true."

David Gallagher interrupted. "We've been watching the news coverage of the commotion at my house earlier and my men claim they're lucky to be alive. The description they gave me of who they think the real rogue agent is apparently matches the description of the gal trying to kill you just now. And, believing the unbelievable has never been an issue with me. Just stay focused on the facts and the money trail and if it seems to unbelievable to be true then check out some more facts and some more money trails. But that's a difficult task for most people and that's precisely why this country is in the mess it's in. No one's minding the store. Now Mr. Windthorpe, tell me what's going on. I'm due at The Press Club in one hour and I won't disappoint my supporters."

Rod quickly filled him in on what Kim had told him as well as what he knew for himself. That Kim was an agent being manipulated through a drug known as CRP-24 and that she had been responsible for the deaths of Dunn and Madsen. The 'hits' of Dunn and Madsen were ordered as a means of eliminating the possibility that these two presidential hopefuls would ever have the chance of being elected by the growing number of citizens who were catching on to the corrupt master plan that existed in government.

That Mick, doing double duty as both Kim's pimp and her boss, had her doing the government's dirty work. And the goal was to ensure that a carefully chosen ringer would be elected to the White House. Someone who could sway the masses long enough to get elected and then be a puppet president with the power elite pulling the strings.

Gallagher and his staff never batted an eyebrow at these revelations. Most of the rest of the country would have. "How did Kim figure all of this out?" Gallagher asked.

Rod continued. "Mick didn't figure there was any chance of the drug wearing off. CRP-24 stands for Can't Remember Past and Twenty-Four Hours. In a nutshell, every memory of her collective past would be erased and from that point forward everything that Mick did not want her to recall in every past twenty-four hour period would be erased from her memory as it happened."

"That's very high-level selective memory manipulation," Gallagher said, quite impressed. "I'd heard rumors about it and never discounted it for an instant. Unless proven otherwise, it's been my experience that where there's smoke there's usually at least a spark of flame. And, if the tiny spark is ignored, well, that's how the big fire gets going but by then it's much harder to get under control."

Rod knew that Gallagher was not talking about fires. He was clearly alluding to an out of control government. Rod then got back to the point at hand. "Kim started having flashbacks about Dunn and Madsen and eventually her own brutal attack and she started to piece it all together. She decided that she had to trust someone so she told her most trusted friends who helped put together a plan. Shortly after Kim got Mick to admit that she was a government-issued assassin, sugar-coating it as serving the best interests of the country, Jay the bartender ended up dead and Angie's lucky to be alive. Sadly, they aren't the only casualties and there was an attempt on our lives as well."

"I assume Kim was the gal I saw in the video? The one jumping over the fence?" Gallagher asked.

"Yes. And as you know, the woman trying to kill her is the same one who tried to kill me in the hallway."

"And she came here to kill me," Gallagher said calmly.

"It seems the plan was actually for Kim to kill you during your press conference. At that point we have to assume that Kim wouldn't leave The Press Club alive and that Lacy, the kung fu bitch from hell, would do what she does best and clean up all the loose ends, those being Street and Angie, and even myself."

"Makes perfect sense," Gallagher agreed, looking at his watch. This simple gesture was the signal that his staff was waiting for. They sprung into action gathering up folders and briefcases, video equipment and cameras, as if there was absolutely no plan to murder Gallagher at The Press Club.

"With all due respect," Rod, clearly frustrated, spoke above the organized turmoil. "I came here to stop you from going to the press conference, to stop you from getting killed. Kim went to your house for the same reason. She's put herself in jeopardy for you. The fact that Lacy's in town tells me that Mick figures Kim may not follow through on killing you, and that Lacy is plan B."

"I agree with your assessment," Gallagher stated as he stared intently at Rod. "But, are you suggesting that I go into hiding?" Gallagher asked.

"Yes," Rod said, relieved that Gallagher was finally understanding. Then Rod would simply have to contact Kim, they could all meet somewhere safe and figure out a way out of this dilemma. The room suddenly went quiet as all activity and conversation stopped.

"Out of the question, young man," Gallagher spoke in carefully measured phrases. "Whether I live or die today is absolutely irrelevant to the cause of freedom in this country. Believe me when I say I'd prefer to live to see the day that 'We the people' take our country back, see our freedoms fully restored, and corruption at the highest levels punished and eliminated, but my preference to live to see that day is not a requirement for that day to come.

"The grass roots movement in this country is at its peak. It's bigger than the powers-that-be would have anyone believe, or even believe themselves. It's grown bigger than I dared to even dream it would. And, make no mistake. It's not because of Madsen or Dunn or myself. It's because of millions of people like you and Kim, and your friends, and these young people," Gallagher gestured broadly around the room to his staffers.

"Millions of people that are standing up and saying 'I've had enough and I'm not going to take it anymore!' This movement has real legs under it Rod, and those legs are going to carry it across the finish line in fine style, whether or not I'm rolling along in the lead. 'We the people' will cross that finish line, and the one after that, and the one after that. And if you doubt it, look to your friend, Kim. When lesser people would give up the fight to reclaim their own lives, Kim dug down deep for the inner strength to keep fighting. She has a very clear understanding that she does not exist to serve a government that's supposed to exist to serve her."

The applause started slowly, building as it went, and Rod couldn't resist joining in. "Enough. Enough," Gallagher said as he set his wheelchair in motion toward the door. "We have a candidacy to announce!"

Rod saw that he was powerless to stop the inevitable.

27

Kim nestled down low in the front seat of the cab. Her bravado about her gunshot wound was fading faster than the bloodstain on her sleeve was spreading. She felt woozy, but not from loss of blood. The thought that they all could have been killed made her feel light-headed.

She knew she owed the cabbie a believable explanation, but gave just an overview so he'd know what they were up against. He'd been an important ally and he deserved to know what was at stake. She wanted to keep him on their side, yet she didn't totally trust him. Neither Street nor Angie gave up any details, either. Despite Jonathon's pointed questioning to get more information, they deferred to Kim's expertise as an agent and let her do all the talking. Jonathon expressed righteous indignation and then fell silent.

Ignoring her trembling fingers, Kim then checked both phones for messages. There was a voice mail from Mick on her phone. She ignored it. Lacy had to have contacted him already so there was no use continuing the game.

On Rod's old phone, there was a text message from him. He was in town. He had seen video footage of Lacy shooting at them, and he was with Gallagher. They were on their way to The Press Club. He and Lacy had had an encounter which he would explain later. *How had he figured everything out?* She felt dizzy and nauseous as she tried to piece it all together.

Angie and Street had been watching Kim closely from the back seat and noticed the color draining from her face. "Jonathon!" Street spoke up, "Pull over somewhere quick. Kim ain't looking too good."

Jonathon had been so busy weaving in and out of traffic to get to the other side of town that he hadn't noticed how quiet and still Kim had become. Stealing a fast look in her direction, he dumped out the doughnuts and napkins from the waxed paper bag scrunched between them and shoved the sack in her direction. Kim grabbed the empty bag and had the door open before Jonathon had come to a stop. The smell of the greasy doughnuts only made matters worse and, since she hadn't eaten in quite a while, what ensued was a gut-wrenching case of dry heaves.

Afterward, totally exhausted, Kim laid down on the cold, freshly-shoveled walkway until some of her energy and color came back. Then, she quietly allowed Street and Angie to check out her wound.

"Hard to believe that a little flesh wound could bleed so much," Street said in amazement.

Angie shot him a shut-the-hell-up look and said, "Well, we're all damned lucky this is the worst of it."

Kim cut in abruptly. "Rod texted. He's in town. He figured it all out but don't ask me how. Him and Lacy had some kind of encounter. He saw the video coverage shot at Gallagher's house and him and Gallagher are on their way to The Press Club."

"I can get you to The Press Club in thirty minutes, tops," Jonathon announced, reaching out a hand to help Kim get to her feet. They were all surprised when Kim ignored the helping hand and continued to lie there.

"Did you hear what the man just said?" Street asked, surprised and annoyed at her passiveness. "It's gonna take thirty minutes to get there. We need to get moving."

Angie was also surprised at Kim's hesitation. "What's the problem, Kim?" Angie tried to be understanding, but her tone of voice gave away her irritation.

"So we get to The Press Club. Then what? Based on what I told Rod, he most likely tried to talk Gallagher out of going and failed, and mind you, he's pretty damned persuasive. If you remember, our primary goal was to talk Gallagher into hiding out until we could figure out the next step. Assuming he won't go into hiding, then what?" Kim looked at each one of them as if she was actually expecting an answer. None came.

"That wasn't a rhetorical question, people. Lacy's so close that I can smell the stench of her breath on my neck," she began, again. "My arm could have been blown clean off, or worse." She let that sink in for a few seconds. "And, I'm not the only one who could have been killed. And, to top it all off, now Rod's involved." She choked on those words and took a minute to compose herself before she continued.

"We're all going to end up dead, and for what? We can't slay this dragon by ourselves. Hell, no one even wants to believe the dragon exists. So we save Gallagher today. What about tomorrow, and the day after? What about his successors? Who's going to take up the torch to protect them? And it doesn't exonerate my actions and it doesn't bring back Dunn and Madsen. It doesn't bring back Jay and Mrs. Murdock. It's not going to give Marie back the innocence that Lacy brutally stole from her, or stop her nightmares. There's no guarantee that we can come out of this in one piece and get our lives back. Or that anyone will believe us. Or that we can put an end to the deception and corruption going on." Kim barely stopped to take a breath. "Where will it all end?" she asked as if to drive the point home. Jonathon handed her a napkin to wipe away the tears running down her cheeks. The ensuing sudden silence was awkward.

"The press conference starts in an hour," Street quietly reminded them as he looked at his watch. It was as if he hadn't heard a word. He thought back to how Grandma Mae had come down off the porch, wailing the tar out of the neighborhood thugs who had pounced on him. She didn't stop to analyze the situation. She reacted to a gut level response and her ingrained belief that "right makes might". And if she had worried, then or later, about the consequences she sure never showed it. It was an attitude that served her well for eighty-eight years.

"There must be a smarter way to handle this without over-analyzing it to death." Street was not about to give up. He had already figured out that it was an all or nothing proposition.

Kim's former conviction, having evolved into total futility and surrender just minutes earlier, now rose to a half-hearted argument. "No matter how many ways we can plan this out, there are too many variables that could throw a monkey wrench into things, putting everyone at risk."

"Then let's all just turn tail and run," Angie said, trying to take advantage of any opening to use reverse psychology. "After all, we can't change a damned thing anyways. We certainly can't change history and most likely can't change the future. We just have to walk away from it like it never happened and then keep running, and running…"

Angie watched for any sign at all that she was getting through to

Kim, but Kim's face was void of all expression as she sat there on the sidewalk. "Maybe your biggest fear is that even if the whole world exonerates you, you won't ever be able to forgive yourself, and if that's the case then you'll never be free. Just don't ever forget that you're as much a victim as anyone."

Long seconds passed as Kim went to some far away place in her mind. *Assuming we can all survive this, and even if Rod and I can have some type of life together, we would always be on the run. We'd all have to assume other identities, always looking over our shoulders, talking in hushed tones about the lives we used to know. Because of me, none of us will know another peaceful day and no one close to us will, either.*

Angie could well imagine what was going through Kim's mind. With a softer tone, she reached out and squeezed Kim's hand. "Whatever you're thinking, me too."

With excellent timing, Street seized the moment before it was lost. "Hey, now don't be thinking that you two are gonna leave me out of anything. By most peoples' accounts I didn't have much of a life before, but at least it was mine, and I'd like to have it back. As they say in New Hampshire, 'Live free, or die.'"

Jonathon said, "Great motto, but New Hampshire betrayed it when they, once again, voted overwhelmingly for someone who continues to inhibit their freedoms."

Kim followed up with, "No, we're not going to run. Eventually we'll run out of places to run to. When that happens, we'll run out of time. When we run out of time, it's over. And don't forget, Angie, you have family that will also be affected. And, what about Grandma Mae?" Kim looked at Street.

"And now Rod's at risk," she added. "And I'm not just talking about all the obvious, immediate risks on a personal level. This goes way beyond getting my identity and life back, or even about getting your lives back. Let's not forget that there's a powerful force behind our government that is undermining us as individuals, and as a country. What we do for ourselves, we do for all. I assume I can count on all of you?" The response was immediate, right down to Jonathon.

"Here's how I see it," Street started, even before being asked. "It's a sure bet that Mick now knows we all know what's up, so Lacy's here to make sure Gallagher goes down, as well as me and you," he looked right at Kim, emphasizing his point. "But now Lacy knows she's gotta deal with Rod and Angie too. She hadn't counted on that and it weakens her position and strengthens ours."

"Hey, don't forget about me," Jonathon said, now feeling fully involved. "Do you think Mick sent a back up for Lacy?" he asked.

"Maybe," Street acknowledged with a crooked grin, "or maybe you been watching too many FBI and CIA shows. Me? I don't think so for a couple of reasons. One. Mick knows that Lacy's a one-man, er... I mean, one-woman demolition team and two, Mick knows the less people involved, the easier the situation is to contain. You know, the less damage control. Can't be a hundred percent sure but I think she's flying solo." Seeing that he had everyone's attention, he continued.

"If we get moving, we still have time to make it to the press conference. Kim, get a hold of Rod and have him stick like glue to Gallagher. Tell him to continue to try to get Gallagher to cancel out, though Gallagher probably won't. We know that Gallagher already has his own security with him, and The Press Club provides its own and all that's a bonus. Rod needs to get word to all of them about what's going on–keep 'em on the watch. The four of us will split up and cover inside and outside watching for Lacy. With everyone on the alert, she may not get a chance to get close enough to him to make a 'hit'. Once we spot her, the security team can deal with her. We'll decide what to do from there." No one but Jonathon spoke up.

"That's it?" Jonathon asked in amazed horror. "That's your plan?"

"Afraid so, my man. Short notice and all."

Jonathon grabbed his walkie-talkie and in seconds he was connected with every cab in the company. "Just be available in the parking lot of The Press Club in thirty minutes. We might have some tires that need changing, so have your tire irons handy."

When Jonathon hung up, the three looked at him and waited for an explanation. "What?" he feigned ignorance and shrugged his shoulders. "It's just cabbie code for 'Bring some back up'."

Street pulled the knife out of his boot. "I brought this."

Angie presented the vial of acid. "Kim and I have these. They'll eat the rust off of steel. It's all I could do."

"Don't forget I now have a gun, courtesy of Mick," said Kim, as she patted her jacket pocket. "And there's a bullet with Lacy's name on it."

Jonathon left the group and started the cab. "Hustle it up! You're on the meter!" he yelled through the open window as Angie and Street pulled Kim to her feet. Before the last door slammed shut, Jonathon was doing a U-turn to get back to the highway leading to The Press Club and when they arrived, the sight of drivers congregating in small groups in the parking lot and surrounding area was a comforting sight. There was a sense of excitement in the air as they speculated amongst themselves as to why they were there. As they saw Jonathon's cab approach, they parted way for him. Within seconds, Jonathon and his passengers were surrounded by a horde of cabbies with one question on their minds.

"What do you want us to do?" asked an older, mild-mannered looking guy.

"Nothing illegal or dangerous," he assured them all, after getting out of the cab and gathering them around. "My passengers are government agents and they simply need some look-outs."

"Are you sure about the illegal part?" a younger guy jeered from the back. "The rules in this country are always changing."

"Yeah, but remember, the rules are always for our own good," piped up a beefy, biker-looking dude as they all laughed at what appeared to be an inside joke.

"Now, now," Jonathon said calmingly sarcastic, "I checked just this morning and it looks like we still have the right, at least as of this morning anyways, to be on the look out for a very hot-looking, fair-skinned gal dressed in black leather right down to black spiky boots, cropped black hair, you know, the proverbial brick shithouse."

"Hey! I was with her last night!" came from the crowd.

"Maybe in your dreams!" was the reply.

The laughter stopped on a dime as Jonathon drove the point home. "Make no mistake, this gal is not the stuff dreams are made of. She's the stuff nightmares are made of." Silence settled over the group as everyone grew serious and waited for Jonathon to continue.

"I can't talk about the details and I don't want to appear melodramatic or anything, but believe me when I say that this is top-secret stuff. This gal has already tried to kill all four of us," he gestured to Kim, Angie, and Street who were sitting patiently in the cab. "And that's just this morning," he added for emphasis.

"She's here to kill the guest speaker, and by extension the country we've all known and loved. To those of you who know of David Gallagher, nothing more needs to be said. To those of you who are unfamiliar with Mr. Gallagher, the time to get familiar is way past due. But, for today, all you need to do is call me on my walkie-talkie the minute you see this badass bitch and give me her exact location. I'll get word to these people," again gesturing to his passengers, "and they'll handle it from there. Don't try to be a hero and don't attempt to communicate with her in any way or you may never live to complain about your new tyrannical comptroller, Omar, ever again." This last comment brought knowing, but nervous, laughs from the crowd as they broke up into small groups once again. In no time they began organizing themselves to watch the entrance into, and exit out of, the parking lot as well as every side of the building.

"Hey, what if she's already inside?" someone yelled out to Jonathon.

Jonathon replied as Street, Angie, and Kim climbed out of the cab, "That's unlikely but, if she is, she'll still need to try to come back out at some point."

"Assuming she can," Street said hopefully, and everyone understood his point. They exchanged contact info with Jonathon and then split up in different directions with each trying to gain access to the inside of the Club. After the morning's incident at Gallagher's house, The Press Club's private security detail was on high–but not impenetrable–alert.

With the sustained downturn in the economy, little chance of recovery in the near future, and a bad attitude about increased taxes to bail out the banksters, irresponsible corporations, Wall Street crooks, and foreign countries, the security guards who wouldn't ordinarily risk their jobs to gain a little tax-free windfall on the side were now open to any side deal they could get. Their attitude was that it was small potatoes compared to the Bernie Madoffs of the world and the big bonuses handed out to Wall Street executives as their reward for screwing the American public out of their retirement funds. They just wanted their piece of the pie. And if their piece of the pie came in the form of a bribe to gain access to The Press Club, then so be it.

Street, Angie, and Jonathon sweet talked their way inside in the form of a sizable donation. Kim gained quick access to The Press Club by clipping her counterfeit security ID badge to the front of the jacket that she had borrowed from Angie to cover up the bloodstain on her sleeve. Her phony ID badge merited a perfunctory glance, at best, from the security guards who never stopped their private conversations to even look at her.

28

Once inside, Kim found herself lost in the commotion. Reporters from all the major news outlets were milling about, networking and vying for the best vantage points for the anticipated press conference. For those who wanted to be selected to have their questions answered, it was imperative to be advantageously positioned for the question and answer segments. Their videographers did likewise, also competing for the best spots as they busied themselves setting up video cameras, lighting, and microphones amidst a tangle of electrical chords. In the chaos, no one took notice of Kim, even as she carefully stepped over and around the obstacles.

Safely tucked away in a corner of the room, Kim surveyed the room then texted her specific location to Rod. She stayed put, waiting for Rod to either show up or text her back. Seconds turned into minutes as she impatiently watched the room come together for the press conference. What appeared to be utter havoc when she arrived, transformed into an organized news conference within minutes. Five minutes passed and no word or sign of him. She pulled the phone back out. Before she could dial, something hard dug into the flesh wound in her upper right arm and she winced in pain.

She turned to face the careless individual who had accidentally bumped into her with some type of video equipment. Instead, she found herself face to face with a long-haired blond dressed in a similar outfit as hers. Pain quickly drew her attention downward, to the hard steel of a gun muzzle bearing down relentlessly on her arm. Braving eye contact again, Kim recognized a cold ruthlessness that was unmistakable. Lacy!

Kim searched the room in a panic. Where was Rod? Someone must see what's going on. But, no one did. They were all focused on their tasks. Kim carefully palmed the cell phone as she looked around again, praying that Lacy hadn't seen it.

"Forget about it, Kim. Nobody cares. Except for maybe your boyfriend. Now, let's see if you care about him as much as he cares about you."

"What have you done with Rod?" Kim demanded, trying to ignore the pain.

"I can think of many things to do with him, in due time. I might even let you watch. Better yet, I might let you join us."

"Not a chance," Kim said, feigning strength she didn't feel.

"Start walking over to the elevator to our far left," Lacy directed her.

Kim's hesitant first few steps invited the barrel of the gun to dig in deeper, a painful incentive to get Kim moving forward. She obeyed immediately in an effort to ease the pain, as Lacy disgustedly chided her.

"Mick was right about you. You're nothing but a little mouse. That's why he handpicked you to do our dirty work. But, do you know what people do when they get tired of the tiny squeaks and nervous scamperings of the little mouse? Yes. They set a mousetrap to get rid of it. Well, consider me your mousetrap, Kim."

The pressure of the gun muzzle had been too much for Kim's fresh wound and it started bleeding again. She tried to ignore the wetness of fresh blood staining her shirt and jacket. Slowly pushing through the room in spite of feeling faint, she managed her way over to the elevator. Lacy reached out and pressed the button. Kim made good use of Lacy's temporary distraction to subtly trigger the vibrate mode on her borrowed phone and quietly slipped it into a pocket. She couldn't risk having her only lifeline taken away from her.

The elevator door opened, spilling its occupants into the main conference room. No one even glanced in their direction. It was as if they didn't exist. Everyone was abuzz about Gallagher's press conference due to start in twenty minutes. Lacy nudged Kim into the elevator. Kim balked, weighing her options.

"Nobody's paying any attention," Lacy hissed in her ear. "You're dead either way, but Rod could live. Your choice."

They rode the elevator up the three floors to the top and stepped into a wide, deserted hallway. Storage boxes were stacked against the walls on each side, stopping short of obstructing each doorway and the large glass partitions that took over where the solid walls ended on their way to the ceiling. Each door led to a small office and inside each small office were labeled boxes of files and manuals all stacked randomly, and somewhat vicariously, about. Old computer monitors and processors, in varying stages of antiquity, were perched on desks and shelves and leaned ominously as if threatening to fall over. In spite of the clutter, Kim's eyes were drawn to the fresh, smeared bloodstain on the doorjamb straight ahead.

"I was hoping you'd notice that. There's nothing like the sight of fresh blood to get someone's attention."

"You're one sick bitch," Kim said, thinking about Jay, Marie, and Mrs. Murdock.

"I do believe that's the nicest thing anyone's ever called me," Lacy laughed, giving Kim a good shove inside.

Kim entertained a fleeting thought about putting up a fight but her arm felt weak and numb from the recent trauma. She knew she would be no match for Lacy. Even with two good arms, she'd be lucky to hold her own against such a formidable opponent.

Kim scanned the room around her but saw nothing to explain the blood. Again digging the barrel of the gun into Kim's flesh wound, Lacy impatiently goaded her through another doorway, also blood-smeared. Kim stopped dead in her tracks. Rod was seated in front of her, tied up so tight that his wrists were discolored from lack of circulation. His face had taken quite a beating.

"Either your man, here, has a real thing for blonds or my attempt to look as boring as you paid off." Lacy slipped the blond wig from her head and, with gun in hand, raked her fingers through her short black hair.

Kim looked at Rod, who shot her a warning look to keep quiet. He had learned the hard way that questions made Lacy even angrier.

"Actually, I'll give credit where credit is due," Lacy continued, as she began to undress in front of them. She proved adept at managing every task in spite of the gun that never left her hand. "I made sure he didn't see my face so that he would think I was you so we can hardly blame him for being a bad boy."

Completely in the buff, Lacy stood in front of Rod and backhanded him hard across the face. It was an act without provocation. Kim recoiled in horror and disgust. Rod shot Kim another warning look and

Kim stood her ground. She had no choice but to trust Rod.

"Bad boys are great fun," Lacy announced, stepping back and stroking her large breasts for her audience of two. "Yes, they're implants, in case you were wondering. Can't have too much of a good thing. But good boys being bad are even more fun," she said, straddling Rod's lap.

Rod turned his head away in disgust, waiting for the back of her hand again. "And of course, I've found that good girls can definitely be bad. They're a different kind of fun but once you get them going the naughty innocence is definitely to my liking," Lacy suggestively said to Kim, as she looked her up and down.

"You're fucking depraved," Kim responded, thinking of Marie.

Lacy's phone interrupted the unfolding scenario, much to Rod's relief. He knew how cold and cruel Lacy could be. He didn't want any of that coming Kim's way. Lacy climbed off of Rod and scrambled to find her phone in the pile of clothes she had thrown to the floor.

"Yes, Mick," she said calmly. "Everything's under control. Kim will do exactly as she's told. Guaranteed."

Mick didn't care to hear the details. His only concern was being reassured that the plan was on track.

"That's correct. I've already booked a return flight and I'll meet with you about four o'clock, your time.

"Why don't I bring a friend and we'll celebrate?" The gleam in Lacy's eyes gave away her intended meaning as she brought the call to a close. Rod and Kim felt repulsed.

They noticed that the clock on the wall indicated the press conference would start in five minutes. Gallagher should be on his way to the conference room. Hopefully, he would wonder what had happened to Rod and would decide to cancel, or at least postpone his announcement that he was running for president until he was reasonably sure it was safe. Rod had already shared with him everything that he knew and it was enough to make most men change their minds. But, Gallagher was not like most men.

"Here's the way this is going to roll," Lacy calmly told Kim and Rod as she squirmed into her tight pants, wriggling them up her hips with gun in hand. "You and I are going downstairs together," she said, looking at Kim. "As a special security agent you're going to approach Gallagher and introduce yourself so he feels more confident. You'll then place yourself in a position directly in front of him so you'll have a good shot at him, and the news people will get great footage of all of it. And remember, I'll never be too far away," she said, waving her gun for added emphasis.

Feeling trapped and desperate, Kim and Rod watched Lacy as she dressed. They were both looking for an opportunity for Kim to gain the upper hand but they were stunned at how fearsome Lacy looked. Underneath her sleek curves was the body of a jungle cat–taut and well-muscled. She was a killing machine. Poor Jay never had a chance. Kim knew she was no match. Nothing short of a miracle would save this situation.

Lacy eyed them both then quickly slipped the tight turtleneck sweater over her head. But, she wasn't quick enough. Before the sweater could clear her head, Kim reacted without thinking and charged at her for all she was worth. Lacy was caught off guard and lost her footing. She awkwardly stumbled sideways, almost knocking Rod over in the chair. Kim regained her footing and jumped on top of her, hoping the element of surprise would be on her side. It was.

Lacy started clubbing at Kim with the gun while at the same time trying to free her head of the sweater. They exchanged blow after blow. Lacy tried to buck Kim off but Kim was straddling her chest like a mechanical bull at a country bar and she was not about to let go. Rod watched helplessly as he tried in vain to break free of the ropes. Then, he remembered the gun.

"Kim, the gun!"

Kim reached into her pocket and pulled out the handgun that Mick had arranged for her. That action cost her the few seconds that Lacy needed to pull her sweater down around her neck. As Kim brought the gun around toward Lacy, Lacy grabbed Kim's wrist. She smashed the gun into Kim's mouth and then took aim at her face.

Rod had used his legs and all of his strength to walk himself, still tied to the chair, over to Kim and Lacy. Using his legs as leverage, he tipped himself over on top of Lacy's lower legs, pinning her to the floor. She screamed in pain and dropped her gun.

"Kim!" yelled Rod, "Shoot her, then get Gallagher out of here! Hurry!"

After a split second hesitation, Kim crawled off of Lacy. She brought the gun up, aiming at the heart, then hesitated again. She didn't know if she could knowingly and cold-bloodedly take another life, even if it was someone's as vile and ruthless as Lacy.

"I wouldn't think twice about shooting your ass," Lacy sneered, confidently daring Kim.

"Think about Jay and Marie," Rod said calmly.

Hearing that, Kim pulled the trigger. The noise was thunderous, but nothing happened. Lacy laughed. Kim fired again. Nothing! With Rod still on top of her, Lacy grabbed her gun and pointed it at Kim. Lacy relished the fear in Kim's eyes.

"You didn't seriously think Mick was stupid enough to give you live ammunition, did you?" Lacy threw her head back and laughed, while keeping the gun trained on Kim. She was a cat toying with a mouse before the kill. It was nothing more than sport for her.

With uncertainty, Kim looked from Lacy to Rod.

"Go, go, go!" Rod yelled as he tried to keep Lacy pinned down. Throwing the useless gun aside, Kim dove headlong through the doorway into the adjoining cubicle and then scrambled awkwardly to her feet while favoring her injured arm. She crouched next to the stacked boxes, using them as cover. Adrenaline was all that was keeping her going.

So I get to Gallagher. Then what? I might save him for today but what about tomorrow, or the day after that? And how about his successors? And what about Rod and everyone else? We all pose too much of a threat to be allowed to go free. Kim knew that the odds were stacked against them but, with renewed determination, she vowed that she was not going down without a fight.

There was nothing Kim could do for Rod at this point. Even Lacy's penchant for violence would not overrule logic. Lacy would need to keep Rod alive so he could be used as the necessary leverage to accomplish her mission. Kim counted on the fact that Lacy would be so intent on coming after her that she would leave Rod alone.

Helpless to do anything more, Kim ran through the cluttered cubicle putting herself briefly in Lacy's direct line of fire, and made a bee-line for the doorway. Clearing the doorway, and safely in the hallway, she bypassed the elevator and ran down the stairs to the first floor, coming out to the right of the stage. She stopped short, trying to catch her breath.

With mild curiosity a few people looked in her direction, but seconds later resumed their tasks. The press conference had started and Gallagher had just been introduced. To her surprise, he was sitting behind a three-sided, bulletproof glass barrier. Fortunately, the day's events had struck a note with him and he was proceeding more cautiously than normal. His entourage of trusted staff stood shoulder to shoulder, directly behind him. Kim surveyed the room and caught sight of Angie and Street milling among the crowd. They had already spotted her and knew from her disheveled looks that Lacy was already in the building.

Kim played out different scenarios in her mind but knew that it was too late to interfere without causing a scene. She didn't know what to do. With the bullet-proof barrier as protection Gallagher would probably survive the day, even without her interference. Maybe Kim should just focus her attention on getting herself and her friends out alive. She looked around anxiously for any sign of Lacy as Gallagher wheeled himself up to the microphone and began speaking. His voice was husky with emotion.

"Ladies and Gentlemen of these tenuously still-united states. I come to you today as your humble servant to fill the void created by the recent deaths of Senator Madsen and Congressman Dunn. Both were assassinated to keep them from not only attaining the presidency of these united states, but even more importantly from spreading their messages of personal liberty and prosperity." Kim, the unwitting assassin of both Madsen and Dunn, was filled with remorse.

"Yes. You heard right," he repeated. "Assassinated. They were murdered. As most of you know I, too, was targeted years ago. I never gave in to the fear and never will. If you're not a target then you're not a threat. It's as simple as that.

"Even in ancient times the power elite of corrupt governments lived in fear of being exposed for what they were and for what they intended to do. Nothing has changed. And make no mistake. There will always be those who ascend to power almost unnoticed until their agenda of self-serving corruption becomes increasingly apparent. Be warned. Those are the truly dangerous. For, by the time their true intentions are suspected, uncovered, and exposed, the damage to each of us, and the country, is near impossible to reverse. *Near* impossible, but *not* impossible. Now, as then, it should be the goal of every one of us, from ordinary citizens to the handful of truly upstanding elected officials, to expose political corruption and eliminate it."

Gallagher stopped speaking and looked intently at the crowd. He wondered how many news stations would edit his speech, or kill it altogether. He stayed on task, determined to make the announcement that would please some and displease others.

"As some of you may know," he continued, "I have spent the past few decades mentoring honest people into positions of power in this country. The goal was to painstakingly reclaim this country for its citizens. Though I never thought I would see it in my lifetime, thanks to the instant world wide communication we enjoy because of the Internet, and the progressively corrupt nature of the powers-that-be, there has emerged a grass-roots movement–rebellion or revolution if you will–that is now decades ahead of where I thought it would be when I took to this wheelchair."

Kim scanned the room, but still no sign of Lacy. Angie and Street were on the move, working their way through the crowd and keeping a vigilant watch for Lacy.

"The murders of Madsen and Dunn," he continued, much to Kim's angst, "are barometers that measure the threat that freedom and personal liberty are to the government of this country. Their deaths are a good indicator that the time has never been better for the citizens of this country to take back what's rightfully theirs–what was guaranteed to them by our founding fathers through the Declaration of Independence, The Constitution, and The Bill of Rights.

"To those who claim we are extremists, I claim that we only appear extreme because this country has veered so ridiculously off track from where it should be. Extreme situations and problems require extreme solutions.

"I stand before you today, certainly not in a literal sense, but figuratively. I stand for our rights to life, liberty, and the pursuit of happiness. I stand for accountability from those to whom we pay our hard-earned money to represent us and make sure that our constitutional rights are upheld. I stand for every one of today's generation as well as generations yet unborn. My fellow citizens, I sit humbly before you and declare my candidacy for the office of President of the United States of America. With great humility, I ask for your support. Together, we can reclaim the inalienable rights that we are all entitled to, not only as Americans, but as citizens of the world. The time has come. The time is right. The time is no..."

The explosion was deafening, resonating in the small space. The fireball blinding. The unmistakable stench of explosives was thick in the air. Most were knocked off their feet, falling into each other and into the equipment which toppled over, pinning them down. Panic enveloped the room and those who could still move crawled, limped, or ran helter-skelter. The less fortunate lay moaning, or lifeless, in the conference hall.

By sheer luck, Kim was practically unscathed. Knocked about by flying debris, the minor cuts and bruises she sustained would heal in no time. She looked toward the stage hoping to see that everyone had survived, but smoke hung suspended over the stage area like a thick velvet curtain.

Members of the security team that were positioned outside of the conference room had descended on the room from everywhere, trying to make sense of what was going on as they started the evacuation process. She started toward the stage, but a movement in her periphery vision caught her attention. Lacy was sneaking back through the stairwell door. She turned and made eye contact with Kim before disappearing from view.

Pushing through the chaos, Kim flashed her badge and commandeered a gun from one of the security guards. She went after Lacy, closing the distance quickly.

29

Halfway up the stairwell Lacy stopped, turned, and fired at Kim. The shot would have hit its mark had Kim not instinctively ducked to the side. Instead, the shot ricocheted off the wall where Kim's head had been.

Out of practice, Kim's shot went wild, imbedding in the ceiling well behind Lacy. Lacy threw her head back and laughed maniacally. Taking up a deliberate pose as if she feared nothing and had all the time in the world, Lacy leisurely took aim at Kim.

Kim ducked down and swung her gun around in front of her. She had a fast flashback to the Bureau shooting range and a comforting feeling of familiarity and calmness enveloped her. With new confidence and composure she stood up and started zigzagging up the steps toward Lacy. Shocked at Kim's sudden boldness, Lacy turned and ran up the next flight of stairs with Kim close behind.

Another explosion rocked the building, knocking both women off balance. In her attempt to grab onto anything to steady herself, Kim released her hold on her gun and it went crashing down the stairs behind her as she fought to gain hold of the handrail. Lacy recovered quickly, never losing grip of her weapon. Within seconds she, once again, had Kim dead in her sights.

"How unfortunate that the fun has to end so fast," Lacy smirked, as she slowly descended the stairs to get closer to Kim. "And we were just getting started," she said, keeping her weapon trained on her adversary.

"Do it! Go ahead and shoot!" Kim ordered, catching a whiff of smoke as it slowly ascended the stairwell. Seeing no way out of the dilemma and feeling defeated, she saw no sense in prolonging the inevitable. She had done her best. There was nothing more she could do. She hoped someone would find Rod as the building was being evacuated.

"In due time," Lacy said sharply. "After all, why rush a good thing? Like good sex, killing someone should be the climactic conclusion of prolonged teasing. I mean, a quickie's okay once in a while if that's all time will allow, but it's just not as emotionally satisfying.

"First, a little foreplay. Allow me the pleasure of telling you why you failed today. Why you failed to save yourself, your boyfriend, your ragtag group of friends, and that sincere but hopelessly misguided Gallagher. You failed because you put emotions ahead of power. My boss and I will win because we know that power strengthens, emotions weaken."

"You and Mick may win today, but you can't win forever," Kim shot back, trying to ignore the smoke. "What you're doing to this country will fail because power for power's sake is always discovered for what it is and overthrown. Me and my friends are just the tip of the iceberg.

"There's millions more out there who are so sick and tired of being afraid and powerless that they're uniting as we speak to bring the corrupt powers-that-be to justice. Historically, that's been true of every revolution. Fear then anger, Lacy. The catalysts that ignite revolutions. So, in the long run it's emotion that wins, not power."

With gun in hand, Lacy started applauding. "Bravo! Very heart-warming! You're as weak as your parents. And by the way, Mick really isn't my boss. He's much too emotion-driven to be superior to me."

"You don't deserve to talk about my parents!" Kim shot back.

"You know what? Since it's just me and you, and you're not leaving here alive, I'll tell you a little story." The gleam in Lacy's eyes was pure evil. If she noticed the wisps of smoke wending their way slowly up the stairwell, she didn't show it.

"Your mom and dad were agents." Lacy baited the hook and then waited to reel Kim in.

"Tell me something I don't already know," Kim sparred.

"Ironically, this whole project has come full circle," Lacy continued. "Mick's dad was the agent in the original plot to stop the growing unrest in this country by taking out Gallagher years ago. You see, there's much more to the Bureau than people realize. There are agencies within agencies. A government-sponsored, multi-level, pyramid scheme."

"I must have missed Billie Mays' infomercial, may he rest in peace," Kim said.

"Sarcastic bitch," Lacy said calmly, and then continued. "As the story goes, your parents somehow found out about the original assassination plot and showed up in the nick of time, causing Agent Jensen to misfire. He ended up crippling Gallagher instead of killing him. Your parents saved Gallagher's life, but it cost them their own."

In spite of Lacy's revelations, Kim found it increasingly hard to ignore the acrid fumes rising up the stairs. Lacy seemed unaware and continued.

"Apparently, no one at the Bureau believed your parents' claim that they had discovered a covert sub-group within the agency. An investigation into the Gallagher shooting concluded that the incident was merely an accidental shooting and nothing more, and a misunderstanding by your parents. But there were those who knew that your parents knew better, so they had to be kept in line.

"With your health and safety as the trump card, your parents minded their own business for quite awhile. If they dared speak of it at all, it was probably in whispered snatches of conversation between themselves, far away from where anyone else could overhear. But, after a number of years, Agent Jensen claimed they stumbled on some very damning information and that they were too big of a threat. Personally, I think he killed mommy and daddy because he grew tired of the constant vigilance, not because they were really a threat. After all, they loved you far too much to place you in any harm, didn't they? Well, I guess we'll never know for sure."

"My parents died in a car accident," Kim argued, choking on the smoke that was now getting thicker.

"Exactly," Lacy agreed, seemingly unaffected by the seriousness of their situation. "A semi truck met them head on as they crossed over the center line of the old bypass highway on their way home. But it was no accident. The whole scene was engineered by Agent Jensen, who forced them into the oncoming lane in front of the truck. I heard it was a delightful mess."

Kim was distressed but determined not to look weak. "You should have been the poster child for birth control. You know, with the caption 'Don't let this happen to you!'" Kim said.

"Cute. But I can think of better things to do with that mouth of yours than to utter such inane comebacks," Lacy said suggestively.

"I wouldn't perform oral sex on you with someone else's mouth," Kim shot back.

"Ouch. Now that really hurts my feelings, Kim. You shouldn't knock it till you try it. I can't imagine where that backbone is coming from."

From a distance, the wail of sirens grew louder as police cars, ambulances, and fire trucks approached The Press Club. The air in the stairwell was a veil of smoky haze but Lacy continued, undeterred.

"No one was really sure if you knew anything and no one could take the chance that you would talk. But killing you would have caused too much suspicion. So Mick offered to monitor you as a possible test subject for some type of future project. He was just coming up through the ranks and was looking for a way to make a name for himself. He kept tabs on you through various sources and once your spunkiness had been tamed down he tagged you as the perfect dupe for use in the project."

"What project?" Kim couldn't believe what she was hearing. The smoke was making her cough and her eyes tear. One way or the other she knew she would never leave the stairwell alive. Still, she had a morbid curiosity to understand everything that had led her to this point.

"Thanks to the wonderful world of pharmaceuticals it wasn't hard to develop drugs designed to make you start thinking about a career in the Bureau. Drugs without the FDA seal of approval, of course, a seal that has been proven many times over to be worth less than the paper it's printed on. It was even easier getting them to you. Our little special division of the Bureau has contacts everywhere who either owe us favors or who want favors which, of course, makes them owe us favors. What a splendidly vicious little circle."

Lacy's story telling was interrupted as sirens heralded emergency vehicles and first responders descending on the Club. Kim was watching for any sign of weakening resolve on Lacy's part that she could use to coax Lacy into trying to save themselves but Lacy seemed oblivious to the threat, as if she was invincible. She merely continued with the story.

"Once you applied to the Bureau, your admission was

miraculously expedited and from there, Mick cultivated a relationship with you, gained your trust, had you drugged with CRP-24, and dispatched you to save the country, one 'trick' at a time. What he didn't foresee were the breakthroughs in your memory, probably caused by some unforeseen, long-term effects of the first drugs you were given after your parents died."

Kim was now choking on each breath and Lacy was doing her best to keep her own composure. Lacy was the epitome of disciplined self-control. Kim hesitated to ask but needed to know. "My aunt and uncle?"

"Natural causes, actually. Purely coincidental that they both died within days of each other, but it saved us the trouble of making sure that no one would ever miss you when you assumed your new identity."

Kim started coughing uncontrollably, gasping for air and Lacy could no longer ignore the smoke. Once again, Lacy took deliberate aim at Kim's head. Between the smoke, the story telling, and the plan to kill Kim Lacy's attention was so focused that she had no idea that Street had stealthily entered the stairwell from the third floor. Kim spotted him and was overcome with relief. Not daring to give him away, she instinctively knew that she had to keep Lacy's attention on herself and keep her talking while Street managed to position himself more advantageously behind her.

"What's in it for Mick?" Kim asked, keeping Lacy distracted.

"For Mick it's simply the satisfaction to know that he succeeded where his dad failed, and revenge for all the years he was ridiculed by his dad as an underachiever. And he didn't just succeed in the original plan to control our elections. Mick has been key in taking the original plan and developing it into so much more. But more on that later.

"For Mick, assuming the power position is important, but secondary. He needs praise, to be thought of as important. Between you and me, that's going to be his downfall. True power players prefer to stay in the shadows, controlling everything at arm's length. It's the control that's key, not the recognition. The need for recognition gets you into trouble."

While Lacy rambled on, Street slowly raised his arm and took aim at Lacy's mid back, just left of center. Hopefully, he would miss the bony part of her shoulder. The sharp blade of his knife would need to cut through the softer, thinner ribs with enough force to hit the heart or some other vital structure. Lacy caught his movement out of the corner of her eye. She turned toward it as Street released the blade.

Lacy's shot went wild as the knife imbedded in her chest. She looked down in disbelief and saw the hilt of the knife sticking out of her left breast, or what was left of it. The ruptured implant was oozing thick silicone down the front of her sweater. In her few remaining seconds of life she seemed more dismayed with the silicon leak than the blood trailing alongside it. In one last futile attempt, Lacy tried to aim her gun toward Kim, but her arm was unsteady and the smoke was growing thicker and more acrid. Kim was riveted to her spot on the stairs as she watched the unfolding drama. She couldn't take her eyes off of Lacy.

With a burst of gunshot, a single bullet entered Lacy's head just above her left ear and sent a chunk of the right side of her head scattering in a reddish pink spray all over the wall. Lacy's eyes went into a vacant stare as she crumbled in a heap on the stairs.

Kim looked behind her in time to see someone scurrying back out through the lower stairwell door in a flurry of smoke. Mick! With Lacy neutralized, Street rushed down the steps toward Kim as Kim sidestepped Lacy who was rolling down each step like a human slinky, slowly at first then picking up speed, finally stopping abruptly at the door below.

"It was Mick," Kim choked out the words.

Street grabbed her hand and pulled her along behind him. They carefully avoided the slippery trail of blood and silicon, stopping briefly while Street retrieved Kim's gun from where it had landed earlier. Thrusting the gun at Kim, he bent over Lacy and grabbed the knife handle and pulled. It held firm. Planting his foot on her chest for leverage, he wrapped both hands around the hilt and, with a great sucking noise, the blade released from Lacy's chest followed by a spray of blood and goo. He swiped his blade clean on Lacy's pants. Marveling at how impotent and unattractive she now looked, Street shoved her lifeless body away from the door and pulled Kim through the opening. A thick wall of smoke stopped them short.

Street pushed Kim down to the floor, to breathable airspace. "The exit near the stage," he ordered.

"No!" she yelled. "We have to get Rod!"

"Angie's got him. They're outside by now." Street's tone invited no argument.

The nearer the stage, the more intense the heat and smoke. There was no doubt that the stage was the epicenter. The intended target, Gallagher. They could barely breathe or see. Staying shoulder to shoulder so they wouldn't get separated, they made their way instinctively across the floor to the remembered exit. Near the stage, they happened upon the carnage. The bomb had hit its mark.

Gallagher's bloody, lifeless form was still strapped into his overturned wheelchair, surrounded by the remains of several of his campaign staff. The American flag lapel pin which had rested so proudly on the collar of Gallagher's suit coat now hung askew, drenched in blood. Kim froze at the sight of the needless devastation.

"Keep moving! Mick's still on the loose!"

Kim didn't budge. She had failed. What was the point? The smoke and heat were getting more intense.

"Mick has to be stopped. Give up and all the future Dunn's and Madsen's and Gallagher's will be dead because you stopped short of succeeding. You'll never get your life back. What about your speech back there about fear and anger and about how emotions win, not power? We got plenty of fear going on here. Just notch up the anger!" Street coughed uncontrollably. Kim still didn't budge.

"With or without you, I'm getting out of this hellhole. Grandma Mae's counting on me and I happen to like my little spot among the living." Still nothing.

"Suit yourself. I'm out of here!" Street crawled toward the exit.

Kim's mind was back in the filthy warehouse. The big guy telling her that she was nothing but a two-bit whore and that's all she'd ever be. If she gave up now she would die as nothing more than that two-bit whore. She had to reclaim her life, even if she died trying.

Within seconds she had caught up with Street. Choking and gagging, they held their breath while they fumbled in the darkness to find the exit. They both feared their lungs would burst as they finally found the door.

Kim tried the handle but the metal was too hot. Street slipped out of his jacket and used it to buffer the heat of the handle as he turned it, but nothing happened. The knob wouldn't budge. The explosion must have knocked the doorframe out of plumb. Street beat on the door with all of the energy he had left, hoping someone would hear. They couldn't breath. They couldn't see.

Again, they sought the few inches of barely breathable space above the floor, their last hope for any oxygen, for one last breath.

"Get back! Back away from the door!" a voice boomed from the other side. Street weakly pushed a near unconscious Kim away from the door. Suddenly, with the collision of the battering ram against metal, the door flew open before them. "They're over here!" the firefighters yelled out as they pulled Kim and Street from the building.

While the two gagged and gasped for air, the EMS carried them to the rescue van and started oxygen. They started breathing easier within minutes. Regaining their strength, they firmly declined a trip to the emergency room and once their conditions were stabilized, the news media descended on them like ants on a picnic basket. With microphones coming at them from all directions and cameras recording the confusion, one question prevailed–had Gallagher survived? Though Kim was anxious to find Angie and Rod and to go after Mick, she stopped to address the questions coming at her.

"David Gallagher has been assassinated, as was Madsen and Dunn over the past week. We found Gallagher and some of his entourage as we tried to find our way out."

"Assassinated?" asked one newsperson in a challenging way. "That's a pretty insinuating statement for something that could simply have been an accidental explosion."

"Any facts to back up that statement?" asked someone else.

A third voice boomed in. "Do you think that candidate Michael Hennessey is in any danger?"

Kim composed herself, then responded. She knew she would be quoted and wanted her statements to make an impact and to be inspiring. "I can assure you that even with the facts laid out before them, most people will choose to ignore the indisputable as unthinkable. But stay tuned folks, because if it's facts you want, it's facts you'll get. But whether your station owners will allow the news to be impartially disseminated remains to be seen.

"However, thanks to David Gallagher, there's a movement in this country, and in the world for that matter, that's fast becoming a force to be reckoned with. I predict that in the very near future the news moguls will be looking to the freedom movement for its stories, for that's the only news that anyone will care about. No one will be interested in being told what to believe in and who to vote for.

"As for Michael Hennessey, he's no threat to the establishment. In fact, until proven otherwise, it's my guess that Hennessey is being put in place as yet another front person to further advance the agenda of the power elite. What better way to convince the American people that there's nothing to worry about and that we're heading in the right direction than to get everyone behind what appears to be a benignly charismatic leader? But, time will tell. In any event, be assured that the times they are a'changing ladies and gentlemen."

"Can we quote you on that, Ms...?" again with a tinge of sarcasm as the reporter tried to read Kim's smoke-smeared ID badge.

"The name's Kim Haven, and as far as quoting me, I insist on it."

Jonathon pushed his way through the crowd, physically tousling with a few bystanders who, thinking him an interloper, were determined to hold onto their precious two square feet of ground space. He grabbed Kim and Street by their arms as he brusquely parted the crowd and started leading them to his cab.

"Interview over!" he shouted rudely to the news hounds who stood staring after them. "Let's move it!" he ordered Kim and Street.

It took a few minutes to dodge their way through the congested parking lot and by the time they reached the cab, Kim and Street were short of breath.

"You sure you don't need to go to the hospital?" Jonathon asked. Both shook their heads firmly from side to side.

"I'm sorry, but no one saw that Lacy bitch come or go." He apologized and started to explain.

"No worries. That bitch is flat-busted dead," Street cut in, sharing the private joke with Kim.

Jonathon looked relieved and didn't ask for details as he continued. "But, I spotted the guy you met at the cemetery. He was in the crowd of reporters. Granted, I only had a glimpse of him at the cemetery, but I'm sure it was him. As soon as he saw that you made it out alive he made a call and then disappeared in the commotion. I looked around for him and that's when I spotted some guy hustling Angie and some other dude out a side door at gun point."

"Mick has Rod and Angie!" Kim said, not sure whether she should feel relief that they were still alive, or dismay that they wouldn't be for long. Jonathon opened the cab door and gestured for the two to get in while he kept talking.

"One of the cabbies also saw it and knew it had to figure into this mess somehow so he pulled around to pick them up and pretended he hadn't seen the gun. With some real good acting on his part, he ignored the tension among the three of them and made the usual small talk. He pretended to call their destination in to dispatch, but instead patched it over to all of us hoping someone would catch on. They're headed to the executive terminal at the airport. Not knowing he was on the cab intercom the guy with the gun, Mick, then used his cell phone to arrange for a return flight to Detroit on a private plane that he had standing by."

"You any good at talking *and* driving?" Street asked.

30

Safely back in Detroit, Mick took his hostages directly to his office. He bound Rod and Angie back to back and shoved them to the floor in the corner. Playing with his captive audience, he took his sweet time as he considered the upcoming scenario of their demise. He pulled the flask from his desk drawer and settled back in his chair, propping his feet up on the desk.

"I've kept you two in the dark long enough. You're probably wondering why I've called this little meeting." He laughed alone.

"The call that I took when we were getting in the cab is what's kept you two alive the past few hours. Apparently, Kim and that third-rate, small-time drug pusher, Street, is that his name? made it out alive. None of you were supposed to survive. It would have been neater if you all had died back there according to plan but, no matter. Your survival is nothing more than a minor inconvenience.

"My contact back there tipped me off that they not only made it out alive but that they were hustled into a cab and got on the freeway in the direction of the airport. The airport manager was only too happy to cooperate with the Bureau and move them to the front of "standby" status when they went to reservations, them being special agents and all." Mick laughed again.

Rod and Angie were testing the restraints as discreetly as they could while paying close attention to Mick. Keeping eye contact would keep his attention focused away from their hands as they were trying to pull and stretch the rope.

"Any questions, class?" Mick could barely contain his amusement as he suddenly lurched forward and jumped up, and then walked over to the far wall.

"This should clear up any questions," he said, pulling aside a heavy velvet drape that concealed the entire length of the huge wall that had been constructed into a large game board.

Even before having the chance to study it in detail, Rod let out a long low whistle at the intricateness of the endeavor. Something this grand had been months in the making by someone obsessed with the task at hand.

"Mother Mary help us," was all Angie could mutter as she stared at the sight in front of her. As her eyes focused on the ghastly details, she made the connection between the broken and blood-smeared female action figure mounted in front of an old warehouse, and Kim. Higher up on the game board was a funeral scenario depicting Kim at her parents' funeral.

Rod's eyes were drawn to the bottom right hand side, to a replication of The Press Club. The building was ablaze and bodies were laid beside it, side by side, The leather-clad doll was a dead ringer for Lacy. But how could Mick have known ahead of time that she wouldn't survive the explosion? A look of sudden comprehension lit up Rod's face.

"I see you're catching on, Rod," Mick said with mock somberness. "Don't make too much out of this wall though. It's really just a hobby, a visual aid, something to pass the time. Let's have a moment of silence, please, for our dearly departed Agent Lacy.

"Agent Lacy was a rare one indeed. There was nothing she wasn't game to try, and I mean nothing." Mick continued on as if he'd been asked to eulogize his twisted partner.

"Sexually, she was unparalleled. I could tell you some stories…"

"Please don't!" Angie spoke out in disgust before she could help herself. She felt sick as she tried to loosen the rope a little more.

As if he hadn't heard a word Angie said, he went on. "But, as sexually depraved as she was, she had the most unique, inventive mind went it came to violence. The more violence, the better the sex. Why, I have to admit that I used to give her carte blanche with her assignments just to reap the rewards."

"Enough, you sick bastard!" Rod thought of Marie and had heard enough. "As much as I'd love to know Lacy's dead, we don't know that. Don't forget she's a loose cannon, Mick. Sometimes a pit bull turns on its own master. She could very well end up being your own undoing once she realizes you intended to sacrifice her."

"Give credit where credit is due!" Mick said sharply, ignoring Rod.

"That's something that my father never understood. This," he said with a grand sweeping gesture toward the wall, "represents my greatest achievement. Something he could really be proud of me for.

"Your concern for Lacy is touching," Mick went on, "but I dropped her like a bird from a tree branch back at The Press Club. She had already taken a knife in the chest so I put her out of her misery before she could kill Kim. I suppose I should have waited a few seconds longer and let her go out in style by taking Kim with her, but Kim can still be useful to the cause. Just as you are, for the time being."

"You never intended for Lacy to survive." Angie was getting the picture.

"Nobody was to survive. But, if by some chance Lacy made it out alive, then I was simply going to suffocate her during our reward orgasms. She so enjoyed living on the edge. Only I was actually going to take it to the next level and actually put her lights out for good. At least she would have died happy."

In the midst of such madness, Rod and Angie strained even harder to loosen the ropes.

"What was your beef with Lacy?" Angie asked, hoping to keep Mick distracted.

"I'm more interested in your cause," Rod asked, stalling for even more time. "To go through all this effort, it must be a worthy one."

"Ladies first," Mick started, turning toward Angie. "Lacy definitely was a loose cannon. Fun but dangerous. When the boss fired her, I kept her on as my secret personal assistant. My plan was to eliminate the boss, and then Lacy. I would then assume complete control of the project. All witnesses would be gone. Nothing and no one to fuck it up. I would finally be on top. But then I caught on to Lacy's dirty little secret." Mick spat these words out as if trying to rid his mouth of the most vile taste. He picked up the opened flask of whiskey, took a long drink, and threw the flask against the wall.

"And now for the cause," he continued, shifting his gaze to Rod. "The cause is to have this government run by a behind-the-scenes dictator, someone with the vision to control every aspect of the economy because, let's face it—it's not love but money that makes the world go 'round. And all the while the puppet president's job is to promote the idea of leveling the playing field to create class warfare.

"Making the wealthier job creators the villains, the 'It's not fair' mantra becomes the battle cry of the lazy, non-motivated underachievers who now believe they're entitled to a share of someone else's earnings. The hero innovators of yesterday who employed tens of millions of people and kept this country humming along are now turned into public enemy number one. I actually coined the term 'one-percenters' to describe the wealthiest of this country and it's really caught on with the ninety-nine percenters."

"Not everyone vilifies the wealthy," Rod argued.

"No, not everyone. But enough to ensure an election. Jealousy is a natural emotion. It's a natural motivator to look better, provide better, and perform better. But human nature is easily manipulated. It was easy to take jealousy to the next step—envy. You see, jealousy is wishing you had what someone else has. Envy is destroying someone for what they have."

"And you're taking credit for that?" asked Rod, as Angie worked discreetly on her restraints.

"Absolutely. Sheeple move in the direction they're led. People want to believe that their government cares about them and has their best interests at heart. When the government tells them it's not fair that others have more and something needs to be done about it, they jump on that bandwagon. While they would not mug someone, they'll let the IRS do it."

"But none of that seized money is going to put one dollar into anyone else's wallet," Rod said.

"Of course not. But they don't know that. Do you know that the average citizen spends infinitely more time each week watching those stupid reality and game shows, reading about the private lives of celebrities, and finding out who the first-draft picks are in sports than they do about checking up on what their own government is up to, if they do at all? Is there really any adult in this country who's actually smarter than a fifth grader?

"Does it ever occur to anyone that these media events that occupy so much thought and time are promoted by the media at the behest of the government because the government is trying to distract everyone from what's really going on? Hell no! People are lazy and trusting. They're too lazy to run their own lives so they choose to put their trust in either the Lord, or the politicians, or if we're really lucky, in both! That way, they don't have to take any responsibility for themselves.

They turn their lives over to allegedly higher authorities and when things go wrong have someone else to blame."

"So, you offer up only presidential candidates that have been pre-qualified by you, such as Michael Hennessey?" Rod began piecing things together.

"And, who are so interested in living at 1600 Pennsylvania Avenue that they'll do anything, and I mean anything, to live there," Mick interjected. "You catch on fast, Rod. We also eliminate all potential candidates that oppose the vision of a unified world existence," Mick finished with an air of proud finality.

"And let me guess," Rod said. "The behind-the-scenes dictator will be you."

"For this continent, yes, temporarily. Taking it further, each of the seven continents will have its own dictator with all seven dictators under the rule of a supreme dictator. It's sort of like the Church, with the hierarchy and the election process modeled after the election of the Pope from the Cardinals. The Klan operates in a similar fashion. Why try to reinvent the wheel?"

"This must be decades off, if at all. You probably won't even be alive to realize your sick dream," Rod reasoned.

"Maybe I gave you too much credit earlier because now you're sounding as stupid and vision-challenged as everyone else. Take a close look at what's going on in this country and in the world. It's closer than you think."

Suddenly remembering he wanted a drink, Mick walked over to pick up his flask. The whiskey had spilled out on the floor. He cursed.

"I could sure use a drink, myself," Angie said.

"Well, geez, I'm fresh out," Mick said.

"I have a small bottle of Russian liqueur that I smuggled on the plane. It calms my nerves. It's tucked in my bra."

Mick walked over to Angie and helped himself. Ripping open her shirt he roughly groped around inside her bra until he found the small vial.

"It isn't much, but it'll do," he said, grabbing a handful of breast. "Ever consider implants?" Laughing at his own joke he quickly moved on, holding the vial up to the light. "Actually, this'll do nicely. What did you say this was?"

"A Russian liqueur," Angie said to Rod's amazement. He

wondered why Angie was offering Mick anything.

"Kim's not going to do anything to help your sick project along," Rod interrupted. "Once she figured out what was going on and that she was being used, she pulled herself together and began fighting the effects of the drugs. She's the strongest person I know and she just wants her life back. You've taken enough away from her. She's going to get her life back, or die trying."

"The dying part? Well, that can certainly be accommodated," Mick sneered, "but I expect her any time now and I'm willing to bet that she'll gladly offer herself to me in trade for you two and that worthless street urchin with her. Keeping you three alive will be the leverage needed to make sure she performs as expected. So, she'll be allowed to maintain distant contact with you so she knows you're alive and healthy and getting on with your lives. Of course, if she won't go along with the plan, none of you will be of any further use."

Rod felt sick. Powerless.

"For you and Kim," Mick looked at Rod, "it will be particularly bittersweet. To be so close, and yet so far away."

"If she makes the right choice though, she can replace Lacy," he went on with renewed purpose, "and assume a power position world wide. With a new drug I've had developed just for this occasion, she may match or, if I'm really lucky, even exceed Lacy's sexual appetites. What's the matter, Rod? You look upset. Jealous?" Mick callously continued on.

"Kim has no past identity. I've erased it. She has no current identity. I erased that when I found out that she had planned her little trip to The Press Club on her own, ahead of schedule. She doesn't exist. If she doesn't exist now, she can't exist in the future, not in her future, not in your future. A classic case of unrequited love, but you'll get over it, Rod. Many people have."

Mick was suddenly distracted, his attention now riveted to the small monitors mounted to the side edge of his desk. He had a clear view of the building's main entrance.

"Right on schedule and without her small-time, small-crime partner. She must have dropped Baby Face Nelson off at the baby sitter's."

For all of their efforts, Angie and Rod had gained only an inch or two of slack in the rope. Both of their wrists were raw and bleeding and their renewed efforts were painful and futile. Kim was alone and walking into a trap.

"Come on up and join the party, Kim," Mick invited through the intercom, as he buzzed the door open for her. She hesitatingly reached for the handle. Finally, she opened the door.

"Why the hesitation?" he cajoled, as Kim stood there. "The secret to a great party is to invite interesting people, with interesting stories to tell, and with a common interest. You three certainly do qualify. I must apologize for lack of refreshments, though. This is all so impromptu. Come on up Kim. Your destiny awaits."

Kim continued to stand there, never looking up at the monitor. Mick wondered if she was actually considering running away. No matter. There was nowhere she could run to that he couldn't find her. There was not a continent on earth that would grant her asylum. The consequences for doing so would be too devastating.

Slowly, head lowered as if walking to her own execution, she crossed the threshold. Mick figured it would take a good three minutes for her to traverse the hallways and elevators and arrive at his door. Due to the elaborate monitoring systems there was no need for human security. Humans failed. Humans betrayed. Electronics were indisputable and loyal.

Angie felt a glimmer of hope as Mick relaxed a little and raised the vial of liqueur. He pulled off the cap and crossed the room.

"A good host always makes his guests feel welcome," he said, opening the door a crack.

Lifting the small vial to his lips, Mick was suddenly thrown backward to the floor with amazing force. The vial went flying and crashed into Mick's game board. "What the hell?" he muttered. He was too disoriented to notice that the contents were melting everything it touched.

He was on his feet in a flash as Kim came through the door armed with the only weapons the TSA couldn't prohibit–her feet and hands. Her leg shot out and landed a blow to Mick's groin. She was off center. She followed quickly with a second try but Mick was on the move. A complete miss. She took a full sweep across the back of her legs and her knees buckled under her.

Mick lunged for the gun on his desk. Kim tackled him from behind and managed to reach the desk top to grasp the handle of the gun and pull it toward herself.

With gun in hand, the tables turned in Kim's favor. Mick bolted from the office. Kim started off, right behind him.

"Stop!" yelled Rod. "Let him go!"

Kim stopped in her tracks. Intent on Mick, she had almost forgotten anyone else was in the room. She locked the door and then rushed over to Rod and Angie and started to untie their wrists.

"Time to call in the big guns, Kim," Rod told her as she worked feverishly on the restraints.

"The big guns are all part of it," she said. "It's all so intertwined that no one can be trusted."

Rubbing the circulation back in her hands and wrists after being freed, Angie said, "We know that it's even worse than we imagined."

Rod pulled Kim over to the game board wall. Kim stood silent as she absorbed its impact, and its meaning.

After hearing about everything that Mick had bragged to Angie and Rod about, Kim was certain their fates were sealed.

"He's just as twisted as Lacy. I can't believe I ever trusted him. That blind trust, just because he's a government agent, has put us all in the spot we're in now. He has no plan to let you live if he confided all that to you," Kim said.

"Quite the contrary," Rod responded. "He has every intention of allowing the three of us to live in exchange for your continued dedication to the project. You cooperate, we live. You don't, we die. By the way. Where's Street? Don't tell me he bailed on you." Rod's displeasure was obvious.

"No way Street bailed," Angie said. "From what little I could see on the monitors, I'm guessing that Street was the blond, camera-shy diva that Mick was trying to coax into the building."

"You guessed it," Kim confirmed. "Street said that those types of monitors don't have good visibility at ground level close to the building and that I might be able to sneak in, on hands and knees, when he opened the door. The element of surprise is key and he was to stall as long as he could before coming in to give me a good lead-time."

"Where is he?" Rod was suddenly worried.

A soft knock came at the door. Kim hurried over.

"Be careful," Rod cautioned.

Kim unlocked the door, opened it a crack, and peered out. She then ushered Street in, checking the hallway in both directions before closing the door.

"Hot babes, direct to your room," Street announced as he pirouetted around the room and fluffed up the long, blond tresses. The three couldn't help but laugh at the sight of Street looking like a diva. It helped relieve the tension, if only for a few seconds.

"Laugh all you want," he said. "I had to give some woman at the airport two hundred bucks for this thirty dollar wig."

"It's called 'supply and demand', Street. It's the way business is done." Rod was enjoying the joke.

"I'll see if I can get away with that with my customers," Street answered.

After being updated on the evening's events, Street gave a whistle of disbelief. "Kim? It's your show. I'm in it to win it," he said. "One way or the other, let's wrap this up tonight. Grandma Mae's gonna be fretting about me soon enough."

"This has been the longest couple of days of my life," Angie admitted, "but I also feel more alive than I have in a long time. I'd rather die feeling alive, than to live feeling dead. If Mick isn't stopped and this whole thing blown out of the water before it can actually be realized, then it will be a mechanical, robotized existence at best. No thanks. I'll pass on that one."

Kim looked to Rod as he spoke. "What those two said? Me too. I had some plans for you and me. Together. Not separately. Let's finish this thing. For us. For everyone."

Kim's mind flashed back to all of the horror she had endured, and then to Mrs. Murdock and Jay. And then to Marie, whose horror would never end. And she knew this wasn't just confined to their little corner of the world.

"But, Mick's just the tip of the iceberg. We need to get to his boss, or at least find out who it is. And, can we even win against a plot of this magnitude? And, is it fair to expect you to fight with me?"

Angie put her hand on Kim's.

"It's not just about winning," she said. "It's about putting up a truthful and courageous fight. It's about doing the thing that will make us proudest of ourselves so that if we go down fighting we go down proud. And if we're lucky enough to survive, we can live with our heads held high. It's about getting our lives back, and our rights as citizens of a free country."

"For David Gallagher and to the first day of the rest of everyone's lives," Kim said. Rod stood by her side and snatched the wig from Street's head as he stood to join them. Angie joined them and pulled the group close together.

"May heaven help us," she prayed softly.

"Very touching! Very touching, indeed!" Mick's angry voice emanated from the intercom system.

"So. This is the way you want to play the game, eh?" Mick continued, angrily. "Then come and get me. I'll be at the pinnacle of my success. I'll be waiting for you."

"Oh," he said calmly, as if an afterthought. "This is a private party. Just me and you, Kim. I'll be watching for your three friends to exit out the front door. They have three minutes. If they don't follow orders, I will be forced to detonate the highest security level for this Bureau and this entire place will implode—and the four of you along with it. By the way, Street, blond is really not your color. Your time starts…, now."

The speakerphone went dead.

Kim pushed everyone through the door and down the hall. Rod balked. "No argument!" Kim ordered, squeezing Rod's hand. "I can do this thing, so get moving!"

One hundred feet from the front door of the trusted government Bureau, a black Mercedes maneuvered into position.

31

Pinnacle, Kim thought, picking up on the clue. Mick had to be on the top floor, a place she was certain she had never been. Only a select few of the Bureau's elite top tier were allowed up there. And, until the last couple of days, she would never have put Mick in that category either.

She couldn't believe that she had been so blindly trusting, taking everything and everyone at face value. She tried to find comfort in the excuse that she'd been drugged. That she wasn't responsible for her actions. But deep down she knew she had to take responsibility for her own naivete.

She started for the elevator then stopped. With no way out, the elevator could be a death trap. It would be better to take her chances on the stairs.

Her vague memory guided her to the hallway leading to the employee stairwell. For security reasons, the visitor stairwell would not have access to the top floor.

She moved quickly, aware that Mick had the advantage of being able to watch her every move via the monitors. She felt like a sitting duck, but she had no choice but to continue on.

Maybe she could play on his emotions, agree to play his game. If he let his guard down, for just a few seconds....

Kim was getting short of breath. Four stairwells. She realized that she was barely breathing. She was too tense. She leaned up against the railing and tried to calm down to regulate her breathing. Sixty seconds later she continued on.

Two stairwells later she was stopped short by a forbidding barricade bedecked with an array of high tech security devices. The sight stopped her in her tracks. *This must be the place. Now what?*

The various high tech devices simultaneously erupted in a visual display of colorful blinking lights and audio tones. Either she was going to be blown up where she stood, or the security was being disarmed. She went with her second guess and took the opportunity to get her breathing under control. She figured she was more important to Mick alive at this point.

One bolt after the other slid aside with a loud bang. One, two, three, four…, ten. The sudden deafening silence beckoned her to continue on. She heaved all of her weight against the steel frame and it slowly gave way. She squeezed through the narrow space to the other side then considered turning back but it was too late. The barricade closed behind her. She now stood between it and a solid door. There was no turning back.

Her hand reached up and felt beneath her jacket for reassurance. Mick's handgun felt alien, but comforting, tucked in her bra. She couldn't afford to let it get knocked from her hand like she did back at The Press Club. Street wasn't going to come to her rescue this time. No one was going to blow Mick away for her. She was on her own.

But the element of surprise was now in Mick's favor, not hers. She was positive that he was intently watching her every move. She was disadvantaged not knowing where he was. He was familiar with the layout of the offices. She was in unfamiliar territory. Would Mick let her near him when there was any chance she was armed? Did he even remember she had taken his gun? Or, had he forgotten in all the excitement? If so, she had one small edge in her favor, after all.

Kim took a deep breath and reached for the door handle. As she did, the door unbolted. She opened it and stepped into a short hallway. This time a thick, steel pocket door with a similar set of security devices lay before her. The lights and noise show commenced then abruptly stopped. The bolts slid aside, one at a time. The heavy door moved slowly as it retracted sideways into the wall. Complete silence. She waited. The continued silence beckoned her in. She took in a deep breath and stepped through. The door slid shut behind her with a noisy finality.

Kim surveyed the room. It was circular and heavily windowed, though the windows were tinted for one-way viewing, from inside to outside. There were seven short, wide, contiguous steel vaults spanning the area from the bottom of the windows down to the floor, each with its own unique series of color-coded dots on the upper left corner.

Kim's eyes swept the room taking in every detail. If she made it out alive, recalling these little details could prove beneficial.

One uncoded vault was mounted away from the others. Its opened door revealed the emptiness within. Above the door, one word–Chimera. *Odd*, she thought, wondering where Mick was. She felt nervous. Her hand reached for the gun.

"It's so true what they say about keeping your friends close and your enemies closer," Mick said, materializing out of thin air. He kept his gun trained on her as he slowly circled her.

"Mind if I help myself?" He ripped open the front of her shirt. "Nice. Not as big as Lacy's but, then, whose are?"

Kim recoiled in disgust. Ignoring that, Mick fondled her unnecessarily before retrieving the gun he had carelessly left behind with her.

"I was going to give you the opportunity of a lifetime, Kim, but now I'm not so sure you deserve it," he smirked, as he stood before her.

"What's that Mick? The opportunity to continue to live a lie? The opportunity to murder on command? To undermine my fellow citizens? My country?"

"My dear short-sighted Kim. Next thing I know you'll be singing *The Star-Spangled Banner*. Actually, I was considering giving you the chance to reclaim your true identity. To be by my side as I join a small, select group of people with the vision to see the benefits of a seven continent sub-government all answering to one supreme dictator."

If he was going for shock value, he was disappointed. Kim registered no surprise as she calmly replied, "You're one sick asshole, Mick. And since I'm not much of a singer, do you mind if I hum you a few bars of *The Impossible Dream?*"

Mick laughed politely. "I'm actually pleasantly surprised to see some spunk from you. You might be a suitable replacement for Lacy after all, especially with some huge implants and regular dosing with…, well, too much info for now. We have plenty of time to get to know each other better." Mick turned to walk away and then turned back toward her with a taunting afterthought. "Your boyfriend's going to be so jealous."

Hearing that, Kim lost her composure and lunged at him, ready to scratch his eyes out. Mick nimbly sidestepped her.

"Is it sick to want to be at the top of the food chain?" he shrieked as he raised his gun as if to pistol-whip her. Kim braced herself for the blow. None came.

"Is it sick to want to rid the world of the confusion that now exists?" He then continued in a much calmer tone. "To bring everyone together under one rule, one monetary system, one healthcare plan—yes," he chuckled, "let's not forget that people worldwide are so concerned about their damned healthcare that they'll sell their very souls for it."

Kim picked up the other side of the argument. "It's sick to want to take away people's basic right to make their own decisions."

"We're not taking away their right to choose."

"You are if you're manipulating the choices they can pick from for elected officials and eliminating anyone who dares to protect and restore their constitutional rights! My God, Mick, you manipulated me to help you in that selection process! I've killed Dunn and Madsen for you and your sick project, and you were willing to let me kill David Gallagher and who knows who else!"

"David Gallagher was too much of a threat to be allowed to live. And by the way, you don't have to call me God," Mick said. "That title really belongs to my boss, the man who masterminded this whole situation. It's true he's young but, damn, the man has vision!"

Kim felt sick. This seemed to be an exercise in futility. Even if she could kill Mick, without knowing who Mick's boss was, it would never end.

Kim turned her back on him and walked over to the desk. Her body language shouted defeat.

"May I?" she asked, pointing to the chair, indicating she wanted to sit down. When he nodded his permission, Kim settled in and took a moment to compose herself. She rested her head back on the headrest of the chair, closed her eyes, and inhaled and exhaled slowly. Mick watched her with curiosity while not letting his guard down. When she finally spoke, Mick noted the resignation in her voice.

"I'm tired, Mick. I'm tired of fighting and running. I thought it might end here, between us, but now I know that it's bigger than that."

"Much bigger," he agreed. "But, while it sounds like you're surrendering, how do I know you're not playing me?"

"You took me in and made something out of me. You gave me direction. Granted, you orchestrated that direction and it's not one I would have chosen for myself had I the chance to freely choose, but...," Kim left her spoken thought trailing in mid sentence and waited for Mick to speak.

"About your parents," Mick started, hesitantly, unsure of how much Lacy had told her.

"My parents are gone, Mick," Kim said, very business-like. "We can't go back and undo the past. Life is for the living. Maybe we just need to move forward into the future. I'm exhausted and I need a drink," Kim said as she reached into her shirt pocket and pulled out the small vial that Angie had given her.

Mick greedily lunged for the vial, grabbing it away from Kim.

"Where did you get this?" he demanded, dying for a drink to calm his nerves.

"Angie gave it to me. She sneaks them on flights so she doesn't have to pay those outrageous prices for cocktails. Is there a problem?" Kim asked, matter-of-factly.

"No. No problem," Mick said, as he uncapped the vial.

"Let me make a toast," he announced, raising the vial. "To the boss. To the man behind the most ingenious political project ever undertaken–*The Chimera Collusion*. A conspiracy against the citizens of the world all living under the sad illusion that what they hope for, and wish for, and strive for in life can actually be achieved. Fools! Each and every one! To the future but hopefully short-lived supreme dictator of the world, not to mention his humble successor." Mick swooped into a low theatrical bow and then straightened up, lifting the vial to his lips. He greedily downed the 'Russian liqueur'. The acid wasted no time doing its job as Mick's esophagus melted shut. His trachea followed suit and he dropped to the floor, gasping for breath. Instinctively, Kim got up and started toward him.

"Thanks for the vote of confidence, Mick. And thank you, Kim, for saving me the trouble of killing him myself."

Kim spun around to the familiar voice. Jay! With briefcase in hand, Jay had silently entered through a false door behind her. Stepping over Mick who lay writhing in agony on the floor–now nothing more than a minor inconvenience–he roughly pulled a stunned Kim toward himself and bent his head low toward her.

"How many times do I have to tell you," he hissed in her ear, "you can't fight city hall."

The barrel of his gun prodded and nudged her slowly toward the window. She let herself be guided to it, her face devoid of any expression, her eyes staring vacantly ahead.

"Snap out of it!" he ordered. "I know it's a shock to see me alive and well and in the flesh, but pull yourself together. That proverbial chance in hell that everybody's always talking about? Well, you're the only chance in hell that your friends have now."

Jay nodded to the Mercedes down below and Kim numbly followed his lead.

"Leave with me, they live. You don't, they don't."

"You're not dead," Kim said softly as she looked at Jay in disbelief.

"You certainly are sharp," Jay shot back.

"But, how...," Kim continued.

"I have a twin," Jay agitatedly interrupted. "Had a twin," he corrected himself. "An identical twin. Hell, even our own mother couldn't keep us straight."

"I don't understand."

"What's that old saying? If I tell you, I'm going to have to kill you," Jay laughed. "But what the hell. If anyone deserves to know it's you so, in a nutshell, here it is. Inquiring minds and all that crap.

"As a teenager, I happened on the story of David Gallagher. His arguments for limited government were largely ignored by those promoting bigger government, even as the consequences became increasingly apparent. He was right. Expanding government heralds in a country's demise.

"I followed everything the man was doing and saying. One thing led to the next and I soon began understanding where this country, and not just this country mind you, was headed. While my twin brother, Matt was playing Nintendo, smoking pot, and trying to get laid I was studying world politics.

"Today, every country is sharply divided with many different factions each clamoring for their own rights at the expense of others. Each also boasts an increasingly excessive bureaucracy bent on taking over private corporations and limiting the rights of its citizens. The governments consume more and more money each year but produce absolutely nothing of value. The populations are becoming more and more enslaved and can do nothing about it aside from meaningless protests.

"Those of us who were paying attention to Gallagher could see it was a disaster in the making but it had picked up so much speed that most assumed that there was no stopping it and, of course, there were those that didn't want it stopped.

"Gallagher continued to speak out against it and then ramped up his efforts to contain the damage for a possible reversal by running for president. His plan to fix this country's problems was rooted in the constitution, common sense, and sound fiscal policy–so simple.

"In time, as the political corruption became more evident, the interest in what he had to say grew exponentially and we all know where that got him. It soon occurred to me, as it occurs to all truly great minds, that I had a decision to make. That I could affect destiny. Let me say from the outset that I admired Gallagher and agreed with him one hundred percent. But, principles be damned! I'm not a patient man. I've always been more interested in short-term satisfaction than long-term gratification. Not in a base kind of way like my twin, but in a broader, success-driven sense. That's when I started working up a plan to be in the right place at the right time." Jay's monologue would have droned on had it not been interrupted by Kim.

"Lacy killed your twin, Matt!" Kim exclaimed with the sudden knowledge.

"I like to think that Matt sacrificed himself for a good cause. It was probably the only worthy thing he ever did. The Library was his pride and joy but let's face it, it had no redeeming social values. It wasn't a means to an end for him, it was the end in itself. The epitome of his short-sighted aspirations was to provide a place for people to drink and shoot pool with others who like to drink and shoot pool because they have absolutely nothing else of any value going on in their lives. Positively pathetic. Besides, it was wreaking havoc on his home life, not that I really cared though.

"So," he went on, "After establishing you in the neighborhood, I started relieving Matt at The Library so he could spend a little more time with his family. He was so grateful and never suspected a thing. Another blindly trusting fool."

"You're insane," Kim muttered under her breath.

"One man's insanity is another man's genius," Jay smugly replied. "I can't believe I'm actually explaining things to a moron like you."

The whirr of rotor blades momentarily caught Jay's attention as a helicopter descended and carefully maneuvered onto the rooftop helipad. Without thinking, Kim seized the opportunity to try to find a way out.

"Where in the hell do you think you're going?" Jay grabbed for Kim's arm but missed as she shot past him. He closed the gap in seconds, tackling her from behind. Ignoring her scream, and the blood from the freshly opened wound on her arm, he rolled her onto her back and straddled her.

"The copter's going to take us to a bunker where I'll orchestrate the rest of *The Chimera Collusion*," he said menacingly. "It's just not safe here anymore. Too many people asking too many questions."

"Go fuck yourself!" she spat at him.

"If only I could. Believe me, I'd rather be taking Lacy. She would have been such a goodwill liaison among my seven continental dictators, but sometimes things just don't pan out," he sighed and then continued.

"Lacy and I let Mick think I fired her from the Bureau and he stayed true to form and hired her on the sly, exactly as we figured he would. He coveted whatever I had. So predictable. I knew that Mick was never going to be happy working for me because he had so much to prove to himself and his father. When Mick caught Lacy in the hallway on her way up to my office Lacy and I both knew he would eventually figure out that we were both using her, sort of like a double agent. At The Press Club she was going to get rid of all of you and then take care of Mick. I certainly didn't want to be always looking over my own shoulder, wondering what Mick was up to."

"If I was you I'd have been more worried about what Lacy was up to," Kim said.

"Chemicals controlled Lacy, and I controlled the chemicals!"

Kim strained to get out from under Jay, but it was useless.

"Did Mick set the explosives?" she asked, now wanting to put all of the pieces together.

"My best guess? Mick and his contact in D.C. Mind you, it's only a guess. If he did, he acted on his own as far as that goes. I don't believe in unnecessary collateral damage. The public frowns on that."

Jay was intent on telling his story and the more he told the less hopeful Kim was that she'd make it out alive.

"It was actually Lacy's idea to set Matt up for the kill, and it was brilliant. I have to admit it didn't feel quite right, him being family and all, but still, it had to be done. I lured Matt back to the bar under the guise of computer issues, Lacy did her thing, and 'Jay's' violent murder should have been all the message you all needed to fall back into line. But, unfortunately, it only fanned your flames of curiosity."

Jay looked to the window where the copter pilot was impatiently pacing back and forth next to the chopper. The wind was picking up and the pilot was nervous. Ignoring the pilot, Jay turned back to face Kim.

"You murdered your own brother! You're a fucking animal!" Kim screamed as she tried to buck him off.

"I prefer to think of it as elevating him to a loftier purpose than he previously had," Jay said. "And just for the record, I had no idea that Lacy had hurt the young barmaid. That's just not my style. I told Lacy that I would kill her myself if she ever pulled a stunt like that again. So you see, I'm really not such an animal after all."

"Maybe we can get your birthday declared a national holiday," Kim said.

"You think?" Jay replied, as he got up and stood over her. "Just don't forget that for the plan to succeed, anonymity is key. Therefore, I'll have to forego the acclaim, though well-deserved.

"The people of this country, every country, must continue to be sheeple, blindly trusting their elected officials, most of whom are nothing more than mindless dupes themselves. They must never find out that elected and appointed officials are nothing more than front people. But thanks to David Gallagher, the citizens of this country are waking up.

"And, after all, we don't want an uprising now do we? Because of Gallagher and the World Wide Web, an uprising is certainly within the realm of possibility. Just think about the American Revolution–what a coup that was. And all without benefit of telephones or computers. Just think about where You Tube, Twitter and Facebook can take a revolution. Utterly amazing!

"If I do say so myself, it takes pure genius to stay on top of everything. And, I intend to do just that. And how, you might ask?

Money. As President James A. Garfield said, 'He who controls the money supply of a nation controls the nation.'" Kim stared in disbelief at Jay's insane ramblings.

The copter pilot had shut down the helicopter and was now heading in their direction. He did not look amused.

"On your feet," Jay ordered Kim, as he climbed off of her, keeping his gun trained on her.

She clumsily staggered to her feet. Jay pushed her toward the windows and grabbed his briefcase as he followed her.

"Aren't you worried about the vaults?" Kim asked, hoping to delay him further as the wind outside increased. Trying to fly a helicopter in this wind could be fatal. Staying out of the copter was her only chance to temporarily survive, and a slim one at that.

"Do I look like an idiot? Everything I need is right here," he answered, shaking the briefcase for emphasis. "The vaults were for future use for vital documents and such for each continent. Hence, the special color-coding. This," he gestured around the room, "was going to be World Headquarters. For an enterprise to be successful there must always be organization and documentation. My plan is for a world-wide dictatorship, not unorganized anarchy!"

Standing at the windows, Jay reached around Kim and gave a narrow glass panel a firm nudge. It magically opened and Jay stepped through, pulling her roughly along behind him. The wind had really picked up, jostling them around as they started off across the roof toward the pilot whose cap had blown off in a sudden gust. Ignoring the hat, the pilot firmly motioned them back inside the building. His demeanor invited no argument.

"Too windy!" he yelled above the wind. "Go back inside!"

Without hesitation, Jay put a direct shot into the pilot's chest and then proceeded on, dragging a speechless Kim along behind him. The front of the pilot's crisp, white uniform shirt erupted in a crimson stain as he crumpled to the rooftop. Stopping momentarily, Jay looked down at the dying man gasping for air, his lungs drowning in blood.

"Just making good on my promise of an early retirement, Captain. My condolences to your family."

The wind was now gusting up to over sixty miles per hour and with each gust they fought to keep their footing. Jay struggled to hold onto the briefcase with one hand, and Kim and his gun in the other.

Fifty feet away, the copter was securely moored in its sheltered area. Still, the rotor blades were flopping up and down with a mind of their own.

"You can't be serious!" Kim screamed above the wind. "We'll be killed!"

"No worries! I've done this hundreds of times on a simulator," he shouted over his shoulder.

As the next gust came out of nowhere, Kim shoved him hard and the wind did the rest. He pitched forward and fell to the deck. Jay hung onto the gun, but the briefcase went flying, settling precariously at the edge of the roof just a few feet away. He looked to the case and then back up at Kim. The split second of indecision on Jay's part was just the break Kim needed. She ran to the edge of the roof and brought her leg back, poised to punt the briefcase over the edge. The warning shot came uncomfortably close to her head. She stopped short.

"Back away from the case!" Jay shouted, watching her carefully while getting to his feet. "Back away now!"

Kim turned to face him, holding her ground against the wind that threatened to sucker-punch her backward into the unforgiving void.

"Get the hell away from that briefcase or you're a dead woman!" Jay was slowly closing the distance between them.

"And we were just getting to know each other," Kim said, feigning regret. "What's in the case? Too light to be gold," she said.

"Something even more important than gold, if you must know."

"Oil?"

"You're one sarcastic bitch, you know that?"

"The blueprint for your success?" she badgered him further. "Your manifesto?"

"In a manner of speaking, yes. Kick the case over to me and we'll forget all about your childish little tantrum."

"What then, Jay? You're going to fly off into the sunset with me by your side?"

"It's your call," he yelled above the wind. "I must say that the spunky side of you is really quite a turn on. You're finally showing yourself worthy to be with me, to help run the country, and then the world. So, I'm going to share the good news.

"What lies at your feet is the carefully crafted constitution for all seven continents as well as the likely candidates to control each one from behind the scenes. Of course, now I'll have to find a suitable replacement for Mick.

"There's also a list of possible pseudo leaders to put in place as figureheads around the world so that people can have the warm, fuzzy feelings they crave–Michael Hennessey being one of them. The plans and timelines to effect the changes–they're all there."

"You've thought of everything."

"There's more. Inside that bag are seven different currency designs and their prototypes. Everything will be merged into one worldwide currency after the big meltdown. The plans for one centralized bank? It's there and ready to go forward."

Kim listened in awe.

"I'm impressed, Jay," she shouted across the rooftop.

"You should be! A unified world existence will bring peace to all, financial stability to everyone."

"Especially to you," she finished for him.

"Yes. Especially to me. And you can be a part of it. Just kick that case my way. There's a decade's worth of work in there and we wouldn't want anything to happen to it, now would we?"

"And I figure into this…?"

Jay rudely cut her off. "You know too much to just let you go. But, then, you probably already figured that out. Kick the case over here and then shag your pretty ass over to the copter. You're not Lacy but you'll do. I believe that once I've had a chance to explain everything to you, you'll see that people everywhere need a higher authority to guide them."

"Control them," Kim corrected.

"As you wish," he said. "But you can only control those who freely give up their right to control themselves."

"You're taking away their right to control themselves."

"Pure semantics!" he screamed. "People who want to retain their rights, fight for them! They stay informed about what's going on in the world! They're more interested in what's going on in politics and currency issues than in texting their god-damned, meaningless vote for the next singing sensation! For Christ sake, Kim, more votes are cast for the next flash-in-the-pan recording idol than in any presidential election."

"Adam Lambert's no flash-in-the-pan," Kim retorted.

"Okay. I'll give you that. One unique talent among thousands. But still, the votes didn't carry him to first place. As in politics, he was just too extreme for most people's comfort."

"Getting back to your point," Kim said, "you're saying that people give away their rights to control their own destinies when they don't prioritize properly," Kim said thoughtfully. "I totally see where you're coming from. What you're saying is that they have no one to blame but themselves. That they deserve what they get. I guess I just never looked at it that way before."

"Now you're talking sense, Kim. A unified world existence. No more wars, hunger, and phony elections that cost billions of dollars."

Jay suddenly noticed that the wind was dying down and wanted to take advantage of that.

"Just kick the bag over here and let's get the hell out of here."

"First, let me make sure I've got this right," Kim said. "Under your plan no one will ever have to think for themselves, ever again. Everyone can concentrate on game shows, sporting events, casino jackpots…"

"Pure utopia," he agreed.

"Except for those of us who function at the higher levels of Maslov's Hierarchy of Need. You named your project well, Jay. Your project is your own Chimera–something you wish for but will never attain. Not if I have any say in it."

Kim then abruptly turned toward the edge of the roof, brought her foot back, and punted the case into the void beyond. An unexpected gust hit her broadside. She barely caught herself from following the briefcase down four stories.

"Noooo!" Jay screamed as he watched his briefcase disappear from view. He took quick aim and fired.

The bullet tore into the flesh and bone of Kim's already injured arm, knocking her sideways to the edge of the rooftop. She teetered precariously at the edge and then collapsed on the roof. She felt nothing as she lay there, bleeding heavily. She fought to stay conscious. She was unaware that Jay was closing in on her, determined to finish the job.

From the black Mercedes, now parked on the sixth floor parking structure above and adjacent to the rooftop heli-pad, Rod, Angie, and Street helplessly watched in horror as the scenario on the rooftop below them unfolded. Rod screamed as Kim fell. Angie and Street had to hold him back as he fought to get out of the car.

From their vantage points outside of the car, Mercedes and his partner raised their guns, took aim, and effortlessly took Jay out just seconds before he could fire the fatal shot.

"What the…," Street said, completely confused.

A distraught Angie tried to comfort Rod as he stared ahead in complete shock.

32

Now early Monday morning, just sixty hours after the start of their ordeal, Street, Angie, and Rod cleared security and were waiting in the visitors' lounge. They were restless, having just come from the hospital where they had kept vigil until Kim was resting comfortably in the surgical recovery room.

They paced around the small lounge, waiting to be escorted into an interview room where they would be asked questions and have theirs answered. The three were tired and hungry. Rod was anxious to get back to the hospital to see Kim.

"Hot damn! I sure didn't see this one coming," Street berated himself as he looked at the large plaque on the wall. "U.S. Drug Enforcement Agency, Forty years of excellence, 1973-2013," he read out loud.

"No one could have seen it coming so don't beat yourself up over it, Street," Angie replied.

"Just be careful who you're doing business with in the future," Rod added.

The door creaked open and they expectantly spun around. A young woman dressed in business casual silently motioned them into the hallway with a nod of her head and led them into a room at the far end of the hall. The agent came quickly to greet them, hand outstretched to each in turn.

"Let me reintroduce myself. DEA Undercover Agent Alex Young. I'm sorry you all had to be kept in the dark about all this. Especially you, Street."

"Hey, if that Mercedes is government issue, where do I sign up?" Street asked.

"It's quite possible that there's a place in the Agency for someone with your street smarts, but we'll talk about that later. First, let me say to all of you that I'm very glad that your friend, Agent Kim Haven, is going to be fine. I know you're anxious to get back to the hospital to see her so as soon as we debrief, I'll get you back over there."

"Well, at least it's all over," Angie said, relieved.

"Not exactly," Agent Young replied, hesitantly. "Your involvement is definitely over. The three key players, Mick, Jay, and Lacy are dead. But, just in the few hours that we've had a chance to go through the contents of the briefcase, it's clear that *The Chimera Collusion* is already much more systemic than we thought. With Mick's and Lacy's help with the day-to-day activities, Jay was able to set his ambitious plans in motion, on all continents."

Rod was curious. "Just how far along did he get?"

"All he had to do was create one basic plan and then recreate it worldwide, continent by continent, country by country. Our computer research whiz found other fairly recent prostitute-related deaths among controversial, constitutional, freedom-loving political figures worldwide. Though a different modus operandi, I wouldn't be surprised if the 2007 assassination of Benazir Bhutto, the Prime Minister of Pakistan, had been part of *The Chimera Collusion*. And who knows, maybe the recent exhumation of Yasser Arafat will prove the polonium murder theory. When you think about it, many of the world's dictators have been killed over the past decade, probably to pave the way for Chimera.

"What Jay didn't count on was Gallagher wheeling himself up to the plate, so to speak, to announce his bid for the White House after Madsen's and Dunn's deaths, or the fact that you all would figure it out. Or, more importantly, that any of you would care enough to try to stop it. People like Jay count on the apathy and complacency of others in order to succeed in their demented schemes."

"I'm still not totally clear on the extent of Kim's involvement," Rod stated, hoping for more information.

"And how did you get involved in another agency's affairs," Street jumped in. "And what clued you in? And why did Donnelly and Branson think you were dealing hard stuff across state lines? And how did…"

"Slow down there, Street," Young laughed, "and all will be revealed. At least the parts I'm authorized to reveal," adding the disclaimer.

They listened intently as Agent Young gave them a general, no names accounting. "Me and my partner had been infiltrating international drug trade in the area for more than a year. Real badasses. Even after a year we were just breaking into the outer fringe of the inner circle. A hooker who regularly serviced the drug dealers bragged to several of them that a gal pal playmate of hers, Lacy, liked to swing in groups. Guess the two of them got it on with Mick once in a while. Maybe Jay joined in, who knows?

"The dealers were intrigued, but leery of newcomers. Thinking it would bag her some extra bucks if she scored Lacy for the group, she defused their suspicions by confiding that Lacy had told her about Jay's plan and about how they had drugged Kim up to use her as an assassin. These types have connections everywhere so it wasn't long before they confirmed the story."

"Weren't they suspicious since Lacy was part of a government agency?" Rod asked.

"And how do you know all of this?" Angie asked Young.

Young continued on, patiently. "Seeing the big picture and how they could profit, the dealers used the info to set up a preliminary meeting with Mick and then, eventually, with Jay. Under Jay's protection, and with his contacts world wide, the dealers could eventually monopolize international drug trade with Jay, of course, getting his sizable cut off the top."

"Sweet," Street interrupted. Angie shot him a dirty look.

"Seeing the benefits of a symbiotic relationship, it didn't take long to seal the deal and the drug dealers then felt free to utilize Lacy to their best advantage," Young continued. "Once in party mode, Lacy was a wealth of information which trickled down to me and my partner and soon we focused our attention on Mick and Jay. We put two and two together, and came up with Gallagher as the next likely target.

"The dealers did, indeed, get both girls in the bargain and after a few hours of partying things got ugly for the young hooker. As if on cue, Lacy went nuts on her. No one even tried to stop it and the hooker was dumped into a trunk and left for dead. My partner and I were called in to get rid of her and found that she was still alive, but barely."

"Is she still...?"Angie asked.

"Alive? Yes. Through surgery, including cosmetic, and sheer will power. She's in the Secret Witness Protection Program and is eager to put these people away. One of the dealers had bragged to her quite a bit of information which, of course, he later regretted doing so she's sure that Lacy was ordered to get rid of her. She was just too much of a threat."

Young looked around the table at the tired, disheveled trio and ordered coffee, tea, and sandwiches brought in. As they gratefully ate and drank, he pressed on.

"I know you're exhausted, so let's get on with it so you can get on with the rest of your lives.

"We've already established the DEA's connection to Jay and Mick. It goes without saying that they were both acting on their own, outside the jurisdiction of their Bureau. Of course, there will be a thorough investigation at the Bureau to make sure, and steps will be taken to better secure operations in the future."

Street was incredulous. "It is f'n unbelievable that all this is going down under the Bureau's nose."

"*Was* going down," Young quickly corrected.

Angie couldn't resist putting in her indignant two cents worth. "And all with taxpayers' money."

Agent Young felt it best to ignore that and move along. "As far as Donnelly and Branson go, they were working with us. With a little detective work we established who Kim was, and where she was living and working. We initiated surveillance and it didn't take long to see a connection between the three of you.

"We then contacted the precinct captain who put us in touch with Donnelly and Branson who already had a relationship with Street. That's when I set myself up as your new dealer," Young said to Street.

"Man. I've been played," Street moaned.

"Like a violin," the DEA agent agreed, "but for a good cause. My cover as your new dealer allowed me to be in the area to keep an eye on things, and Donnelly and Branson could check in with Street to see if anyone was catching onto anything and then relay that info back to me.

"It was crucial that my status as your dealer remained intact so my cover wasn't blown while I was also handling the investigation."

"Sort of like a double agent," Rod added.

"Sort of. And very stressful. Instead of working between good and evil, I found myself caught between two evil factions—the drug cartel and the renegade agents–joining forces to enact a diabolical, fraudulent, but very profitable scheme against the citizens of the world."

"This is just unbelievable," Angie said, completely stupefied.

"And that's exactly why it just may have succeeded," Rod spoke up. "The more unbelievable something is, the more people tend to dismiss it as conspiracy theory. It's hard for people to believe that those they trust to act in their best interests are really only acting on behalf of their own."

"In reality, we're actually giving them carte blanche to victimize us," Angie said.

"They're not all crooked," Young said.

"No. Not all of them," Rod added. "But I actually started delving into some of what's referred to as conspiracy theories–the Internet makes it so easy– and I was shocked at the inter-relatedness of so many things. When I started connecting the dots of some of the most famous conspiracies…"

"I want to caution all of you," Young warned them sternly, "that not everything you read is factual so don't start jumping on the conspiracy bandwagon."

"But, if only some of it's true…" Rod pointed out.

Young shrugged his shoulders. "I'm not at liberty to comment on that."

The phone rang. Young took the call and then started to bring the session to a close. "As you were told before you were brought in here, this meeting was monitored by my superior who feels that your questions have been adequately answered. I want to finish by saying that the international drug dealers are going down and thanks to our secret witness we have a slam dunk case against them.

"Kim probably figured she was dead either way but she still risked her life by kicking the briefcase to the street. By doing that she gave us the information needed to pursue the key players, world wide, and that plan is already being worked up. We're not wasting any time.

"As for the chemicals that Kim was dosed with, our chemists are confident they have the antidotes to completely and permanently reverse their effects.

"Needless to say, through our advanced identification systems, we have positively confirmed her identity as Kim Haven, right down to her repaired broken nose and dislocated elbow suffered at the start of her ordeal. Apparently, she was supposed to think 'Kim Haven' was an alias since it was far easier to alter her mind than her actual identity. She was offered a totally new identity under the Secret Witness Program, but she firmly declined.

"She'll also have to go through an intense debriefing and complete psychological evaluation before being reinstated to duty, assuming she wants to stay with the Bureau. It may be hard for her to reconcile her role in the deaths she caused even though she's been completely vindicated. And, she's certainly redeemed herself. I hope she can come to terms with everything because agents like her are hard to come by."

"Just one more thing," Street said. "How did you know we were at the Bureau headquarters last night?"

"Jay called me and told me to bring my partner because he had five bags of trash to take out. Judging by the time he called me, which was well ahead of your arrival there, it appears that Jay marked you four and Mick for elimination ahead of time. Of course, I played it up some, saying we were dealers not the sanitation department. I had to play it cool so we wouldn't look too eager. He said we'd be cut out of the worldwide drug trade if we didn't cooperate so I begrudgingly gave in. You were all being closely monitored so we were already on it, anyway."

"Damage control," Street muttered and then suddenly remembered that he had turned his phone off hours earlier.

"Geez, Grandma Mae! I have my own damage control to deal with," he said.

"Not this time," Young assured him. "When she hadn't heard from you she started calling the precinct station worried that something had happened to you. The dispatcher relayed it to Donnelly and Branson who were on duty in the neighborhood. They went to see her and assured her that you were fine, telling her that you were helping out the police department on a special assignment. She said something about your destiny being inevitable. Anyways, she'll rest easy till you see her." Young rose from his chair and announced that he would escort them to the underground parking structure.

"An agent will take you back to the hospital to see Kim. I'm sure you want to check up on her. Especially you, Rod. The agent will be at your service. Let him get all of you safely where you need to go and then I suggest all four of you get on with your lives like this never happened. And I mean, like this never happened." The added emphasis was clear.

"I doubt that's going to be possible," Angie said quietly, exhausted from the weekend's events.

"Then let the experience and what you've learned in the past few days change your lives for the better. Like they say, be the change you want to see," Agent Young said.

They walked in silence to the underground parking structure. A government car pulled up to meet them. When it stopped, Young leaned through the window and told the driver, "Take them back to the hospital and when they're finished there, take them wherever else they want to go."

As Rod, Angie, and Street piled into the back seat, Young handed Street his card. "Give me a call if you're seriously interested in a career with the Agency. Undercover could use your street savvy."

"Damn right it could. By the way, how do you know the four of us aren't going to talk?" Street asked.

"I don't know. But even if you did, who'd believe a preposterous story like this?" Agent Young laughed as he turned and walked away. "You'll just look like four more idiotic conspiracy freaks," he yelled back over his shoulder.

Angie, Street, and Rod buckled their seat belts, anxious to see Kim. From the car radio, the disc jockey cut in with a special announcement. "In a strange turn of events, yet another presidential candidate has died. We've just learned that Michael Hennessey was the victim of an apparent suicide late last night–a single gunshot wound to the head. He was found by his wife when she returned to their Washington D.C. home. The coroner has ruled it a definite suicide but the police are looking for the driver of a flower delivery truck that was seen near the house at the time of his death...."

"Well, it certainly is true what they say. Things are seldom what they appear to be," the driver said, turning to face his passengers for the first time. With his collar up, his hat pulled low, and sunglasses on, no one had recognized Jonathon, but the voice was unmistakable. With a smile at the stunned trio, he turned off the radio and slowly drove away as he leisurely pulled up the lapel of his coat and sniffed the blood-red carnation.

33

Jonathon ignored the barrage of questions coming at him from the back seat. *You're an agent, not a cabbie? What is going on? Did you have anything to do with Michael Hennessey's death? Do you think Hennessey was murdered?* He just laughed his low, guttural laugh and said, "The Lord moves in mysterious ways, my friends, in mysterious ways indeed."

The rest of the trip back to the hospital was made in uncomfortable silence. Though none of his passengers gave voice to their fear, Jonathon was certain that each was worried about their own safety at that point. *How could they not wonder if they were going to be driven to some secluded spot and shot to death?* He also wondered if the carnation had been a mistake, then just as quickly dismissed the thought. *No. They need to be kept on their toes. They can't put blind trust in anyone or anything ever again.* When he finally turned into the hospital parking lot and proceeded to the visitors entrance, he stole a fast look in his rear-view mirror expecting to spot looks of relief pass between them. Instead, the three sat stone-faced—the picture of self-restraint.

"I'll be parked over there," Jonathon gestured toward a parking spot with a stab of his finger. "And take your time. You're not the only ones who've had a rough few days. I'm getting too old for all this excitement. I'll probably be sound asleep before you can get to Kim's room."

Rod, Street, and Angie silently obeyed Jonathon's unspoken command to get out of the car. Though they were all privately speculating about what was going on with Hennessey's death, they remained silent as they entered the hospital. There would be plenty of time to talk things over later.

Within minutes they located the Information Desk and, armed with visitor passes, found Kim's new room. She was sound asleep in spite of a nurse's awkward fumbling with her IV set-up. Spotting the three visitors the nurse stopped in her tracks, syringe in one hand and IV bag in the other, poised to inject the contents of the syringe into the bag. That is, until they walked in. Her trembling fingers withdrew the needled syringe. "I..., I'll just come back later," she stammered nervously.

"What's in the syringe?" Rod demanded, stepping into the space that would block her from leaving the room.

"Hey, take it easy, Rod," Angie said. "She's just doing her job."

"That's obvious," he answered. "The question is, who does she work for and what's in the syringe?"

Street grabbed Rod's arm to get his attention. "It's understandable that we're all a little paranoid right now but, Jesus Rod, this is a hospital, she's a nurse."

"Nothing's as it's seemed up to now, why should we blindly accept that this is?" Rod's question was stated more as a fact. "Because she's wearing scrubs and Nurse-Mates shoes?" he asked Street and Angie. They conceded the point with silence. They didn't want to cause a scene or wake Kim from her much-needed rest.

"Haven't we learned a god-damned thing?" Rod's voice was low, but firm, in his reprimand.

"She's got a hospital ID badge on," Angie offered in a small, apologetic voice.

"A dime a dozen," Rod countered. "The picture's so small you can't even see it from here. How many times do we just take shit like this for granted? Like it's all official?" Angie was clearly wounded by Rod's sudden change in demeanor. Street shot her an understanding look.

"You've been watching too many movies. You're over-reacting," Street said to Rod, while motioning the young nurse toward himself. She'd been standing still, nervously watching the interaction between the three, unsure what to do.

"Let's look at your ID and then you can be on your way," Street assured her in an attempt to placate Rod. She hesitantly complied. Street looked at the photo and then at her, and back at the photo. "It's a match," he announced to everyone. "Though I must say, the camera doesn't do you justice," he said soothingly, looking into her eyes. "So, you're still in training. That would explain your nervousness. A little stage fright maybe?"

"A lot, actually," she said. "It's my first day without direct supervision. I was just supposed to inject her antibiotic into her IV. Guess I'm more nervous than I thought."

"We'll step out if you want a little privacy," Street offered.

"No. It's okay. I'll just be a minute, then I'll be out of your way." With slightly more confidence, the nursing trainee succeeded in her task and then hurried past Rod and Angie as she gave Street a thankful look.

"By the way," she said, stopping in the doorway. "Ms. Haven is still being sedated so she'll probably sleep soundly for a couple more hours. You can stay here if you want, or I can let you know when she wakes up."

"We'll wait, thanks," Rod answered kindly. "We'll use the time to unwind a little. We're all a little uptight."

"I understand," she graciously accepted Rod's oblique apology, as she walked from view.

"Though I must say, the camera doesn't do you justice," Angie mocked Street after the nurse left. "Real smooth."

"You know, I just might get into a different line of work. A real nine-to-five. It'll free up my evenings for more important things."

"Get a grip on reality, Street," Angie said. "Even as small as it was, that diamond on her finger means she's taken."

Kim groggily scanned the room through half-opened eyes. *Am I dreaming?* She tried to partially sit up but her bandaged, immobilized arm restrained her. She focused her medicated thoughts as best she could and within seconds her mind quickly replayed the events that put her there. She wondered where her friends were.

She looked at a large floral display perched on top of her bedside tray. Though it partially blocked her view of the corner of the small room, the three pairs of legs extending below it on the other side were an unmistakable and welcomed sight. The heavy breathing told her that her friends were sleeping. Kim couldn't believe they were still there. Not wanting to wake them, she closed her eyes and settled back trying to make sense of the recent events. Seconds later, a large warm hand covered hers.

"I was wondering if you were ever going to wake up. How's the pain?" Rod asked Kim in a hushed tone.

"Maybe a three out of ten. It's do-able. Have you been here the whole time?" she asked quietly.

"No. Once we knew you were out of surgery and stable, we were taken to the DEA for a de-briefing with Agent Young."

"DEA? Agent Young? I would appreciate a de-briefing, myself, considering my ass was also on the line."

Realizing that he was privy to much more information than Kim had, and knowing how strong she really was, Rod pulled a chair up beside her bed. While he was filling her in on everything they had found out from Alex Young, Angie and Street woke up and joined them.

"I still can't believe that all of this corruption was going on for so long, completely unnoticed, and on such a world-wide scale," Kim said.

"Thank God for the good guys," Angie said, hesitantly adding, "including Jonathon."

"Including Jonathon?" Street challenged. "I'm not going to let his agent status give me a false sense of security."

"Jonathon saved our butts on more than one occasion," Kim agreed with Angie. "What's with the attitude?" she asked Street.

"Apparently, Rod didn't get to the part about Michael Hennessey's death last night," Street answered, looking at Rod.

"I'm not sure that it has any bearing on anything," Rod defended himself.

"Michael Hennessey's dead?" Kim interrupted. "Well, don't look at me, I have an airtight alibi for last night." Kim laughed awkwardly before continuing. "Bad joke, but seriously, what happened?"

Rod told her about the radio broadcast, the coroner's preliminary ruling of apparent suicide, and the police search for a flower delivery truck. He hoped it would be left at that.

"You conveniently left out the best part," Street added, not letting it rest. "Don't forget about Jonathon's red carnation. Circumstantial evidence, but damning nevertheless."

"And the part about him saying that the Lord moves in mysterious ways," Angie said solemnly, feeling a little braver. "I like Jonathon and owe him a lot, but I have to admit that the whole episode was pretty creepy."

Kim's pain medication was wearing off so now, though her pain was escalating, her mental acuity was as well. "Are you saying that Jonathon had something to do with Hennessey's death?"

Rod gave everyone a signal to stop talking as an older nurse came in to check on Kim. Rod held himself in check as he scrutinized her ID badge and said nothing as she pumped some pain meds into Kim's IV. When she left, Street closed the door behind her and then sat on the end of the bed as he started to speak.

"As I said days ago, we need to stay out of what's none of our business. But, none of us heeded that advice and so we're all lucky to be alive. We did our part, but now it's the government's job to finish it. And, don't forget that Agent Young suggested we forget everything that's happened and get on with our lives. Let me re-phrase, he *warned* us to forget about everything and move on."

Angie spoke up. "I agree with Street. Enough people have been hurt or murdered because of us. I don't want to be responsible for any more."

"The only people responsible for hurting or murdering anyone are the people who did it or who manipulated others to do it. Not us." Street reasoned. "But I don't want to put myself, or people I care about, in the line of fire. No sense pressing my luck."

"Let's get back to Hennessey," Kim looked at Rod, wanting to stay on point. "Do you really think Jonathon killed him? And, why?"

"Well, he did have means and opportunity. Hennessey lived within five miles of the airport, right off the freeway. Jonathon could have commandeered a flower delivery truck to be at his disposal on behalf of the Agency. Who would have refused someone flashing government-issued credentials? Aren't we all conditioned to accept badges as a sign of legitimate authority? To trust unconditionally? Nowadays, anyone who questions authority or doesn't blindly follow along is called unpatriotic, tased, or arrested in an effort to bring them back into line. In my opinion Gallagher was right. The real patriots are the ones who question the hell out of everything that flies in the face of the Constitution. And, let's face it, catching a last minute flight back here would have been no problem since everything's at the command of the government."

"But what about motive, my man?" Street challenged. "With

Chimera going down in a counter-plot, Hennessey was really a moot point. Neutralizing his future position as the hand-picked, puppet, presidential candidate would have been just as effective as neutralizing him."

"And far less suspicious," Kim pondered thoughtfully. "If he was neutralized then the only justification for raising suspicion like that would be that he was still seen as posing a potential threat."

"Because he knew too much," Angie added, realizing what Kim was alluding to. "But if Hennessey was going to be the next puppet for the powers-that-be, then he was one of the bad guys so why should we even care? Or maybe Jonathon was simply doing his job, tying up the loose ends." Angie was clearly conflicted and clinging to the hope that her loyalty to Jonathon was justified.

As the pain medication began to work its magic, Kim closed her eyes and tried to relax. Being stressed would only enhance the pain. But her mind was in overdrive and she couldn't shut it down. Nothing made any sense.

Rod sat there, frustrated but grateful, as he watched Kim close her eyes and fade away. Thinking Kim was sleeping, Street kept his voice low as he echoed Angie's last words.

"Maybe Hennessey *was* just a loose end that needed to be eliminated. Works for me. If this country lost someone like David Gallagher, why should we care about someone like Hennessey?"

"In theory, I don't have much of a problem with Jonathon killing Hennessey," Rod said, "if that's what happened. He's authorized to act on behalf of the government. And yet something about it doesn't feel right to me," Rod said.

Kim opened her eyes on that one. "It doesn't feel right because it isn't. If the so-called good guys act no differently than the bad guys, they're no better. Actually, they're worse. They're blindsiding people who trust them, and abusing their power."

"Maybe killing Hennessey instead of letting any aspect of the Chimera live on is just the lesser of two evils," Angie said.

"The lesser of two evils is still evil," Kim replied. "And don't forget that my Bureau is under fire because of a rogue agency operating within it. If it can happen at the Bureau then why not at the DEA? Or any other agency for that matter."

Even through her sedation Rod saw a renewed fire in Kim's eyes.

It was one of the things that he loved about her, but right now it was scaring the hell out of him. He knew that, once Kim made up her mind, there was no stopping her.

At Kim's request, Rod rolled the head of the bed up slightly so she could sit up to face her friends. "I like Jonathon too. But, if he killed Hennessey in cold blood, it was pre-meditated murder. A crime." Kim stopped to let that fact sink in. "I don't think it was coincidental that Mrs. Hennessey was away from the house at that time of night. Okay, a point in his favor if he planned for no collateral damage. But no one is above the law. Not even those who are paid to enforce it. Not even when they try to justify it by arguing that the end justifies the means."

"Agreed," Rod said with finality. "And as soon as you're feeling better, we'll figure out who can be trusted and we'll tell them everything and they can take it from there."

"No deal," Kim said. "My job is to uphold the law and expose corruption, not just corruption on one side, or corruption that I don't politically agree with. I'm going to call my new supervisor and move up my debriefing so I can get back to work. We have important information that warrants follow up. Hennessey's death doesn't totally wash with me either. On the outside chance our suspicions about Jonathon are wrong, and it was a suicide, why would Michael Hennessey kill himself? Was he afraid of something? Or someone? Or maybe it was guilt. If he was murdered, which is how it's looking, was someone afraid of him? Or getting even?" Kim paused to catch her breath.

"Could Jonathon be part of a bad element operating in the DEA? Right under Agent Young's nose?" Angie asked.

"Maybe *not* under Young's nose," Kim said, giving everyone time to chew on that thought for a few seconds. "Maybe Young's in it up to here." For emphasis, her free hand made a slicing gesture across her neck.

"Hand me my phone, Rod. As soon as you guys leave, I'm calling my new supervisor." The look in her eyes told Rod that arguing would be a waste of time.

"In the meantime, what are we going to do about Jonathon?" Angie asked. "He's waiting to take us all home."

"Then don't leave the meter running. Just act naturally," Kim said, "and leave the rest to me."

34

Jonathon chauffeured his three passengers around and tried to pick up on any clue that they were harboring new suspicions since coming back from visiting Kim. But the three were noticeably exhausted and, surprisingly, completely disinterested in pursuing Hennessey's death.

They engaged Jonathon in polite small talk and invited him to lunch at a local restaurant because it would look odd if they didn't. He declined, as expected, but not before cautioning them to stay out of trouble. While Rod went in to get a table, Street and Angie lingered on the sidewalk and made phone calls.

While Street made his excuses to Grandma Mae, Angie took a minute to call her parents to do the same. Her prolonged absence would cause them to worry. Still, she could hear doubt in their voices when she told them she was staying with a sick friend. She wondered if her nocturnal activities had been discovered.

Quitting her evening receptionist job had been a difficult decision when her mother had become ill, but the medical bills were piling up and the strain on her family was taking its toll. Angie had needed a lot of cash, and fast. Now that the finances were under control, she thought it might be time to give up her covert lifestyle before she was found out.

Joining Rod, the three ate and talked in a secluded booth. All were mindful that they were now suspicious of nearly everyone. Anyone who looked their way might be eavesdropping, but anyone who was ignoring them might well be trying to not look suspicious.

"I have real mixed feelings about Jonathon," Angie quietly said. "I know how things are looking, but I can't help but like the man. He saved our asses."

"I like him too," Street said, "but Kim's a trained agent. Based on what we told her, if she says Hennessey's death looks suspicious then that's good enough for me."

Rod ate more from need than enjoyment and kept the conversation light on his end. Street and Angie noticed his quietness but took it for an effort at discreetness as well as fatigue and concern about Kim. When he was done, he picked up the check for the three of them and excused himself. He was anxious to get back to the hospital and talk Kim out of any further involvement. But, judging from the earlier determined look in her eyes, he knew he would be up against a formidable force.

Rod stopped short of the hospital room. Even with the door closed to within an inch, he could hear the conversation between Kim and another female. Judging by the conversation, Rod figured it was Kim's new boss who had wasted no time getting to her bedside. He restrained himself from barging in. If he went in, the talk would stop. He wouldn't learn anything that way.

Looking up and down the hallway, there was little activity. The old days were gone. No longer were hospital halls bustling with nurses, doctors, and orderlies. One-on-one nursing was largely replaced by an unthinkable eight-to-one, patient-to-nurse ratio aided and abetted by machines that monitored patients from an impersonal distance. But, fortunately for Rod, that left the hallways nearly deserted. When the coast was clear, he edged closer to the door and cocked his ear toward the crack.

"I promise you would be nothing more than a decoy, Kim. Everything you just told me about your suspicions that Jonathon had something to do with Hennessey's death means that the Bureau may not be the only agency gone rogue. If we can use you as bait, we might be able to confirm those suspicions and find out why and whether he acted on his own or on orders by the DEA. Under the circumstances, no one would blame you for declining. But remember that the Bureau will have your back at all times."

Rod wanted to put a stop to the insanity, but held himself in check. Surely Kim wouldn't hold her own feet to the fire again, after barely escaping the first time.

"You can count on me," Kim said.

Rod saw red. She was in no shape to be signing on for such things. He was wondering how he could get her to someplace safe to recuperate and come to her senses when he was startled by the sounds of her visitor preparing to leave. He couldn't be caught listening in.

He looked up and down the hallway to make sure he was still alone and slipped into the empty room next to Kim's, ducking into the bathroom for good measure. He peered around the door frame and watched Kim's visitor leave. She was not at all what he expected. About sixty years old, petite, with a slight limp.

When he heard her footsteps fade away, Rod walked into Kim's room as if nothing had happened. Wanting Kim to volunteer news rather than coercing it out of her, he forced himself to be casual.

"Hey you," he greeted her, pulling a chair closer to her bed and taking her hand in his.

"Hey you, yourself. Too bad you weren't here a few minutes ago. You could have met my new boss."

"It sure didn't take long for her to get over here," Rod said, as nonchalantly as he could.

"And I didn't even have time to call her. She just stopped by to check up on me."

Knowing that checking up on Kim was not the only item on boss lady's agenda, he found it hard to play it cool. "Well, she wouldn't be much of a boss if she didn't, considering you were nearly killed."

"Do I detect a little resentment there? I know you're worried, but I swore an oath to serve this country. It's my job."

"But you can't serve it if your dead."

Ignoring him, she continued. "I told her I was concerned that Jonathon may be involved in Hennessey's death, and why. She said it really does sound suspicious and wants to use me as a decoy to ferret out info whether he was involved or not, and if he acted alone or under orders from the DEA. And probably most importantly, *why* Hennessey was killed. I mean, using me makes perfect sense since Jonathon and I have already established a relationship. You look upset."

"Just concerned for your safety," Rod forced an even tone.

"My safety is pretty much guaranteed."

The absurdity of the situation was too much for Rod. He knocked over the chair in his haste to stand up. Kim was startled by his sudden change of demeanor which now had her full attention, even through her drug-induced lethargy. As Rod stood staring out of the window Kim advanced her argument, but it fell on deaf ears.

"This isn't just run-of-the-mill Bureau business," he finally said. "If it was, that would be bad enough. But you've been instrumental in uncovering and exposing a massive network of world-wide government corruption, aided and abetted by outlaw federal agents. A conspiracy that would have had grave effects on the entire world. And even though Agent Young said a complete counter-plan was in place, no one can really be certain how far the corruption extends. But you can bet your ass that if even one person escapes detection that one person will make every effort to maintain a position of control. And not even your new boss's claim to have your back at all times…," Rod stopped, instantly realizing he had said too much.

"You were listening?" Kim asked.

"No. More like overheard. If your boss didn't want anyone to hear she should have closed the door."

"Whatever." Kim had her back up and then instantly regretted it. Rod had been nothing but loyal and supportive in spite of the horrible things she'd done. He had even put his life on the line for her and now all he wanted was for her to be safe.

"Look, Kim. You've done one hell of a job. No one should ask you to do more. A chunk of your life was taken from you and your fight to get it back uncovered an unthinkable conspiracy against all of us. It almost got you killed."

"It could have gotten us all killed," she interrupted. "And let's not forget that a lot of innocent people were badly hurt or murdered. All things considered, we came out of this okay."

"Yes, but I agree with Street. Why press our luck? I'm just asking you to think about me and a future together."

Kim was careful not to get caught up in the emotion of the moment. Emotions got in the way of good judgement. She proceeded, sounding cooler than she really was, considering his awkward attempt at a relationship commitment.

"Look, I can at least hear what she has to say and then base my decision on that. If it's just a little game of 'I spy', then I really don't see any harm in that." Her tone suggested there was little wiggle room.

"Any chance I can talk you out of it?" Rod said.

With Kim's few seconds of hesitation, Rod's jaw tensed in anticipation of the answer he dreaded.

"I'm sorry but, no chance at all."

Rod's look was an odd mixture of resignation and sadness, anger and fear. Silently, he held her for a minute and then walked out. Wordlessly, Kim let him go. Caving in would mean she was still letting someone else control her and, regardless of her feelings for him, she was determined to live her own life.

Shifting around to take some pressure off her bad arm placed the floral arrangement in direct view, less than three feet away. It was spectacular. Kim realized, for the first time, that she had neglected to thank Rod. *How rude*, she thought, and vowed to make it up to him.

The bouquet was a welcome harbinger of spring with daisies and mums of various colors and sizes expertly arranged to look completely casual and unstructured. She allowed herself the luxury of taking it all in, appreciating each blossom and the wonderful scents.

Odd, she thought, staring at a larger mum tucked into the middle of the bouquet. The entire surface of the eye of the mum was not smooth and fuzzy-looking like the rest. It was shiny. Using a trick she had learned from her parents, she squeezed her eyes tight and then re-opened them. With her vision momentarily sharpened, she stared at the center of the flower again. *Am I seeing things?* She employed this trick again and then realized she needed to get closer as well, and propped herself up on her good elbow to lean toward the vase.

Not quite flush with the surrounding area was a tiny imbedded microphone. *Why would Rod do such a thing?* Then she realized her assumption was probably wrong. *Jonathon! Now he knew they were on to him! They were all in danger!*

Kim placed a frantic call to her new boss but there was no response. She left a message and then tried to call Rod. No answer. Within minutes she decided to try Street and Angie. *Where was everybody?* She patiently waited for a return call. Twenty agonizing minutes later she tried calling everyone again. This time, she turned up the volume of urgency in her pleas for return calls and then waited again. Still nothing. She rang for the nurse.

"I need that shot of morphine after all," Kim declared, wasting no time once the nurse walked into the room.

"I don't think you're due quite yet. How about a couple of aspirin to hold you over?"

"I only had half a dose earlier. I thought I could make it through, but I can't. I want the other half so I can get some sleep."

"Yes, well I see your point. I just came on shift so let me check your chart. Then it'll take about twenty minutes to come up from the pharmacy. When it does I'll log it in on Meditech and bring it in along with a fresh IV bag."

"I don't want it in the IV bag this time. I want a direct push. I need fast relief."

"That'll take a smidgen longer, then. Your doctor has to okay the change in administration route so I'll have to track him down."

"That's fine. And the sooner the better."

How did Agent Young not suspect that Jonathon had his own agenda? Kim wondered as she lay there, trying to keep her mind off the pain and anxious to leave. Nothing made sense. *How was it that Jonathon just happened to be around whenever he was needed? Somehow, he was on the receiving end of vital information which paved the way for him to orchestrate his plans. But how was he getting his information? Where was that morphine! I have to get out of here!*

The hospital wheels grind slow, but sure, and twenty-five minutes later the nurse returned with the syringe. Immediately after the direct push, Kim's pain subsided and within minutes she was feeling no pain at all. When the nurse left, she removed the existing IV from her arm and applied pressure till the bleeding stopped. Her first effort to sit up failed as dizziness took her back down to the bed. When her head cleared, she tried again and found that she could dress slowly with one arm.

She hoped no one was sitting at the nurse's station, but no such luck. Watching the nurse's back, Kim snuck into the room next door. It was empty. Behind the nurse's back she then went into the room on the other side of her own.

"Who are you?" the bed-ridden elderly woman defiantly demanded.

"I'm sorry," Kim said, slowly and deliberately. Her mouth felt like it was stuffed with cotton balls. "I must have misunderstood the room number. I'm looking for my Aunt. Here, let me fluff your pillow while I'm here." She had to pronounce her words carefully so they wouldn't slur.

"I don't need no pillow fluffing, Florence Nightingale. I need something to sleep."

Ignoring the protests, Kim awkwardly fluffed the pillow while hitting the "call" button and then went back to her own room before the nurse could see her. When the nurse responded to the diversionary call, Kim made her move. The morphine made her feel like everything was happening in slow-motion. She could hear the nurse and patient arguing back and forth over whether the "call" button had been activated or not. She cautiously moved past the deserted nurses' station, down the elevator, past security, out the lobby door, and into the crisp afternoon air.

35

"What the hell's wrong with you?" Agent Young yelled at the woman standing before him. "You were supposed to discreetly retrieve the damned microphone, not cast suspicion on the DEA! Now Kim won't trust anyone!"

"I told you. She was pretty alert when I got there so trying to pull the microphone would have looked suspicious. And keep in mind that I wasn't the one who caused the suspicion. Thank Jonathon for that. But don't worry. She thinks I'm her new boss so it will look perfectly natural for me to go back and try again. Next time I won't fail."

"There won't be a next time. I'm putting a pro on it."

"I may only be your secretary, but I'm not stupid, Mr. Young. Don't think for a minute that I don't see there's something weird going on here, but just keep me out of it. I want to be able to claim plausible deniability if whatever you're doing blows up in your face, just like the President can do. And don't forget, I didn't drive Kim to any conclusion about who I was, I merely went along with assumptions made on her part that she was eager to embrace, no questions asked. She did all the talking and I simply responded appropriately. And brilliantly, I might add."

Disgustedly, Young dismissed her telling her she was finished for the day. Upset at the dressing down she had just received she slammed the door behind her, never bothering to say good-bye.

"Yes, thanks to Jonathon, they'll all be sniffing around here," he mumbled to himself. "And I can't afford that. I'm this close," Young gestured to himself with nearly-closed thumb and forefinger, "and no one's going to fuck it up. And I mean no one."

Alex Young stood at his office window and made a hurried phone call. "About five four, thin, sixty, blond, glasses, and a slight limp." He watched the employee parking lot across the street. Within minutes he made a second call.

"I want to report a hit-and-run," he said into the phone as he watched his secretary bounce off the front end of a fast-moving, silver, run-of-the-mill domestic car that was pulling into the lot. Alex flinched slightly as she landed grotesquely, face-down and motionless, on the asphalt.

A small crowd quickly gathered around the secretary. No one paid any attention to the car as it sped through the parking lot and exited onto a side street and out of view. Alex suspected that she would not survive given her age and small stature but if she did, plastic wrap held over her face in the hospital would surely finish the job.

He ignored the guilt that washed over him. "Like I said. No one's going to fuck this up. No one," he muttered.

Agitated, Alex made another call as he walked away from the window. *Where the hell are you?* he wondered. Then, when the call was finally answered, "I have another job for you.

"My secretary just got hit by a car in the parking lot across the street and the paramedics will be there shortly. In case she survives her unfortunate accident, get some plastic wrap and get on top of it."

Frustrated at having to explain himself, Alex said, "What do you think I mean? Do I need to spell it out for you? Decommission her.

"Listen up, I'm only explaining this once. When I sent her to retrieve a bug I planted in Kim's flower arrangement, Kim assumed she was her new supervisor at the Bureau. And, because you were stupid enough to put that damned flower in your lapel, in her and her friends' minds you're now the number one suspect in Hennessey's death, a fact that she reported to my secretary. Now that whole mess links back to me. So take care of it. If she's not already dead get her there, and fast! She's probably going to County General. Take the initiative to solve the problem, just like you did with Hennessey. You sure didn't need me to spell that out for you though a fatal car accident next month would have been far less conspicuous."

Alex listened, then said, "Now that you ask, they're being taken care of as we speak. And since you're going there anyway to give my secretary the send-off she deserves you might as well discharge our guest of honor. Just make sure you don't arouse any more suspicion. Are you familiar with the abandoned steel warehouse on Fort Street, near the river?"

Rod came to, in the trunk of a car. His head was pounding. In the darkness, he could see a sliver of daylight leaking through a crack overhead. Car trunks were getting smaller these days, so his tall frame was contorted into an unnatural position. He wasn't tied up but he could barely move anyway. His legs were in bad need of circulation. He tried to shift position but the tight confines wouldn't allow much movement. He cursed.

"Shut up!" the voice commanded, followed by a sharp rap on the trunk lid. Seconds later, the trunk popped open. Rod closed his eyes to block out the daylight until he could adjust to the brightness. The guy was masked but, based on size and voice, there was no mistaking him. It was Kevin, Agent Alex Young's sidekick. Two beefy hands grabbed hold of Rod, roughly pulled him out of the trunk, and set him on two wobbly legs.

"I don't know what all the fuss is about," Kevin said, giving Rod the once-over. "You don't look like much to me."

Rod ignored the insult, deciding it would be smarter to assess his surroundings than exchange banalities. The situation didn't look hopeful. Obviously-abandoned warehouses in all directions. Broken windows, if there were any left at all. Old stained mattresses and grimy appliances lay wherever they happened to fall when shoved out of the back of a pick-up truck. A movement caught Rod's attention and he found himself staring as a couple of guys huddled next to a debris pile, helping each other tie tourniquets around their arms.

"Hey you! Call the police! I've been kidnapped!" Rod yelled.

Kevin bellowed with laughter then walked over to the pair, peeled a wad of cash from his money clip, and tossed it in their direction. The pair eyed it hungrily but went back to work. Rod felt sick.

"Payday for the security guards," Kevin said, laughing loudly as he walked back to the car and then pushed Rod toward the warehouse door.

"Why are you doing this Kevin? What's in it for you?" Rod asked.

With his identity in the open, Kevin pulled the mask off and threw it in the trunk. "To answer your first question, money. To answer your second question, money. What else is there?"

"Who are you working for?"

"Whoever pays the best at the time. I don't get tangled up in loyalties. Loyalty is totally over-rated."

"But you're a federal agent."

"That I am. Got my own tin badge and a gun to prove it."

"You don't know anything about me but I'm confident I can buy you out of your present contract. Name your price and I'll make arrangements for payment and we'll go our own ways and forget this ever happened."

"Unless you can print your own endless supply of worthless money, you can't possibly buy me out of this contract."

"Do I look like the U.S. Treasury?"

"Politically savvy," Kevin said. "I'm impressed. Now shut the fuck up. Ever shoot up?"

"What?" Rod asked, confused.

"Ever shoot H?"

"H?" Rod looked as appalled as he felt.

"Horse. Smack. China White. Heroin. Don't play coy with me. Wealthy types like you take advantage of all the pleasures life has to offer. But then again, H is for poor folk. You're probably into cocaine."

"I don't do drugs."

"No? Well I might just be able to persuade those two over there to hook you up. You've all been working so hard lately that you all deserve a little party before the fireworks start."

"What do you mean, *all* of us?" Rod asked the question he feared he already knew the answer to.

In response, Kevin pushed Rod toward the rusted door of the warehouse office.

"Why are you doing this?" Rod demanded again.

"I told you, money. Also, there's the little business about the hit and run number I did on Young's secretary. What's that poker expression that's so popular these days? I'm all in."

Once inside the dusky dimness, the two forms bound to the chairs were instantly recognizable. Street and Angie shot him a look that was both hopeful and apologetic.

"There's no reason to hurt anyone else," Rod said to Kevin.

"Actually, no one's going to feel a thing," Kevin's laughing comment wasn't lost on Street or Angie, who shot Rod a questioning look. Kevin waved his gun and motioned Rod into a chair. Trying to be a hero could cost all three their lives so Rod acquiesced in hopes of buying enough time for the three to come up with a plan.

Within minutes, Rod was securely tied to a chair. As Kevin busied himself nearby, but just out of sight, the three talked in whispered tones. When Rod told them about Kevin's intentions, Angie was speechless, but Street was resolute. "I'm not leaving this world on an overdose, so let's come up with a plan."

36

Jonathon arrived at the Emergency entrance just prior to the arrival of the rescue squad who came in without sirens blaring. *Dead, or in stable condition?* he wondered.

He was glad he had contacts on the inside, people who owed him favors and who he could trust. But he wouldn't approach anyone unless he needed to. The less people involved, the better.

He lingered outside the entrance door, pretending to make a phone call, hoping he wouldn't attract unwanted attention. The EMTs took their time opening the back of the van and then they pulled the gurney out, set it on the ground, and engaged the wheels. From his vantage point, Jonathon could see her face. Even with the oxygen mask on, he could tell it was Young's secretary. She looked pale and peaceful—probably highly sedated.

He watched patiently as the EMTs closed the back door of the van and locked it. He stood aside as they wheeled past him and followed them into the Emergency Department, keeping a respectable distance so as not to attract suspicion.

"This is the DOA we called in," they announced to the staff as they maneuvered her into a vacant side room. Respectfully, they pulled off her oxygen mask and pulled the sheet up over her face.

With nothing more to be done there, Jonathon casually left the area and got back in his car. He drove around to the front entrance of the hospital and parked. He couldn't botch the job with Kim. Too much was at stake. He sat for a minute, going over his plan, then got out of the car.

He hadn't walked more than a few feet toward the hospital visitor entrance when he saw her walking out of the door. He ducked for the safety of the closest parked car and watched. She was slow moving and unsure of her footing, and as conspicuous as a drunk trying to drive home from the bar after last call. *Injured and drugged. This is going to make things a whole lot easier,* Jonathon thought.

But still, he had to be careful. If she spotted him walking toward her it might spook her and cause unwanted attention from onlookers. After all, she didn't trust him now and who could blame her? He kept low and hustled back to his own car, where he continued to watch her from a distance. With any luck she'd wander into a more secluded area, away from the front lobby and prying eyes.

She stopped and made a couple of calls. From where he was sitting, it looked like she left no messages. Appearing disoriented, as if she had no idea where she was going or how she was going to get there, she looked around and tried to focus on a bench off to the right, by the AIDS Memorial Tree. She felt light-headed and needed a place to sit down. She wondered if she could make it that far and then decided to try. She was making progress in a slow-motion kind of way when the black car pulled up alongside her.

The passenger door swung open in unspoken invitation. She glanced toward it with detached curiosity, trying to focus on the driver as he got out of the car.

"What are you doing here?" she slurred, as he walked toward her.

"Lucky for you I just happened to be in the area. You don't look too good."

Kim was too weak, physically and mentally, to fight him. In short order, Jonathon made quick work of picking her up and strapping her into the front seat of the car.

"Why are you doing this?" she mumbled.

"As I told the others, 'The Lord moves in mysterious ways'."

The black coffee was strong, bitter, and hot. Kim spit it back into the cup. Jonathon patiently poured a second cup and added some water. He needed her awake and alert. And he needed it quickly. She eyed him warily, noting the gun in his waistband, then surveyed the hotel room. Two doors and both were bolted. Even without her injury, she was no match for the older man with his imposing size.

"Not exactly the Ritz, but not a flea-bag hotel either," she observed, eyeing her surroundings and taking the coffee from him. He let the comment pass as he gently changed the dressing on her wound. An arm sling was laid out on the bed. A deli sandwich sat next to it, untouched.

"You can do anything you want with me, Jonathon. Kill me like you killed Hennessey. Just leave my friends alone. They're no threat to you."

He grunted and adjusted the straps of the sling after eye-balling her up for size.

"Eat something," he finally said, motioning toward the food. "You need to keep your strength up."

"And the condemned woman was offered a last meal," she said.

Ignoring her, he placed the sling around her neck and carefully lifted her arm into the cradle. His gentleness belied his size and occupation. He showed no sign of uneasiness as she stared at him. He made a further adjustment to the sling and then, satisfied, pulled the handgun from his waistband and placed it in the sling, the handle positioned within easy reach for her to grasp with her other hand.

"Check out the positioning of the handle," he ordered. Confused, Kim looked at him but made no move toward it. *Probably a set-up,* she thought. *I went for a gun so he had to kill me.*

"Go ahead," he encouraged her. "Reach for it like you're going to use it. Like your life depends on it. If it doesn't feel right, change it to suit yourself. Just make sure you can get to it in a hurry. And yes, it's loaded, so please be careful."

He answered her bewildered look. "None of you are a threat to me, Kim. And I'm certainly no threat to any of you. I know what you're thinking but I haven't gone rogue and I didn't kill Hennessey."

In a show of trust, he turned and walked away from her. He was testing her. When he got to the door that adjoined their room to another, he unlocked it. As if on cue, it opened wide. "Kim, meet Michael Hennessey." Kim stared in disbelief at the man who stood in the doorway. If he wasn't Michael Hennessey, he was a dead ringer for the presidential candidate.

"In the flesh," Hennessey assured her.

"We don't have much time. We'll talk on the way," Jonathon said.

"On the way where?" Kim asked, giving Jonathon a puzzled look as the two men scurried around gathering up the few things that were strewn about.

"To put an end to Chimera, once and for all," Jonathon said.

"I thought that was being taken care of," Kim said, confused.

"I regret to say that my boss, Agent Alex Young, is an unexpected loose end that must be tied up."

"Loose end? He's part of Chimera? How did you know? About any of this?"

"We don't have time to backtrack the whole story," he said, peering around the parking lot and surrounding area through a crack in the closed drapes. Satisfied that they were alone, he faced her. "Suffice it to say that I know what you know, and then some. When Young's behavior changed drastically, I followed my instincts and employed the best surveillance tools in the world–devices with such sensitivity and specificity that I could monitor Alex while he was monitoring everyone else. I was privy to conversations on all sides and it didn't take long to get the drift of what was going down. When I was confident I was right, I positioned myself to protect and help you and your friends the best that I could while also setting Alex up for the fall. Granted, none of it was the perfect plan but I did the best I could given the circumstances and timing, and you're all still alive, and we're closing in on Young."

"And you're sure he's involved?"

"Positively. And, if that's not enough, his little story about turning in the Chimera documents and about a plan being underway, well, let's just say that a story is all it is. My sources tell me that the documents about Chimera never made it beyond himself. We can assume he's positioning himself for a take-over."

Hennessey broke in, nervously looking at his watch. "Unfortunately, there's a new development, something time-sensitive."

"Something that involves you," Jonathon directed at Kim. "But you'll have to trust me."

"What are we waiting for?" she asked. Halfway out the door she reached over and took the sandwich from Jonathon. "I assume you can talk and drive at the same time."

Across town, Agent Alex Young had secluded himself in his office, waiting for the call. He placed his gun on the desk, within easy reach. He needed time to think.

When did I cross the line? he wondered, replaying the past events in his mind. *All I wanted to do was make the bust of a lifetime. Something that would make the DEA sit up and take notice so I'd get promoted to a top spot even without belonging to the Freemasons. But, what Mick was doing looked so easy, I just wanted a piece of the action. Now I stand to lose what little I have left,* he thought as he looked at the framed picture on his desk.

His ex-wife and kids were smiling at him from a photo that was taken as a Father's Day gift two years ago. *How could things have changed so drastically in two short years?* He wondered if the youngest had gotten in her new front teeth and tried to imagine what she looked like. He blocked out images of his son playing catch with his new step-dad. It was too painful, and too late. *Guess it's true what they say—it's lonely at the top,* he thought.

The office phone rang, but he made no move to answer it. His secretary was not going to be picking it up and he feared it was her husband, wondering why she wasn't answering her cell phone. He couldn't face what he'd done to her in a moment of panicky self-preservation. *That's when I crossed the line,* he decided. *What the hell was I thinking? You weren't, Alex. You weren't thinking. Up until the very instant she was hit, this whole mess was salvageable!*

37

Jonathon took the freeway as far as he could before switching over to a series of one-way surface streets until he was on a service drive running parallel to the Detroit River. With the downturn in the economy, the years hadn't been kind to the downriver area. The aborted beautification projects were evident all along the waterfront—abandoned, ghostly reminders of better times and campaign promises not kept. Once the main talking point at election time, the once-thriving warehouse district was now reduced to a blight on the landscape, and losses on the city's tax rolls. Yet they did serve a purpose for those who wanted to do their deeds away from prying eyes and ears.

The morphine had worn off, so the ache in Kim's arm was ramping up. *Better a clear head, even with the pain,* she thought. She shuddered at the horrible memory that block after block of the skeletal remains of once-thriving warehouses evinced. *I've come full circle since that awful night.* The irony was inescapable but she was determined not to dwell on it. It could cloud her judgement and jeopardize the plan.

Jonathon sensed Kim's growing discomfort and handed her a prescription container, followed by a bottle of water. "Take two and call me in the morning," he said. It was an awkward attempt to ease the tension they were all under. "It's not morphine but it'll do. And eat something, for god's sake. That sandwich set the taxpayers back a pretty penny."

She looked at the bottle–Tylenol 3. She took two and swallowed them down then forced herself to eat a few bites of sandwich while she listened to her companions fill in some of the missing pieces for her. She wasn't sure if she should feel hopeful or hopeless.

Jonathon turned off the service drive and pulled into a pot-holed and trash-strewn warehouse parking lot near the river. He drove cautiously, weaving his way around broken bottles as they all kept a vigilant eye on the surrounding area. Satisfied that they were alone, he tucked the car into a small space under the bridge facing the razor-wire topped cyclone fence meant to cordon off the sharp drop to the river.

"We'll hold up here," Jonathon said. He kept the engine running and adjusted the heater temperature. The air was always colder near the river.

The fence's state of disrepair sent cold shivers down Kim's spine. Once a symbol of safety and security, it could do nothing now to prevent the curious or stupid from getting dangerously close to the river with its legendary, treacherous undertow. Kim looked with uneasy respect at the fast-moving cold water with its choppy whitecaps.

Jonathon continued, "Once we take care of this situation and Young, we can get the Chimera documents into the right hands. Once it becomes clear what's at stake and the international intelligence community grasps the magnitude of Chimera and it's potential ramifications, we believe everyone will cooperate."

"Short of a nuclear holocaust, there's never been so much at stake," Hennessey added, intently. "We get it right, or the world as we know it will cease to exist."

Kim suddenly felt colder than she'd ever felt before, and it wasn't from the cold, damp Detroit weather. "Then we need to get moving on this," she said. "But first, I'd like to know how you got involved in all of this." She looked at Hennessey.

"Ego and greed. Jonathon and I go way back together. When, out of the blue, I was approached to consider a run for the White House I couldn't wait to brag to my old college buddy, here. He thought it came from left field and suggested that I exercise some caution making my decision."

"Who approached you?" Kim asked.

"Some Political Action Committee that claimed they liked what I stood for. There's hundreds of PACs so I didn't think much about it. Well, that's not entirely true. I did think about Jonathon's advice to use caution but just the idea of a possibility of living at 1600 Pennsylvania Avenue and sitting behind the historic *Resolution* desk...," Hennessey's voice fell off in embarrassment before he continued.

"My ego embraced the idea. Other inexperienced unknowns like

Jimmy Carter and our present leader made it to the White House, so why not me? Within days, a box was delivered to my office, via courier. It contained a prepaid cell phone with typed instructions that it was to be used only to receive a phone call two days later and then discarded in the Potomac River at a specified time and location. Two days later I was contacted by a man who demanded anonymity and loyalty in exchange for the Oval Office. All I had to do was follow orders and not ask questions. He said it was the way business gets done in D.C. and that anyone who thought otherwise was naive. As instructed, I tossed the phone into the river at the specified time and remote location.

"I then received another phone with the same instructions and we continued to communicate like this. Thank god I finally came to my senses. As if the secrecy wasn't enough, I'd been watching the polls and faced the fact that they were clearly being manipulated to look like I was an up-and-coming favorite. After all, I was previously unknown at the national level so my sudden popularity made no sense. Then press releases were being issued that I had no idea about, with radical ideas that weren't mine. On top of that, I found myself endorsing ads that I wasn't allowed to preview. I was nothing more than a political whore. That's when I put my pride aside and called Jonathon again. We put the pieces together from there."

Hennessey stopped talking as a car pulled into the area. Jonathon pulled his gun from its holster and Hennessey awkwardly handled the one Jonathon had given him earlier. Kim's agent's instinct took over and she rested her hand on the gun hidden in her sling. They silently watched and waited. The car drove cautiously toward them and parked. A middle-aged Asian man got out and opened the trunk of his car. The three let out sighs of relief as he pulled out a tackle box and fishing rod.

"With the fence broken down it's an open invitation to fish, but we can't take a chance on him getting hurt," Jonathon said as he opened his car door. He holstered the gun and pulled his badge from his pocket as he walked toward the man. Showing the man his badge, Jonathon claimed official business and asked him to leave the area.

"Fish for dinner. No break law," the man explained in broken English. "Need fish, feed family."

"You must leave quickly. Not safe." Jonathon pulled his wallet out and handed the man money. "Buy dinner. Fish, chicken, whatever you want. But you must leave. Now!" Jonathon waited and watched the man drive away. Returning to the car, he opened the trunk and pulled out two vests and handed them to Kim and Hennessey. "Kevlar. Put them under your shirts like I did. And don't get too cocky, the vests can only do so much and you still have vulnerable kill zones."

They did as they were told, then Kim continued. "So, for his own safety, Hennessey's death was staged."

"That's correct. What little he might know, or suspect, would put him in jeopardy if he tried to back out of the deal. But his death allows him to hide in plain sight and since no one knows he's still alive, he's our ace in the hole."

Jonathon looked at his watch. "Almost showtime. Once I realized how deep Alex was involved, I had to convince him that we shared some of the same beliefs as far as how the world should operate. He'd been drinking so it was easier than I thought. He boasted that there was a plan in place to drastically alter the way business gets done. I said I wanted in. Surprisingly, he bought my bullshit, lock, stock, and barrel and I soon found myself privy to some of the plan, which allowed me to come up with a counter-plan. So now you know almost everything up to this point." He then turned to Hennessey. "Your role isn't mandatory, so last chance to back out, my friend."

"No chance in hell you're doing this without me," Hennessey answered. "Remember, I'm your ace in the hole. And, after how they tried to use me, I have skin in the game."

"Same here," Kim said.

Jonathon laughed. "That's great, because I've been a little busy the last few days so there's no plan B." Then, more seriously, "Kim, I said you knew almost everything. Now I'm going to tell you the rest. But, don't panic. I'm confident we can pull this off. We have to."

Jonathon then pointed to the structure about a block away and closest to the river. "Rod, Angie, and Street are being held in that warehouse."

"What!" Kim yelled. "And you're just now telling me! Are they okay?"

"From all indications, yes. I delayed telling you because I needed you to focus on everything prior to this in case you're the only one of the three of us to make it out alive. Someone has to get the truth out."

"You haven't called for back-up?" she screamed.

"The only people I completely trust are in this car. But think about it. How do you think I knew what was going on here? Alex was using Kevin because of his inexperience and willingness to do whatever he was told. Knowing that, I had Kevin followed by two undercover agents who disguised themselves as junkies and positioned themselves near the warehouse. In the interest of national security, they're following orders on a need-to-know basis. We can't have everybody and their brother knowing what's going on. So pull yourself together and listen up."

Kim wondered, if she were in his shoes, who she would have trusted enough to call and came up empty. She knew Jonathon was right to keep the loop as tight as possible. *If this story got out, the effects would be disastrous. The stock market would crash, anarchy would reign, the rest of the Patriot Act measures that the government had put into place to control the people, with 911 as the excuse for it, would be implemented to completely repress the citizens. The President would use the kill-switch to shut down the Internet which would effectively shut down everything dependent on it–banking, healthcare, defense, education....* Kim shuddered at the thought as Jonathon continued.

"It would be best to take Kevin by surprise but the only other entrance, the receiving dock, is padlocked. And without a ladder and some rope, the windows are too high to access."

"Not to mention dangerous, with the broken glass jutting out of the frames," Hennessey added.

"Yes, the windows are out of the question," Kim agreed. "Do your agents have sniper capabilities?" she turned to Jonathon.

"They're top notch. But there're two catches. One, we don't know where everyone is being held and we don't want our friends in there to be collateral damage. Two, Kevin was an explosives expert with the army and volunteered for three tours in Iraq. Judging from what the two agents could see, Kevin carried explosives materials into the warehouse. So that's upped the ante on taking him alive. We not only need him to testify against Young, but if he's booby-trapped the place then he may be the only chance for everyone to leave there alive. For him to get out alive, he'll have to guide all of us out safely."

"All of us?" Kim asked.

"Young ordered me to pick you up and deliver you to Kevin. While I'd prefer to take Kevin by surprise, that's not an option. And he's expecting me to bring you in through the front door so that's what we're going to do. Once you and I are in there, here's what we're going to do."

Kim and Hennessey paid close attention to Jonathon's plan, knowing everyones' lives were on the line.

"And once we clean up this mess, we go after Young," Kim said with conviction.

38

When Kevin disappeared from view, Street turned to Angie. "Got any tricks up your sleeve?"

"Just the ropes tying me to this chair, smart ass."

Rod looked around, sizing up the remnants of tools and machinery that were left behind when the warehouse was abandoned. A few small tools lay scattered about, unclaimed by the local scavengers who took everything they could carry away when it closed. Even if he could get his hands on the smaller pieces, they were too small for adequate self-defense.

"Well, I don't have much to offer in the way of hope," Street said, "but I can feel some rough, sharp, metal burrs on the back of this chair that might be used to cut through the rope if I can twist my arms enough to get some sawing action going."

Angie and Rod immediately set about trying to feel any sharp edges on their own chairs, but came up empty.

Street grimaced in pain as he forced his arms into an unnatural position and started a repetitive, short, up-and-down motion. The physical strain was obvious as a sheer veil of perspiration erupted on his forehead and above his lip. Rod and Angie watched helplessly while keeping alert for any sign of Kevin returning. In Kevin's absence, unfamiliar sounds echoed through the empty space, punctuated by occasional cursing.

Kevin's continued disappearing acts for brief spans of time piqued the hostages curiosity and kept them on their toes. Like a little mouse scampering to and fro, he busied himself just out of everyone's range of vision, but well within earshot. The three speculated in hushed tones. They couldn't connect the noises with a recognizable activity, but they instinctively knew whatever he was up to wouldn't bode well for them.

Occasionally, a shout of self-satisfaction could be heard, or a string of obscenities. The cursing gave the three a glimmer of hope as it signaled things not going according to plan. They took their victories where they could and when things grew quiet they knew that he would soon make an appearance to check up on them.

Since Street freeing himself was their only hope, they stayed alert for any sign that Kevin was returning. But, as alert as they were, Kevin managed a surprise appearance and threw Street a curious look as he worked feverishly on his restraints.

"My circulation is cutting off. Can you loosen these up a little?" Street's quick thinking paid off and Kevin ignored the request and left him alone.

"I demand to know what you're doing in there," Angie said indignantly, nodding toward the warehouse.

Rod silently watched the interactions, looking for a chink in Kevin's armor that could be used against him.

"You're in no position to demand anything. But since you all were determined to blow the lid off of Chimera, I'm creating an appropriate send-off for you."

Rod picked up on the inference immediately and was thankful that at least Kim was safe.

"And just what does that mean?" Angie persisted, oblivious to the threat.

Kevin smirked at the trio before turning his attention to the five rapid knocks on the warehouse door. "Don't go anywhere. Be right back," he laughed as he walked away from them.

They watched him open the door and then quickly step outside, closing the door behind him. Once alone, Rod told Angie and Street about his hunch. "Don't freak out just yet, but I believe Kevin's wiring the place with explosives."

"Say what?" Street frantically renewed his efforts to free himself. "Is that drug overdose option still on the table?"

Rod did his best to comfort Angie. "Once Street is free he'll untie us. Kevin's no match for the three of us."

Outside, Kevin impatiently listened to the man explain. "I do like you say. I saw car by river, under bridge. Two men, one woman. Driver had gun and badge."

"And did they think you were just going fishing?"

"Yes. I made look real. He gave money to buy fish. Said too dangerous there. He watch me leave. I did good?"

"Describe the driver."

Satisfied that it was Jonathon, Kevin pushed his fist out. "Here's the rest of your money along with a word of caution. You open your mouth about this to anyone, *anyone*, and you'll be fishing your family out of that river, instead of walleye. Understand?"

The man nodded vigorously.

"Now get out of here."

Alex paced anxiously back and forth, waiting on Kevin's call that everyone and everything was in place. If the plan went wrong, Alex had no back-up plan, which could put him in jeopardy. *But, even if everything goes according to plan and Kevin walks out alone, what's my guarantee that Kevin can be trusted? At some point, he could prove to be a liability. No one can leave the warehouse alive.* Alex holstered his gun and started off on the short drive to the warehouse.

39

Under cover of surrounding buildings, Hennessey made his way to the back corner of the warehouse and watched Jonathon park the car at the door and get out. He took what little comfort he could in the thin Kevlar flak-jacket hidden under his clothes. Jonathon assured him that, though getting hit would knock him on his ass and hurt like hell, it would unlikely prove fatal. He watched Jonathon open the door for Kim. When the two agents started their charade he stepped backward, out of view.

"Hey you turncoat bastard! Watch the arm! You don't have to pull!" Kim yelled loudly. The two tussled back and forth and Jonathon turned in a convincing performance by threatening and pushing her toward the warehouse.

Hearing the commotion, Kevin stopped what he was doing in the warehouse and went to the door. Opening it, he looked at Jonathon and Kim and then cast a cautious glance up and down the length of the structure. Satisfied they were alone, he stepped aside to let them in.

Angie, Street, and Rod listened with curiosity to the commotion and then watched in horror as Kim tripped and stumbled into the room ahead of Jonathon, whose gun was trained at her head. Kevin was following close behind. Street stopped his efforts to free himself just in time. Kim helplessly looked at her friends.

"You fucking traitor!" Street screamed, spitting at Jonathon.

Angie was too shocked to speak.

"Hey! Take it easy on her arm! You don't need to be so rough," Rod spoke up. He tried to catch Kim's eye, but she looked away. He felt a sense of futility as the very thing he tried to prevent was happening before his eyes. He thought back to the last time he saw her in the hospital and wished he could take it back.

Jonathon ignored Rod and tried to engage Kevin in conversation hoping to distract him, but Kevin's only response was sullen silence accompanied by kicking a chair and some rope toward Kim. Jonathon took the cue and pushed Kim into the chair with more force than he wanted, but it needed to look real. He could feel the hatred directed at him from the captives.

"How could you turn against us?" Angie asked Jonathon.

"He didn't turn. He always was. He played us for fools," Street said disgustedly. "We were just too trusting to see it."

Kim spoke as loudly as she dared to still be heard and worded things in a way she hoped they would get without being too obvious. "It's true that sometimes things aren't what they appear to be."

She briefly caught Rod's eye as she said this. With a subtle wink from her, his confused look was replaced with a fleeting look of understanding. She had a plan. He wondered what it was and hoped she could pull it off. He had gained a great deal of respect for her in a short time, but four unarmed hostages were no match for Kevin and Jonathon.

"Don't be getting all philosophical on us, girl. What got us through everything over the past few days was you showing some righteous ass! Don't get all candy-ass on us now!" Angie scolded, unaware of the exchange between Kim and Rod. "Have you forgotten what we've been through, and why? You can go back to life as a sheeple if you want, but count me out."

"Count me out, too. Looks like Jonathon's another turncoat selling out to the highest bidder, and Kim's lost her will to fight," Street added. "But as long as I've got an ounce of energy left in me..."

Jonathon went about his business in silence, but Street had given Rod an idea. "If this is about money, I'll give you whatever you want, after you let the rest go. You don't have to do this thing. It's not too late," Rod bargained with Jonathon.

Jonathon responded loudly. "I appreciate your position, Rod, I really do. And I would do the same in your shoes. Hell, I'd sell my soul for the woman I love. But Kim knows way too much, and while you three don't know everything you know too much to let you walk out of here." With that, Jonathon jerked the rope, securing the last knot, and shot Kim a hard stare. She returned it. He then took a position near Kevin.

"We can't just leave them behind," Jonathon told Kevin in a

subdued voice. "We need to cover our tracks real good. No evidence leading back to us, or Young. Any ideas?"

"No worries. They're definitely going to be left behind. Here, there, everywhere," Kevin chuckled as he motioned around the room. A shiver went down Jonathon's spine.

While Kevin was distracted, Kim attempted to get a coded message to her friends. "It's freezing cold in here. I'm glad Jonathon gave me time to dress for the occasion. I mean, the lacy stuff is sexy but I'm glad that for today's activities he helped me choose function over fashion."

Angie's jaw dropped. "Have you lost your mind? We're about to get wasted and you're talking about clothes?"

Street added, "You better get your fight on, girl, cuz that's the only shot we're gonna have."

Rod noticed that Kim looked unusually flat-chested and a little bulked up. *A bullet-proof vest would account for that and it was something Kevin would never notice from a distance. And, there's no way Jonathon would have missed that when he subdued her and tied her to the chair. That can mean only one thing. If my hunch is right, Jonathon and Kim are in cahoots which means we all just might get out of this alive.*

"When have you ever known Kim to make idle chit-chat?" Rod asked softly. "Read between the lines." Making sure that Jonathon and Kevin were at a safe distance, Rod took a chance to confirm what he was thinking.

"Are you and Jonathon wearing bullet-proof vests?" he asked, quietly. With her affirmative nod, Angie and Street looked toward Jonathon with a glimmer of renewed hope. They saw that he was trying to engage Kevin in conversation, but Kevin was clearly distracted.

Jonathon had been sizing up the situation with Kevin. Taking him out was a tempting thought, but Kevin's testimony against Agent Young was crucial. Then, there was the issue of the explosives. With the place booby-trapped, if Kevin had already activated the detonator then he was their only ticket out. But now Kevin was acting wary. Jonathon had to exercise the greatest of caution. One wrong move on Jonathon's part could blow the whole plan. He had to get all of them out of this alive.

Unexpectedly, Kevin turned and walked toward the hostages. He bypassed the rest and walked over to check on Kim's restraints. He shot Jonathon a disgusted look as he tightened them. Kim flinched in pain. "You're getting soft, Jonathon. She's injured, not dead. Anything short of her being dead makes her a continuing threat. She's already proven she's not your average woman. She takes a mauling and keeps on hauling."

"My mistake. I'll be more careful next time."

Something had Kevin on guard. Maybe it was simple paranoia coupled with the gravity of the situation. Maybe it was something more. Kevin listened intently for a few seconds and then shrugged it off. He pulled out a small, hand-held device and typed in a series of numbers. "Fully activated. Except for a one-time de-activate/re-activate on the office door, there's simply no way out of here alive." He tucked the device into his pants pocket.

The movement behind Street's chair was slight, but caught Jonathon's attention. Street looked directly at Jonathon and then as discreetly as he could, moved his bloodied hands and wrists freely in the rope. Jonathon nodded ever so slightly that he understood. With Kim now securely restrained, Street was Jonathon's only chance for help to overpower Kevin. But Street had proven himself over the past few days to be a force to be reckoned with. Jonathon knew he could count on him.

"Then again, you might be giving her too much credit," Jonathon said. Playing the game until he was sure the timing was right, he pointed his gun at each captive in turn. "All good things must come to an end, my friends. I've enjoyed our brief time together, but a higher duty calls. You must know that you all know too much to leave here alive, but Kevin's gone to great pains to make the end as painless as possible."

"Touching," Kevin said, turning his gun on Jonathon as he shoved a chair in his direction. "Sit down! You've had a last minute invite to the party, courtesy of Agent Young."

Instinctively, Street jumped out of his chair and lunged toward Kevin. In one sweeping motion, Kevin turned toward Street while raising his gun and taking aim. A shot rang out. Kevin screamed as the gun flew out of his bloodied hand. While Jonathon readied to shoot again, Street quickly retrieved Kevin's gun, training it on its owner.

"My fingers are in bloody shreds too," Street told Jonathon, "so you're gonna have to do the honors while I make sure this son of a bitch doesn't try anything cute."

"It's just a flesh wound," Jonathon told Kevin, tying his hands behind him. "It could have been a whole lot worse."

Jonathon then freed everyone else. Kim, Angie, and Rod stood on shaky legs, rubbing the circulation back into their arms. Quick hugs were exchanged all around and Rod and Kim held onto each other an extra few seconds before the barrier of the kevlar vest grimly reminded them of the severity of their situation.

Jonathon pulled the hand-held device from Kevin's pocket. "What's the code?"

Silence.

"Do the right thing and get us all out of this building."

"Fuck you!" Kevin said defiantly.

"It's your last chance to do right and live to tell about it," Jonathon offered again.

"What you really mean is, it's everyone's last chance, but no deal!"

"You guide us out of this warehouse safely, and I promise you a nice plea bargain in exchange for your testimony about Chimera, and Young's role in it," Kim spoke up. "Federal prisons are the country clubs of the penal system. You could do a whole lot worse."

"No dice. I'd rather go up like the Fourth of July than look over my shoulder the rest of my life. Chimera is too big for the power players to walk away from. Anyone who gets in their way won't be for long. Think about it. Would you easily give up the opportunity to control the world and everything in it, and the wealth that would come with such power? And don't think it's such a crazy idea. Chimera is closer to becoming a reality than anyone dares to think. And do you know why? Because no one's minding the store! Just look at the unprecedented bold moves governments have already taken. From taking over the largest private sector companies including the auto industry and health insurance, to further regulations of the stock market, to more gun regula..."

"But the people are getting wise to it, and protesting," Angie interrupted.

"That's right," Street said. "Right makes might. Power to the people."

"Don't be naive. The protests are being put down by police and military who have been given authority to use extreme measures on their fellow citizens in the name of national security," Kevin said. "And remember that the media are the lap-dogs of the rich and powerful so the little folk only know what the power-brokers want them to know, and the conservative talk-show hosts who dare to tell the truth are discredited at every turn as conspiracy nut-jobs."

"Drop the gun and kick it this way." Everyone turned toward the commanding voice at the doorway. Alex Young stood there, gun in hand. He lined up a head shot between Jonathon's eyes. With no other choice, Jonathon did as he was told. As the gun slid across the floor, so did everyone's last hopes of escaping.

Young turned his attention to Kevin. "If my hands were free, I'd give your little speech a standing ovation. I'm touched by your loyalty. I had no idea that you were so invested in the cause. But unfortunately, like my secretary, you've become too much of a liability. So, as soon as you're free," he nodded at Jonathon, who begrudgingly complied with the implied meaning and moved to set Kevin free, "you will tie Jonathon in a chair so I can wrap up my business here."

"Don't be stupid, Young. I have a shit load of evidence against you in a safe deposit box. Call it life insurance if you want. If you kill me, you're done!"

"You're the stupid one, Kevin. Once Chimera is fully implemented, I'll control the government which controls the banks which will control the safe deposit boxes and everything in them. The stupid little key you're holding will be worthless."

"That would be true if no one outside our little group, here, knew what was going on. Like in Vegas, what goes on here, stays here. But, you made the fatal mistake of turning over the Chimera documents and now there's a counter-plan in progress."

Young laughed. "You're just as naive as the rest. Do you really think I'd be foolish enough to let the blueprints for world domination out of my sight after Kim was nice enough to kick them my way? That whole de-briefing bullshit was just that. Bullshit. Once again, you were all too eager to trust that your best interests were being served by your government."

The captives listened to the exchange in horror. There was no plan in progress to stop the insanity.

"Then it looks like we've got ourselves a good old-fashioned Mexican stand-off," Kevin said. "And please, pardon the pun, but what with illegal immigration such a hot topic and all, it just seemed so fitting. Now, believe me when I say that this place is wired to blow to hell and back and I'm your only way out."

Jonathon kept quiet as he held onto the programmed hand-held device. It would be their ace in the hole.

"Knowing of your affinity for explosive booby-traps, and even as distasteful as I find torture to be, I came prepared to get you cooperating in short order if the need arose." For emphasis, Young stepped backwards and kicked a small duffel bag forward. It clinked and clattered into the room. The small group of hostages cringed at the thought of what they would be forced to witness.

"Kind of like Jack Bauer in an episode of *24*," Alex said to the group. Then to Kevin, "Once everyone is tied up, you'll either render the explosives harmless or you'll wish you had."

"Just go out the way you came in," Kevin challenged.

"I'd like to, but I was already in here when you set the detonator. I know that opening the door will trigger the explosion so I'm stuck here until you do the one-time deactivate you mentioned. Let's both walk out of here."

"I have a feeling I wouldn't get too far."

Young nodded threateningly toward the duffle bag. "Torture is such a protracted death. But, then again, I'm a patient man."

"Your patience is going to get you killed along with the rest. It's true the place is booby-trapped, I just couldn't resist. Old habits die hard. But that was for fun. To really get the job done, though, there's a timer ticking off the remaining few minutes of everyone's lives, second by second. If my watch is right, the main detonator has now over-ridden the hand-held. I didn't plan on sticking around this long."

"You bastard!"

As Alex took aim at Kevin, Kim turned slightly away from them.

"Where do you think you're going?" Alex yelled at her.

"I'm kind of squeamish when it comes to cold-blooded murder."

"Isn't that the pot calling the kettle black? Perhaps it would be more acceptable if I was fucking him while I was killing him."

At the insinuation, Kim's jaw tensed with anger and resolve.

"I swear, they just don't make undercover agents and politicians the way they used to," Young smirked. "But, then, maybe I didn't really kill Hennessey with the other two a few minutes ago." He laughed again as everyone choked on the reality of what he had said.

With her sling-supported arm lined up in a new angle, Kim discreetly slipped her hand into the sling and felt the comfort of the cold, hard steel Jonathon had placed there earlier. Wrapping her fingers around the handle, she did her best to covertly line up a shot from her disadvantaged position. If she failed to hit Alex, she wouldn't get a second chance. She was counting on the others to overpower Kevin. After that, their only way out of this mess was to convince Kevin to disarm the bombs. It was a slim chance, but better than none at all.

Taking a few seconds to compose herself and concentrate, Kim squeezed off a round. In a flash of gunpowder, a piece of her cast and sling disappeared as Alex's jugular exploded along with half of his neck. The sight was sickening, but mesmerizing, and everyone stared long and hard for a few dazed seconds until Jonathon sprang into action, taking Kevin down. Street piled on for good measure while Rod checked on Kim.

Kim was ashen-colored and visibly shaken. "You did what you had to do," Rod comforted her.

"I almost missed," she said quietly.

"Missed, hell. A clean shot to the neck. And backwards I might add," Jonathon said as he retrieved his handgun from across the floor. "I'm impressed."

"It was a lousy shot," Kim yelled. "I was aiming for the heart." She squeezed Rod's hand and walked toward Kevin. Standing directly over him, she took aim at his kneecap. "Now let's talk about that deal I offered you earlier. I can almost hear that timer ticking away. It's making me nervous so I'm pretty shaky. Kneecap first, then your family jewels." She pointed the gun at his crotch.

Angie and Street exchanged uncomfortable, shocked looks at the coldness in Kim's eyes and voice. They had never seen her like this before. Rod stood in silent support knowing she was their best chance of survival. Jonathon, too, held himself in check, confident in her abilities. She fired, and Kevin screamed as the tip of his shoe disappeared.

"That was a warning shot," she told him, once again leveling her gun at his kneecap.

Angie stepped forward, pleading, "Kim. There's been enough violence. There must be another way."

"It was only the tip of a toe," Kim said, icily. "Kneecaps hurt a hell of a lot more. And, of course, explosives are totally debilitating." With that said, Angie stepped back and out of Kim's way.

"What'll it be, Kevin?" as she turned her attention back to him. His eyes grew larger as she placed the barrel of her pistol smack up against his kneecap.

Rod stepped forward. "Don't think she won't. And, after what the agency put her through, no one will even blame her. Take the plea-deal she offered before she changes her mind. You still have an opportunity to do the right thing–to honor the badge you swore an oath to."

"I don't know if there's time," Kevin said softly. Based on years of experience, Jonathon stepped forward, sensing Kevin's faltering resolve. He reached a hand out to help Kevin to his feet.

"How much time is left?" Kim asked, cocking her pistol. "How much!" she screamed. Jonathon pulled Kevin up. Kevin favored his injured foot and flinched in pain as he wiped the blood off the face of his watch with his good hand. "Seven minutes."

"Lord have mercy," Angie prayed.

"I'm counting on it," Street added, shoving Kevin in the direction of the warehouse he had been busily in and out of so many times earlier. "Lead the way."

40

Hennessey had been getting anxious. Jonathon and Kim had been in the warehouse too long. Something was wrong. Young showing up wasn't part of the plan and now he'd lost sight of him.

Minutes earlier he'd watched Young warily circle the warehouse before parking his car and getting out. He edged as close to the corner of the building as he dared in order to keep tabs on Young, but Young was soon out of sight. Veering from the plan, Hennessey worked his way around the building, weaving his way around the stacks of debris littering the vast property. If he could reach the undercover agents, he was confident they could come up with an alternate plan.

He snuck up to within twenty feet of them, hid behind an old refrigerator, and signaled to get their attention. Nothing. Keeping low, he darted to and fro until he was within a few feet of the two men. Even at that distance he could read the hastily-scrawled, blood-stained note that lay on top of one of them. *Long live Chimera.* A sound, and he whirled around. He was face to face with Agent Young, and staring into the silenced barrel of a gun.

"You!" Young gasped. "But you're..."

"Obviously not dead," Hennessey said with more calm than he felt.

"Not yet," Young said, just as calmly.

Remembering his kevlar vest, Hennessey hoped Young wouldn't go for a head shot. Either way, he prepared to get knocked on his ass and hurt like hell. Hopefully, playing dead would give him a chance.

You sure as hell weren't kidding, Jonathon, was the last thing he remembered thinking as the impact of the slug knocked the gun from his hand and the wind from his lungs. He was knocked backward, lost his footing, and hit the ground.

He lay stunned, until he was sure he was still alive and Young was gone. Rolling over to get to his feet, he found the pain in his chest excruciating. Betting on some broken ribs, he moved as carefully as he could to not puncture a lung.

Getting on his hands and knees, he noticed his gun several feet away. He slowly retrieved it and stuck it in his belt. He crawled past the bodies of the agents and used the old, grimy stove to hoist himself to a standing position before painfully making his way toward the warehouse.

The main detonator was tucked into a cross beam supporting a steel walkway used by plant foremen in the old days to oversee operations from above. With two good hands, wedging it into place earlier had been easy, but now it was stuck tight. Kevin tried to wiggle it back and forth, but it held firm. Despite the cold, beads of sweat ran down his face as he listened to the seconds tick away.

In the same way that he had installed it, he lay flat out on the walkway, hanging over the edge. His large fingers fumbled nervously at the attached wires, but he couldn't disconnect them.

Kim nudged her gun impatiently into the back of his neck. They were running out of time. "What's the problem?"

"It's wedged in so tight I can't get it out."

"Then just disconnect the wires," Jonathon said.

"I'm trying. I can't get a good enough hold on them from this position."

"Five minutes," Street warned.

"The windows aren't rigged," Kevin offered, nodding toward the nearest one, "but we're a good three stories up."

"You three try the window," Kim told Rod, Street, and Angie.

"Four and a half minutes," Street interjected.

Jonathon spotted something hanging by the window, something overlooked by the scavengers who looted the place. "We're *all* going out of the window," he shouted, nodding toward an old rope emergency ladder hanging by the busted out window. "It's old, but it should hold long enough to get some of us to the ground. Those on the ground can break the fall of the others."

"The lord does help those who help themselves," said Angie, already on her way to the window.

"Four minutes," Street said, looking at his watch, "should be enough time for *all* of us to get out, but only *if* we hustle."

"He's right," Angie yelled over her shoulder as she took her shoe off and began smashing out the sharp shards of glass from the window frame. "No reason for anyone to die here today. Move your asses, people!" she shouted.

Street's fingers quickly moved back and forth under the window framing and his hunch paid off. Two large old hooks that had been screwed into place decades ago, for just such an occasion, were still in place. He looped the rope ladder into the hooks and threw the ladder over the sill. It untangled in a cloud of dust. He pulled Angie toward the window. She looked down, then back at Street. "It's not long enough!"

"It's longer than no ladder at all! Move your ass!"

She stood back away from the window. "You first, and make sure you break my fall."

Kim looked at Rod and said softly, but with unmistakable urgency, "You go ahead with the others and wait for me at the bottom. I love you and I promise I'll be right along."

Rod shot her a confused look.

"I'm not leaving without that duffle bag," she explained.

"Duffle bag?" Rod asked.

"The one Young came in with. I'll bet the Chimera papers are in it. Like he said, he'd never let them out of his sight."

"The hell with the papers! Kevin can back up your story."

"I'm not putting my trust in someone who was going to blow us to kingdom come! I need that bag!" Kim thrust her gun into his hand. As he reached out to hold her back, she slipped out of his grasp and was gone. In spite of her bad arm, she was soon awkwardly shimmying down the metal structure toward the ground floor.

Rod started after her, but Jonathon grabbed his arm. "Let her go. We need to get our key witness down the ladder," he said sternly.

"I'm going after Kim!"

"She's not helpless! If you really love her, let her to do what she needs to do. This may be her last chance to reclaim herself. Give it to her."

Rod hesitated. He knew Jonathon was right, but feared he may never see her alive again. When he looked a few seconds later, she hit the floor running and disappeared through the doorway into the office.

"Three minutes!" Street screamed, as he disappeared from view with Angie close behind.

Now, with everyone and their extra weight off the walkway, Kevin was finding that he could jiggle the box back and forth a little. With enough time, he might be able to pull it out. "I think I've got it!" he yelled, still working feverishly to extract it. "And, with two minutes left!"

"Forget it!" Jonathon yelled. "No time! We're going out the window!" Yanking Kevin from the floor, he pushed him toward the ladder. Kevin moved fast, despite his injury. He was on the sill in a flash and turning around to make the backward descent. Jonathon held back to let Rod go ahead. That's when they saw Kim coming back around the corner.

She was holding her bad arm protectively across her chest, while her sling cradled the duffle bag on her back. Before Jonathon could stop him, Rod was running to meet her. Knowing that they would need unimpeded access at the ladder–if they made it back in time, Jonathon followed Kevin out of the window.

Kim fought hard to pull herself frantically up the structure, using her injured arm as best she could. Utterly exhausted, the additional weight she carried on her back threatened to pull her down. With each step she felt heavier. So close to the walkway. To the window. To the ladder. She wasn't sure if she really saw Rod running toward her or if it was just wishful thinking.

Rod braced his lower torso against the framing above her and thrust his arms toward her. Kim held onto a supporting post with an arm that ached so badly she doubted her ability to sustain for more than a few seconds. She looked into his eyes. He seemed so far away. She reached up to him and tried to grasp his hand. They barely touched fingers. She strained forward as far as she could and the effort was rewarded as they clasped hands.

"No good. We need to lock wrists, Kim," he stated with urgency.

"I can't."

"You can. I'll meet you halfway. Trust me," Rod encouraged her as he leaned further toward her in a careful balancing act that defied the laws of gravity. His lower body and legs strained every fiber to stay rooted behind the low barrier that barely kept him from toppling forward.

She pulled back and repositioned herself for stability and then struggled against the weight on her back to draw herself up even taller, balancing on tip-toes. She extended her free hand as far as she could, then a little further. First, fingers touched once again. Then, palms slid across each other as they locked wrists. Rod's other hand circled her wrist as well and, once he was sure he had her, he strained for all he was worth and slowly pulled her the rest of the way up with a strength that surprised him. Once both of her feet were on the walkway, they wasted no time as they breathlessly bolted for the window.

Just short of the ladder, Rod reached into the sling on Kim's back and wrestled the duffel bag from inside. With a firm grasp on the handles, he lowered the bag to his side and swung it backwards behind him and then brought it forward letting its own weight propel it out of the window ahead of them.

He followed the bag out of the window and once securely on the second step he pulled Kim out, keeping one arm around her waist. In unison, they quickly worked their way down the frayed rope steps. Kim hung on with both hands as best she could to keep them anchored on the ladder as Rod worked his way down with one free hand. Close to the last step, the old roping began disintegrating under their combined weight. Without warning, the step gave way and they awkwardly dropped to the step below.

The unexpected fall caused rope burns on their hands as they instinctively grabbed tighter. Their weight, combined with the force of gravity from the short fall, proved to be too much for the next step. It gave way as well. With no strength left to hold on, Kim and Rod helplessly plummeted the last ten feet.

The pile of grimy mattresses broke their fall and they lay there in an exhausted stupor for a few seconds. "Over here!" Street yelled, motioning frantically from behind a pile of debris. He looked at his watch, counting down the seconds. Street's urgent screaming snapped the pair from their exhausted state and, within seconds, Rod scrambled to his feet and pulled Kim after him. They started running away from the warehouse when suddenly they both stopped short. Something was missing. *The bag!* Rod broke free and ran back to get it.

"Forget the bag!" Kim screamed after him. Ignoring her, he quickly breached the distance there and back in record time. Locking hands once again, they bolted for the safety of the debris pile. Rod flung the bag in ahead of them, and they dove head first right behind it as the warehouse exploded in an ear-shattering, earth-shaking concussive blast.

For a brief moment they felt as if they were suspended in space before landing clumsily, with bits of debris raining down on them from every direction. Kim had managed to twist her body into her fall just enough to protect her bad arm from further damage when she hit the ground, but the impact was still jarring on her recent injuries. The pain took her breath away. She lay where she landed and looked around. There was a new face among them, and everyone was accounted for, alive and well. A lengthy silence ensued as they all appreciated the gravity of a situation barely avoided.

Finally, Street broke the silence. "Kevin, you ever think about a career in demolitions?"

"Smart ass," Angie laughed in nervous relief as she slowly sat up while taking inventory of her parts, making sure she was in one piece.

Rod and Kim looked at each other. No words were necessary to convey the gratitude they felt.

The newcomer among them spoke next. "When I saw the ladder flying out of the window, a little short of the mark, it seemed a shame to waste all of the discarded mattresses laying around," Hennessey said. "I dragged a couple over for these two," he gestured toward Street and Angie, "and they added a couple more for the rest of you."

"Lucky for us, you happened by," Street told the man.

"No luck involved," Jonathon intervened. "He didn't just happen by. For those of you who haven't met him yet, this is my old college buddy and good friend, Michael Hennessey." Seeing the surprised look on everyones' faces he quickly added, "Looks like I owe all of you an explanation." Suddenly, the warehouse ignited into a blazing inferno. Staring at the raging fire, they were each thankful to have made it out alive.

Hennessey gestured to a nearby location. "Unfortunately, the two undercover agents over there didn't fare as well as the rest of us. Young murdered them in cold blood. He tried to kill me, too, and left me for dead. All I got out of the deal was a broken rib or two."

"I've seen enough death and carnage in the past few days to last me a lifetime. What possesses people to act that way," Angie asked sadly.

"I can tell you," Kevin said as he sat up, his voice tinged with remorse. "Power and money. The more power, the more money and the more money, the more power. It's more seductive than a beautiful woman and never enough. And Chimera was going to be the mother-lode of both. Regretfully, my momentary lapse in judgement cost me a hell of a lot more than the skin off my hand and the tip of a toe."

"Sorry Kevin, but I'm fresh out of sympathy and I doubt that Young's secretary, or her family, would have any for you either." Kim then shifted her attention to the duffle bag.

She eyed it warily. Opening it would be the moment of truth. Would her instincts be proven right? What if she was wrong, as she'd been about so many things over the past few months? Her instincts had failed her and she'd placed her trust in people and agencies she shouldn't have. Sensing her inner conflict, Rod crawled over to retrieve the bag. He put it in her lap and, still, she just sat there.

"You risked your life for it twice, trying to make sure it got into the right hands," Rod prompted her.

"You risked your life for it too," she said.

"No," he said. "I risked my life for *you.*"

She acknowledged his meaning with a grateful smile. "Well, it was the least I could do to try to undo some of the damage that was caused by my errant gut instincts. We're lucky to be alive and in one piece. Others haven't been so lucky." Everyone knew she was talking about Jay's brother, Marie, Gallagher, Mrs. Murdock, the helicopter pilot, Madsen and Dunn, and countless others who had been injured or killed.

"You can't blame yourself for being taken advantage of," Street offered.

"Thanks for the vote of confidence. But at some level I must have given the impression that it was okay to take advantage of me. Maybe it was nothing more than my complacent unquestioning of authority that I fell into after my parents died. It was easier that way. Just go along to get along because no one except my parents appreciated a teenager who had a mind of her own."

Because Street had been privy to the stairwell drama that had unfolded between Lacy and Kim at the Press Club, he knew that Mick had purposely taken advantage of her in her weakest moments, recruiting her to do the unthinkable. As much as he wanted to argue the point with Kim, he knew that she would gain strength and confidence from reconciling her feelings on her own terms.

Angie touched Kim's arm in a show of support. "Your parents would be proud of you today for turning this situation around."

Kim said, "Well, we don't know about that yet, now do we? Without those documents to prove Chimera is not just some conspiracy theory, it's just us against the establishment."

"Then what are you waiting for?" Jonathon prompted.

Rod understood. "You're afraid to open it, and just as afraid not to. But remember that once you did start trusting your gut instincts again, it was you who forced this whole episode into the open."

"Yeah. I sure did," she said with more confidence, pulling the bag toward her.

Everyone was curious, including Kevin, so they all gathered in a little closer. Taking in a deep breath, Kim reached in the bag. She brought out a taser, a wire cutter, a pliers, and a wrench. One by one, she tossed them to the side and they clattered to the ground. Kevin shivered. Would Young really have used those on him?

After a moment's hesitation, she hefted out the manuscript and pushed the bag aside. She placed the heavy tome on her lap. Still afraid that she was wrong, she let it sit. What if Rod had been killed needlessly as he waited in the warehouse for her to retrieve it, or as he ran back to get it earlier?

"You won't know till you know," Angie urged her on from the sidelines.

Kim held her breath and slowly opened the cover. On the first page, her vindication in one word–Chimera.

"Unbelievable," was all she could mutter, as she randomly leafed through the hundreds of pages and fingered the coded CDs in the back. Everyone kept silent, giving her the space she needed to take it all in, to reconcile her part in it, and in stopping it.

"It's all here, and probably duplicated on these CDs as well," she finally said, in a reverential tone. "Everything from the chemical indoctrination of agents like me to do the dirty work, to the intentional collapse of all major monetary systems, to the takeover of private enterprises and health care, to the manipulation of media events that would sway the public opinion of the ignorant, and the list goes on and on. And all to control the people for a one world government, under one currency, and one supreme leader. Just like David Gallagher has been predicting for decades, and trying to stop."

"And what good people like him and your parents died for," Street said.

"It's a shame that it got as far as it did," Jonathon said. "And right under the noses of trained agents like me and Kim. We've got one hell of a job ahead of us if we're ever going to regain the public trust of all the people on this planet, not just Americans."

"Maybe we just need a whole new paradigm," said Street. "I'd opt in for anything right about now."

Angie couldn't resist. "Other than the two dimes in your pocket, just what do you know about paradigms?"

Distant sirens could now be heard as firefighters and other first-responders raced to the scene of the explosion and fire. Jonathon pulled Kevin to his feet. "Agent Haven is going to escort you to FBI Headquarters so you can corroborate Agent Young's role in Chimera. There might be a deal in it for you. That'll be Kim's call."

He tossed his car keys to Rod. "Get the five of you out of here before the local police get here and try to take all the credit. Hennessey and I will handle damage control."

"Thanks for your help, Agent...," Kim faltered. "I'm sorry Jonathon, I don't even know your last name."

Jonathon just smiled a tired smile.

Hennessey spoke up. "It's Lourde. L-O-U-R-D-E. Agent Jonathon Lourde."

Everyone began talking at once. "You sure had us fooled," Street said to Jonathon. "I would have bet my last nickel bag you killed Hennessey, and that we were next."

Angie said, "Especially with that red carnation. Why did you try to make us think the worst about you?"

Jonathon shrugged. "Probably not my best idea, but you needed to lose a little of your naivete. People and events aren't always as benign as they seem–they're just made to look that way to advance a hidden agenda. And I happen to like red carnations and one was handy."

Kim ignored the chatter going on around her. Was she remembering it clearly? Or, perhaps she'd been dreaming? *The lord moves in mysterious ways.* That's what Jonathon said as he put her into his car at the hospital. "The lord moves in mysterious ways," she said out loud as the sirens grew louder. She could tell by the look on the faces of Street, Angie, and Rod, that they were making the connection as well.

"Time to go, Agent Haven," Jonathon urged. "Vindicate yourself, avenge Chimera's victims, and put a stop to it, once and for all. "

A gusty, cold wind came out of nowhere and sent paper debris from old discarded books and magazines flying in all directions. Kim looked down at a weathered page that had landed on her shoe. She started to kick it away, but something deep inside told her to pick it up. She obeyed her instincts. It wasn't the damp Detroit air that sent chills up her spine as the printed words spoke to her, beckoning her onward.

"The very word 'secrecy' is repugnant in a free and open society; and we are as a people inherently and historically opposed to secret societies, to secret oaths and secret proceedings..."

— President John F. Kennedy
    April 27, 1961

22165934R00145

Made in the USA
Lexington, KY
15 April 2013